“

in

“Ooh, do
she slipped into the car. Richmond stroked her cheek and brought his lips down on top of hers in a slow and gentle kiss.

“As long as I can do that again, I’ll stop.”

Blinking, she looked up at him and sighed. “We’d better get going.”

“Right. But you should answer my question. Will I get to kiss you again?”

“All I’m going to say is maybe.”

Also by Cheris Hodges

Just Can't Get Enough

Let's Get It On

More Than He Can Handle

Betting on Love

No Other Lover Will Do

His Sexy Bad Habit

Too Hot for TV

Recipe for Desire

Forces of Nature

Love after War

Rumor Has It

I Heard a Rumor

Deadly Rumors

Published by Kensington Publishing Corp.

Strategic Seduction

CHERIS HODGES

Kensington Publishing Corp.
www.kensingtonbooks.com

To the extent that the image or images on the cover of this book depict a person or persons, such person or persons are merely models, and are not intended to portray any character or characters featured in the book.

DAFINA BOOKS are published by

Kensington Publishing Corp.
119 West 40th Street
New York, NY 10018

All Kensington titles, imprints and distributed lines are available at special quantity discounts for bulk purchases for sales promotions, premiums, fund-raising, and educational or institutional use. Special book excerpts or customized printings can also be created to fit specific needs. For details, write or phone the office of the Kensington Special Sales Manager. Kensington Publishing Corp., 119 West 40th Street, New York, NY 10018. Attn: Special Sales Department. Phone: 1-800-221-2647.

ISBN-13: 978-1-4967-0930-1
ISBN-10: 1-4967-0930-6
First Kensington Mass Market Edition: May 2018

eISBN-13: 978-1-4967-0931-8
eISBN-10: 1-4967-0931-4
First Kensington Electronic Edition: May 2018

10 9 8 7 6 5 4 3 2 1

Printed in the United States of America

Acknowledgments

Thank you to everyone who's ever picked up a book with my name on it. I can't help but be humbled and thankful that you have read and enjoyed my work. Your emails and messages on social media have warmed my heart and keep me going no matter how dark it gets.

Black love will always matter, and thank you for spending time between the pages with me!

Chapter 1

Alicia Michaels walked across the campus of Clark Atlanta University with a smile on her face. Being back on the yard made her think about the carefree days of undergrad. Even though she was having a good time with her girls, she was tired of hearing the *Alicia, girl, you're next* refrain as soon as someone noticed Serena Billups's wedding ring or when Jade Goings showed off her pictures of Jaden or her growing baby bump.

"I figured I'd find you out here," Kandace Crawford, one of her best friends and business partners, said as she and Richmond Crawford approached the library. "Still hiding from people?"

"I'm not hiding from anyone. Well, not really." Alicia locked eyes with Richmond Crawford, Kandace's brother-in-law. This was not the man she'd met a few years ago in New York with the glasses and pudgy belly. And was he smiling? She'd never seen this man smile before. *Why am I paying attention now?* Alicia thought as she turned away from him briefly.

"Hi, Alicia," he said, once again blinding her with his warm smile.

"Hi. What are you doing here?" She didn't even try to keep the shock out of her voice.

"Looking to start a new business venture down here in Atlanta, and Kandace was nice enough to show me some of the city," he said.

"And Solomon figured I needed a bodyguard, since he had to stay in New York for a meeting." Kandace nudged Richmond in the side.

"I'm not a bodyguard," he quipped. "Solomon knows that you can't wait to get back to him."

Kandace blushed. "True. So, Alicia, why are you hiding out at the library?"

"Just tired of the same questions. Richmond, what kind of business venture are you working on out here? I'm actually in the process of moving back to Atlanta."

"Laying the ground work for some new hotels. I hear Atlanta is the place to be."

She nodded. "I can't wait to make it home again. I've been hanging out in Old Fourth Ward and I think I'm in love."

Kandace folded her arms across her chest. "Your girl Jade is not happy about that. She even tried to enlist me in helping her talk you into staying in Charlotte." Shaking her head, she added, "I'm staying out of it. But, Richmond, if you're looking for someone to help you with marketing, you're looking at a genius right here."

Alicia stood up and smiled. Moving to Atlanta

meant that she would be starting over. She'd been laying the foundation for her marketing firm by visiting the city and reconnecting with old friends who were in powerful positions. Atlanta had changed a lot since Alicia had moved to Charlotte to start Hometown Delights with her friends. Neighborhoods had been gentrified and new businesses had popped up all over the place.

A few of Alicia's college friends were launching businesses or were looking to expand what they had going on. She'd made some important contacts already and couldn't wait to hit the ground running. She'd even signed two small clients and would be meeting with them next week.

"She'll get over it. What time is the awards ceremony? I can't believe we're getting honored after all the hell we went through in school for being forward-thinking women," Alicia said.

"Maybe they had no idea that you ladies would grow up to be this fine and successful," Richmond said. Alicia felt her cheeks heat up as Richmond looked at her and winked.

Weird, so weird, she thought as she turned her head. *Isn't he married?*

"Want to head to the Busy Bee Café?" Kandace asked. "Richmond needs to experience some real soul food. Especially if he's going to be meeting with folks around here about those hotels and doesn't know the difference between collard greens and kale."

"Oh yeah. Where's Jade and Serena?" Alicia tore her eyes away from Richmond, deciding that he was being extra flirty because his wife wasn't around or maybe he'd been drinking.

"They headed to Miss Maryann's bakery." Kandace winked at her. "You know how Jade is about that woman's icing."

Alicia shook her head, thinking that Jade was just going to get icing to use with her husband later. She was sure that Maryann, Jade's mother-in-law, had no idea that Jade and her husband, James, used that icing on each other and not cinnamon buns. "All right, let's go." When Richmond extended his hand to Alicia, she took it without a second thought. She didn't miss the side eye that Kandace shot her way.

"We'd better get a move on if we want to get a seat this century," Kandace said.

Alicia dropped Richmond's hand and smiled. "This place is small, but the food is amazing."

"That means a lot coming from you guys, since you have your own restaurant."

Kandace laughed. "This place is historic to us and was the reason—"

"One of the reasons," Alicia interjected.

"That we started our restaurant."

"What were the other reasons that you guys went into the restaurant business?" Richmond asked, then focused on Alicia. "Kandace said you have a background in marketing, right?"

Alicia nodded. "I handle the marketing for the restaurant and I'm starting my own firm here in Atlanta."

"And Alicia would definitely be a great asset

for the boutique hotels project," Kandace said. "Everybody in the Southeast will be making reservations."

"I am that good," Alicia quipped.

"So that's why you ladies started your restaurant, just because you were good at it?" Richmond asked.

Kandace and Alicia exchanged a knowing look. "Revenge," Alicia replied. "Jade had been involved with a loser who tried to open a restaurant in Charlotte, and we bought the spot from underneath him."

Richmond looked toward Kandace, who nodded in confirmation. "We're not that way anymore, but people know better than to cross us."

"I hope Solomon knows that too," Richmond quipped.

"Pretty sure he figured that out when she stabbed that crazy . . ." Alicia glanced at Kandace, then let her statement die. Though years had passed since the death of Carmen De La Croix at the restaurant, Kandace was still uncomfortable talking about it. The woman had been obsessed with Solomon and followed the couple to Charlotte. She'd attacked Solomon with a meat cleaver and Kandace saved their lives when she'd stabbed Carmen in the chest.

That had been one of the morbid headlines that made their restaurant, Hometown Delights, one of Charlotte's most popular dining destinations. Then, there was the time when disgraced movie director Emerson Bradford tried to kill Serena in the restaurant.

The notoriety had died down since then and the

restaurant was finally known for its award-winning menu and great service.

Alicia worked hard behind the scenes to make that happen. The community involvement and donations the restaurant made to major events changed the narrative about the place and turned it into one of Charlotte's premier eateries. She wasn't too egotistical to realize that part of the successful restaurant had to do with Jade's relationship with James Goings, the brother of Carolina Panthers wide receiver Mo Goings.

Then there was Marie Charles, the former socialite who married chef Devon Harris. Marie's influence also helped the restaurant because she mentioned it in her popular *Mocha Girl in Paris* blog all the time.

Alicia wanted a challenge and Atlanta was it. Things had changed since Alicia and her girls ran their business in Georgia. Many of the power players they'd known were gone and the landscape had changed a lot. Alicia knew things were going to be different, but at least she didn't have to worry about blind dates every week.

She glanced over at Richmond and wondered if Kandace would try to do that setup trick that their other friends were becoming famous for. Though, she'd be interested in bouncing some business ideas off him, maybe even help Richmond get his footing in Atlanta. There was no way she was attracted to this married man. But there was something under the surface that had piqued her interest.

* * *

Richmond noticed Alicia's glances as they walked to the café. Maybe he was just imagining things because he was looking at the ebony enchantress with new eyes. When he was married, he'd ignored Kandace and her friends. But over the years, his admiration for Kandace and her crew grew when he saw how they handled their business and turned every controversy at their restaurant into gold.

He could've used some of that magic after the scandals that happened in his life over the last few years.

When they arrived at the café, the line was wrapped around the block and the smell of fried chicken perfumed the air.

"If the food tastes as great as it smells out here, then I'm going to love it," Richmond said.

"Oh, you're going to love it," Alicia said, then nudged Kandace. "Remember how many times we ended up here, eating away our blues?"

"That was you and Jade. I just came for the biscuits. Remember, I was in love." Kandace twirled around. "Foolish, but in love. And Devon could cook anything I wanted."

Richmond laughed, wondering what fool would've broken Alicia's heart. He could only imagine what a knockout she was in college, because like fine wine, she'd gotten better with time. Her body reminded him of the classic Coca-Cola bottle—curves for days. And she was smart. That didn't happen overnight. Remembering the vapid women he'd attended NYU with, Richmond wondered what it would've been like to be around women who were focused like Alicia and her friends.

At the awards luncheon, he'd been impressed when he heard about their investment group and the after-hours café they'd opened during their freshman year. Of course, it had been an illegal setup, but the school administration had been so dazzled by their business plan that they had given the group a permit to run the café for a year.

"Are we going to wait in this wave of humanity?" Richmond asked as he glanced at the line.

"It's worth it, Mr. No Patience," Kandace said. "This food will melt in your mouth. You'll be here every day, once you move to Atlanta."

Alicia turned to Richmond. "You're moving to Atlanta?"

He nodded. "We're looking at expanding the Crawford Hotels franchise further south. I'm going to be heading the project. Can't do that without being a part of the city."

Alicia rubbed her throat. "Atlanta can be hard for a newcomer. Or someone who's been away for a while."

"I've been in tougher situations," he said as the line inched forward. "As they say, if you can make it New York, you can make it anywhere."

"Good luck with that," she said with a smile.

"When you have talent, you don't need luck. I've researched this city and I'm ready to take it by storm. And I'm going to have a great team to help me out."

Alicia smiled brightly at him. "That confidence is awesome. You're going to need it."

"Maybe you can be a part of my team." He winked at her and Alicia's knees went weak.

Kandace rolled her eyes. "It looks as if there is an open table. Praise the Lord. Let's move, and quickly."

Following her lead, Richmond and Alicia got to the table before a couple who were moving a lot slower.

"Savage," Alicia said as they sat down. "You know those two were waiting for this table."

"If you're slow, you blow," Kandace said. "Besides, when is the next time we will be together here?"

Richmond glanced at the couple as they shot them an evil look. Turning away, he laughed. "Real estate in this place comes at a premium, huh?"

Kandace nodded as Alicia picked up a menu.

"How are things in New York?" Alicia asked as she glanced at Richmond over the greasy menu.

Snorting, he shrugged. "So great that I'm moving to Atlanta. You'd think our family was the Kardashians or something."

"Tell me about it," Kandace muttered. "Kiana shouldn't know what the paparazzi are, but she does. Thank God her dad taught me creative ways to hide her face."

"That's why you should let her take a giraffe every time you go out."

Alicia raised her right eyebrow. "A giraffe?"

Kandace shook her head. "This man is obsessed with stuffed giraffes and has turned Kiana's room into an African safari. And she loves it."

"Guessing that you don't," Alicia said.

"Overkill." Kandace pulled out her phone and showed it to Alicia. "See what I mean?"

"Come on," Richmond said. "Those stuffed animals are beautiful. Even Solomon agrees with me."

Alicia shrugged because she did think the room looked amazing. And it wasn't the typical princess design that most little girls had.

"Whatever. I'm ready to toss all of those damned things, but she's going make her own choice soon enough. I can't wait until she gets into Barbie dolls."

"I'm hoping that never happens," Alicia said. "Those dolls are self-esteem killers."

Kandace waved her hand at her friend. "Says a woman who looks like a damned doll."

Richmond definitely agreed that Alicia looked like a doll, only with more realistic curves. And those thighs. Richmond had always been a leg man, and he couldn't help but wonder what they would feel like wrapped around his waist.

Their eyes met and she smiled, then pulled her skirt down over her thick thighs. "I know what I want," Richmond said as he looked down at the menu. But what he wanted was not on that greasy paper.

Alicia turned away from Richmond. Was he really staring at her legs like he wanted to dive between them? And why was she shivering with want? Had it been that long since a man showed her attention, that she found herself wanting Richmond Crawford? Now, she couldn't deny that he was looking a lot different than he did when she'd met him years ago. He was chiseled, his face slimmer, and those eyes. Hypnotic brown orbs that seemed to penetrate her soul.

She pulled a napkin from the dispenser and dabbed her top lip. "It's a little warm in here," Alicia said as she looked toward the counter. "We'd better order and get out of here before someone snatches this table from us."

It wasn't long before the trio was chowing down on crisp fried chicken, fresh cabbage, and cornbread.

After finishing his plate and Kandace's cornbread, Richmond patted his stomach. "I'm going to have to spend about three hours in the gym tonight to work this off. Maybe if my ex could cook like this, I wouldn't be divorced now."

Alicia inhaled sharply as she thought about sweat dripping down his chest. Did he wear compression pants or gray sweatpants? And he said he was divorced. Was the universe giving her a green light?

What in the hell is wrong with me? Alicia turned away from Richmond and rose to her feet. "We'd better give up this table before we get thrown out."

"Wouldn't be the first time," Kandace muttered as she and Richmond stood up.

"Don't tell me you ladies were rowdy college students," he said with a smirk.

My God, this man has dimples. Why have I never noticed this before? Oh, he never smiled before. Who knew Richmond Crawford was human? Alicia thought as they headed for the exit and Kandace recounted the time that Serena had cursed out a waiter at the café because he'd had the nerve to ask her for her phone number.

"And Alicia didn't help the matter," Kandace said, breaking into her friend's thoughts. "She tried to help Serena assault the man with chicken bones. We were so young and silly."

"That's not what happened!"

"Don't try to rewrite history now."

"So, you're forgetting that you were tossing cornbread?"

Richmond laughed. "Is that why you didn't have a problem with me eating yours today?"

Kandace shrugged. "All right, whatever. You messed with one of us, you messed with all of us." Then she looked from Richmond to Alicia. "And that hasn't changed."

Chapter 2

Richmond caught what Kandace was throwing his way when she said her friends looked out for each other. The hint was taken, but Alicia was fine as hell. Kandace didn't have anything to worry about because his focus was on work and building the hotels. Though it would be nice to . . . *Stop it,* he thought as he turned his attention to the traffic signal in front of them.

"This neighborhood is going through a revitalization, huh?" Richmond said.

"Gentrification is more like it," Alicia muttered. "It's happening all over the city. Hipsters are moving out of their parents' basements and into the city."

"I'm wondering if this might be the best spot for the first hotel," he said as he folded his arms across his chest. "It would be a great way to pay homage to Mom and D-Elliot's vision for the Crawford hotels. They started in the community and look how our empire grew. I think I can do the same in Atlanta."

"Things aren't like they were in the sixties," Alicia said. "Image and location is key to everything now.

Hell, you have people hiding who really owns things just to keep a buzz going."

"That isn't how we're going to do business. But giving back is always a good way to get in good with the right people." Richmond smiled. "Don't you think so?"

Alicia stared into his eyes, not really remembering what they'd just been talking about. Marketing. They were talking about marketing. She couldn't give him all of her knowledge for free. Maybe if she took him on as a client, she would be able to push her growing attraction to him deep down. One thing Alicia never did was mix business with pleasure.

"Umm, when are you moving to Atlanta?"

"Did that last week. I'm renting a place in Dunwoody until I decide where I want to live, or if this is going to be my new home. It's interesting how everyone out here wants to be outside of the city limits. I'm not sure I'm ready for yard work."

Alicia nodded. "I'm thinking that I'm going to live in midtown, that way I can take that MARTA."

"A woman who actually wants to take public transportation. That must be a Southern thing."

"Well, the moment you get caught in that traffic on I-285, you will learn to love the MARTA as well."

Richmond shrugged. "Or I can just get a really good car service and just read the paper while my driver deals with traffic."

"Guys," Kandace said. "Can we speed this along? I want to get back to the hotel and relax a little before this mixer tonight. And these shoes have to go."

Alicia laughed as she gave Kandace's heels a cursory glance. "Scared you're going to break it?"

Ever since famed photographer and Richmond's other sister-in-law, Dana Singleton-Bryant immortalized Kandace in her photo book with a broken shoe and a smile, Alicia and the girls always did a shoe check for her when she wore heels.

"I don't see how you and Serena march around in these things without breaking your necks."

"Practice makes perfect," Alicia said as she kicked her leg out. "Besides, these shoes make my legs look good."

"Yes, they do," Richmond muttered as he gave her outstretched leg a long glance.

Alicia dropped her leg and turned away from him as her cheeks heated. "Well, we'd better get back to the hotel."

Kandace shook her head as she glanced at Richmond and Alicia. "Let's go, people."

Walking in silence, Richmond tried to keep his focus on everything except Alicia's ass and those shapely calves. He failed. Every time they stopped at a crosswalk or for a traffic light, Richmond couldn't tear his eyes away from her.

"Atlanta's a really clean city," he said after getting caught looking at Alicia again.

Kandace crossed over to Richmond and nudged him in the side. "Whatever you're thinking, stop it."

"What are you talking about?"

"Alicia isn't your rebound chick."

"I'm not trying to make her my rebound anything."

"Make sure you remember that. Because I'd hate to have to kick your ass if you hurt my girl."

"Kandace, we're adults and there is nothing going on. But you can't deny that having her on my business team would be a win for the hotel."

She narrowed her eyes at him. "Keep it that way. As tough as my girl tries to pretend she is, she's not and . . ."

"What are you two whispering about?" Alicia asked.

"Nothing," Kandace said as she pulled out her phone. "I'm calling an Uber, I'm tired of walking."

"Such a privileged New Yorker," Alicia quipped. "You guys go ahead and take your Uber. I'm going to walk on."

"I'll keep you company," he said.

"You two be careful. This is still southwest Atlanta. Crime is down, but y'all look like tourists right now."

"See you in a few hours," Alicia said as a black car pulled up in front of her friend.

Richmond jogged over to the car to make sure the U symbol was visible. "All right, sister-in-law, text me when you make it to the hotel. I'm going to walk with Alicia. If that's all right with you."

"Funny. You just remember what I said. Don't play the rebound game with her. I know that you and . . ."

"Kandace, just let me know you made it back to

the hotel safely so that Solomon won't keep texting me about what you're doing."

"Is he really doing that?" She dug into her purse and pulled out her iPhone. "He should've come down here with me."

"And who was going to keep my beautiful niece?" he said with a smile.

"Adrian and Dana had volunteered. Richmond, remember, you two are just taking a friendly walk."

"Be safe, Kandace," he said as he closed the door. When Richmond turned around, he noticed that Alicia was standing inches behind him.

"That was a first," she said with a smile on her lips.

"What are you talking about?"

"Normally, my friends are trying to make me believe that every single man they know is the perfect guy for me." She laughed. "Richmond, do you know how many blind dates these women have tried to set me up on in the last six months? You just wait, you're going to get that same treatment from people now that you're single. I really want to jump in that car and kiss Kandace for not falling into the Jade and Serena trap."

He laughed, pretending that he didn't want to be one of the men sitting at a table across from her to be that blind date. "I guess your friends just want you to be happy."

She sucked her teeth. "People act as if single folks can't be happy alone."

"You're right. Now that I'm officially single, I'm starting to understand why my brother enjoyed those years of being a playboy."

"How long were you married?"

"Eight years. Vivian and I married right after college and . . ." Richmond stopped talking about why he married his ex. Everything started with a lie. He knew that now, but at the time he'd overlooked what everyone said Vivvy was, because he thought that he loved her and would have a marriage like his parents.

Too bad he hadn't known how big of a lie their marriage had been at the time. When Vivian said she was pregnant, Richmond knew he had to do the honorable thing and marry her. He thought, at the time, that he couldn't be the one to bring shame to the Crawford name. However, two months after their marriage, Vivian said she'd suffered a miscarriage. With their child gone, he'd had his way out, but he'd wanted to try again with his wife and have a child in wedlock, but it had never happened.

"Richmond? Are you all right?" Alicia asked, breaking into his thoughts.

"I'm fine, I was just thinking about where to break ground on our first hotel," he covered quickly.

"All right, but I think this isn't going to be the right place. And I can't believe you, of all people, are acting on emotion and not research."

"I've been doing business that way for a long time, and you know what? I'm about to try something new."

"What? Losing money?"

"No. Making business personal. I could come into this city as just another businessman looking to make a profit or I could become a part of the community and make a difference."

"That's a novel idea. But what happens if you

don't become a part of the community? After all, you're a New Yorker and things work differently in the South."

Richmond placed his arm around Alicia's shoulders and heated shivers rushed up and down her spine. What in the hell was happening? She eased closer to him, inhaling his masculine scent and feeling heady with desire. When his fingers brushed across her lips, Alicia smiled. "Richmond, what's going on here?"

"Just two people walking and talking about Atlanta. I'm new to the city and you know this place like the back of your hand, right?"

She sighed and told herself that she would buy his logic. They were simply walking and it was just her imagination that the warmth of his body wasn't turning her on like a light switch.

"What do you think of Atlanta so far?" she asked, needing to cut the tension between them. She inched out of his embrace and pointed to an old building. "That spot right there is where we originally wanted our first business. At the time, we had no idea what that business would be. After Devon and Kandace broke up, a restaurant wasn't in the cards."

"So, how did it happen? You ladies own one of the most successful restaurants in the Southeast and you're telling me that it wasn't your plan?"

Alicia grinned. "It all started with a newspaper article and humiliation."

"Huh?"

"Stephen Carter was dating Jade at the time and she was working as his bookkeeper. They seemed to be an Atlanta power couple, but he was going to marry someone else and planned to expand his restaurant into Charlotte."

"So, you all acted on emotion and not a business plan?" Richmond quipped as they crossed the street.

"If you want to say it like that, yes. But the principle behind all of that was that Jade deserved better and she'd invested in a man who treated her like crap. And look how it all turned out. Stephen is dead broke and our restaurant is everything he wished his could have been." She winked at him. "Never underestimate a woman with an investment plan."

"Let me make note of that," he replied.

"Things worked out for us for a number of reasons, but if we had to do it again, I'm sure we would do things a little differently."

"Or maybe the way you guys did your business is a new blueprint."

She tilted her head and looked up at him. "Really?"

"I'm not trying to have an experience like your friend Jade, but I'm looking to do things differently. Maybe we can work together on this," he said. "This project is really important to me and I'm looking to make sure this hotel will be one of the most successful in the Crawford chain."

"Means a lot to you, huh?"

Richmond nodded. "You have no idea. I'm definitely trying to make sure I'm surrounded by people who know how to be successful."

"As long as you know I don't work for free."

He stroked her forearm. "Now, you know I wouldn't insult you like that. I need a consultant, and since you're someone who knows this city, I want to hire you."

"Really?"

"How much of a businessman would I be if I didn't hire an insider?"

She smiled. "That's a good idea, and I'd be glad to help you."

"Thanks. Why don't we get together next week and have dinner? A business dinner," he said as he held his hands up. "You bring your contract and we'll go from there."

"All right. Where do you want to meet?"

"You know the city better than I do, so you tell me where and when." Richmond's smile made her heart skip a beat.

"Restaurant Eugene is a nice place, so I've heard. Keep in mind, it has been a while since I was a resident here. I don't want you to think that I have all the answers, but I do have most of them."

"Why are you coming back when you guys have such a great thing going in Charlotte?"

Alicia sighed. "I've never been the kind of person who wanted to take the easy route, and that's what Charlotte is starting to feel like. I know I'm good at what I do, but everything can't be this easy. I want to strike out on my own and see if I'm as good as I think I am."

"So, the lady likes a challenge?" Richmond smiled. "I should've had you by my side in New York this past year."

"Were things that bad?"

"Let's just say I missed the days when Solomon was tossing supermodels out of his bed and making Page Six every week."

Alicia folded her arms across her chest. "That's cruel."

"I didn't say I wanted him to go back to those days, but his headlines allowed me to stay in the shadows for a long time. Not a fan of that New York spotlight."

She nodded. "It can be hard, I'm sure. But you just jumped into another fishbowl. You're in reality-show central. Just wait until the right woman gets a look at you and finds out that you're *those* Crawfords, then it's going to be on."

"I doubt that's going to happen," he said. "From what I understand, Southern belles don't take too well to New Yorkers."

"Someone told you wrong," she said with a wink. "We'd better get back before they send a search party out here."

Richmond closed the space between him and Alicia. "You know, you're a beautiful woman and I can't believe I never noticed that before."

"Well, at least you're paying attention now." She flashed him a smile and walked a step ahead of him. "Make sure you get a good look."

Richmond laughed as he caught up with her. "You're funny, but it was a great look."

After they arrived at the hotel, Alicia saw that her friends were sitting in the hotel bar. "I guess they have questions," Richmond said with a wink. "I'm going to see if I can figure out the MARTA. See you later."

She almost leaned in and gave him a kiss on the cheek, but knowing she was being watched, Alicia decided against it.

"Well, well," Serena said as Alicia walked into the bar. "Looks as if you and Richmond were pretty cozy."

"That was about business, thank you very much."

"Keep it that way," Kandace said as she took a sip of her merlot. "I love my brother-in-law, but he is dealing with a lot right now and I don't want you caught in the crossfire."

Alicia raised her right eyebrow at her friend. "I'm a grown woman and I can handle myself. Besides, you guys know that I don't mix business with pleasure. Richmond and I are going to work together on the marketing for the new hotels; that makes him off limits. Besides, I'm going to show him around Atlanta, introduce him to some people who can help with finding the best locations for the hotels and whatnot."

Jade cleared her throat. "I said something like that once."

"You slept with that man in Las Vegas, so when we started doing business with him, you were already hooked." Alicia shook her head.

Jade rolled her eyes. "Whatever. I'm just saying, we all have eyes and saw the way you two were looking at each other."

"We were sharing a joke about MARTA. Now, can y'all stop seeing things that aren't there?"

"We just want to make sure that you aren't getting into something that's going to break your heart," Kandace said.

"I'm a big girl and I've been through worse, including blind dates at Jade's house."

Serena laughed and Alicia shot her an icy look. "And that coffee ambush the other week."

"It really was Jade's idea," Serena said.

"Don't throw me under the bus like that," Jade said. "Besides, we failed and she's ready to move back to Atlanta."

Alicia waved for the bartender. "Can we just enjoy the rest of this reunion weekend and stop worrying about my life?"

"Sure. Did you happen to see Felix Thompson?" Jade asked. "When you hightailed it out of the conference room, he was looking for you."

Alicia rolled her eyes. "He can keep looking, that asshole."

Kandace glanced at her friend. "What happened between the two of you that has you holding a grudge this long? Even Serena was nice to her former nemesis Yolanda Perkins. This is so unlike you."

"I don't want to talk about it or him." Alicia turned her attention to the bartender and ordered a vodka and pineapple juice.

"Fine, but if you see him tonight, please don't cause a scene," Jade said. "We can't get an award and then have you get arrested."

"I wouldn't give him the satisfaction." Alicia crossed her legs and thought about Felix Thompson, the man who ruined her senior year in college.

It had been her senior year at Spelman, and Felix, a Morehouse student, had been one of the most attractive guys in the Atlanta University Center.

He'd been a star basketball player and chemistry major.

Over the last two years, Alicia had been trying to downplay her attraction to Felix, with his curly black hair and caramel brown skin. She'd gotten a chance to get to know him when they'd worked together in a study group. His brilliance made her fall deeper for him. They had grown closer, and one night in the library, Felix asked her to come back to his room and watch a movie.

Everything in her screamed yes, but she'd said no. He smiled and she'd thought everything was fine. She was wrong. When he'd offered to walk her to her dorm, Felix had tried to kiss her. He'd been forceful as he'd pushed her against a tree. She kneed him in the crotch and pushed him to the ground. Alicia almost stomped him in the face; instead she ran to her dorm room and vowed to never tell anyone about what had happened.

She'd dropped out of the study group and for the first time in her scholastic career, Alicia made a C.

Because she knew her friends would've been livid, Alicia never told them about what happened with Felix. Now that he wanted to talk to her? He could really drop dead.

"Are you going to have a drink with him? He's still fine," Jade said.

Alicia rolled her eyes. "I'm good with that."

"But you used to have a huge crush on him, if I remember," Serena said as she reached for her drink. "Whatever happened with that?"

"There was nothing ever going on with us and . . . Just know that I don't want to talk to or about him." Alicia rolled her eyes and took a big gulp of her drink.

The ladies exchanged confused looks. "Doesn't sound like nothing to me," Jade said as she stroked her growing baby bump. "Maybe this could be your second chance and . . ."

"Leave it alone," Alicia said, then rolled her eyes. Her mind went back to the next time she'd seen him.

"Alicia, can we talk?"

"No." She kept walking, but he caught up with her and grabbed her elbow. She snatched away from him and prayed someone else would walk through the quad.

"About the other week . . ."

"When you tried to assault me?"

"Girl, please, you know that it wasn't even like that. I need you to not tell anyone about it. I'm already on probation and I don't want to—"

She hauled off and slapped him. "You son of a bitch. Don't you dare stand there and ask me not to tell people that you're a sexual predator!"

"I'm thinking about you. No one would believe your story. It's not as if you're Serena; no one is beating down your door. People are going to think you came on to me and I said no. It's going to look like sour grapes."

"Go to hell, you piece of shit." Damn him for tapping into her insecurities when she was the victim. Alicia knew that people looked at her differently than her best friends, in image-conscious Atlanta. She'd heard all of the You're pretty for a dark-skin girl *comments, and she was sick*

of it. But for this bastard to wrap his assault in colorism was the lowest blow she'd ever received.

She gave him a sardonic grin. "You're right, I'm not Serena." Alicia kicked him in the groin and as he fell to the ground, she delivered a blow to his face. "And I'm guessing you're not going to tell anyone where you got this black eye from either!" She stomped away and vowed that if she saw him again, she'd give him another black eye.

Alicia never reported the assault, but Felix never approached her again either. He'd made comments about her to his friends, though. That became clear one night when Alicia sat in the library, studying for finals, when Keith Brown sat down across from her.

"What's up, brown sugar?"

Alicia looked up from her books. "What do you want?"

"A taste of you. Felix said you got that fire." He winked at her and licked his lips.

Alicia slammed her book shut. "If you don't get out of my face, I'm going to slip this pencil through your eye."

"Hold up, babe," he said as he threw his hands up. "I didn't mean any harm, but I love me some dark chocolate."

Alicia tossed a pencil at his head. "Go drink a bleach cocktail. Better yet, go get some from Felix. He's had a crush on you for years." Packing her things, Alicia headed to her dorm room and slammed the door behind her. She was pissed and ready to knock Felix out. But Serena walked into the room and started talking about how she was so over finals. They spent the rest of the night drinking tequila and counting down the days to graduation.

Alicia finished her drink, then rose to her feet. "I'm going to freshen up and get ready for this event tonight." She sighed and thought about facing the demons that she'd kept hidden for so long.

As she walked away, she heard Kandace ask, "Is everything all right with Alicia?"

Chapter 3

Richmond flipped the channels on the TV in his bedroom, hoping to fill his mind with something other than Alicia Michaels. Nothing was working, not even his favorite pundit on CNN. All he could think about was his walk with Alicia.

Make sure you get a good look.

Sassy and classy. She's the kind of woman who made men stand up and take notice, and Richmond was definitely on notice. Rising from the bed, he crossed over to the closet and pulled out his tuxedo. He was going to attend the AUC gala because he wanted to meet some of the movers and shakers in the city. Seeing Alicia again was going to be the icing on the cake.

He hoped she wore something strapless.

Richmond was about to make a quick meal when his cell phone rang.

"What's up, Solomon?" Richmond asked when he answered.

"Nothing much. Just wondering how things are going in Atlanta."

"How things are going, or how Kandace is doing?" Richmond chuckled. "Your wife and her friends are some badass women. It's amazing what they did as college students and how they got started in their business."

"Nice, but are there any exes lurking around my wife?"

"Get over yourself. There are a lot of people who are in awe of your wife and her friends. And I think folks are a little scared of your wife."

"They should be. Anyway, what's going on with the business plan? Adrian and I were wondering if we should add a club to the hotel since Atlanta is a hub for entertainment."

"Let's get the hotel up and running first. But that is a great idea. They do like to party and eat around here." Richmond laughed as he thought about dancing with Alicia tonight. Because he was going to dance with her and hold her real close.

Richmond couldn't understand why everyone thought he and Alicia would be such a terrible idea. All he wanted was to get to know the beauty, and the city of Atlanta. She knew her way around and Richmond knew he was going to need some assistance making headway in a town that didn't, according to what he'd heard, take kindly to strangers. But if they were going to be in business together, he would have to tamp down his want for her.

He had to admit, though, he liked being a stranger. Since he'd been in Atlanta, no one had mentioned Elliot Crawford, the man who he thought was his father, Adrian Bryant, Elliot's secret son, or even Solomon. Richmond felt revitalized and ready to take on the world. Richmond felt as if he could do anything in Atlanta once he made the right connections.

It was a new venture for him that would allow him to create a legacy for himself that wouldn't be tarnished by the lies his family created. He'd be able to remake his image and make some money at the same time. Smiling, he realized this would be the first project that he and Solomon would have created without the influence of Elliot. Failure was not an option.

Turning his attention back to his brother, who had been going on and on about the Pamela Bryant project—named for Adrian's mother—that he and Adrian were heading up in Los Angeles for single mothers looking to go back to school, Richmond realized he needed to get off the phone if he was going to make it back to midtown in time for the gala.

"Hey, I have to get off the phone and get ready for this gala," Richmond said. "And for the record, I'm not going to the grand opening of whatever y'all are doing in LA."

"Did you just say *y'all*?" Solomon chuckled. "You haven't been down there long enough to be talking like a Southerner."

"Whatever. Saying *y'all* is the best way to make friends down here. You already know that, being that you slip in and out of Southern drawl all the time."

"Blame my wife. You're just trying to make Southern women fall for the new Richmond Crawford."

Richmond smiled, thinking there was only one woman he'd actively try to impress, but now wasn't the time to pour on the charm. "Whatever. My mind is on business right now. I'm going to get ready for the gala and I won't tell your wife that you're checking up on her."

"For the record, Kiana was asking about her mother and her uncle. That's why I called."

"I hear that lie and I don't believe it at all. I'll send you my market report in the morning, and do me a favor: Don't call me until after eleven."

Solomon chuckled. "Got it. You're going to kick her out around ten."

"Everyone isn't a player like you used to be. Get your mind out of the gutter."

"Former player. I'm just trying to see how the game is played these days."

Richmond laughed, thinking how the tables had turned. Solomon was the happily married man, and he was the single one who could have any woman he wanted. But the only woman who'd caught his eye was Alicia.

"I'm not even getting involved in games."

"I'll talk to you later. I need to get a quick bite to eat before I head out."

After hanging up with Solomon, Richmond ate a quick dinner, then showered and dressed. He was kind of wishing that he had stayed in the city for the weekend. It would've given him a chance to see how hospitality worked in Atlanta and what he could do to make the Crawford hotel stand out. There was always next weekend. Since food was such a part of the landscape in Atlanta, he had to make sure the Crawford hotels had the best. Maybe

Alicia had some other famous chef friends. Shaking his head, Richmond knew that he was just making excuses to find reasons to get closer to this woman. It could be so simple for him to hire a headhunter and find a chef. He didn't need Alicia—he simply wanted her.

But how was he going to make that happen when he couldn't understand what was happening between them? Was there an attraction there or was it in his head?

"I need to focus on my business," he muttered as he stripped out of his clothes and headed to the shower.

Once he was dressed and ready to head to the gala, Richmond headed out the door, got into his waiting Uber and started toward the Georgia World Congress Center. He wondered if he was making a fool of himself, going to this gala. The main reason he was going was to see Alicia again. Of course, hobnobbing with the cream of the crop in Atlanta was a good idea, but how much business would he get done tonight, when no one even knew him? Yet.

Supposing the evening didn't go as planned and Alicia ended up reconnecting with some ex from college? This wasn't supposed to be about romance, but there was something about Alicia's smile and her sexy walk that had awakened something in him that he thought was dead. Not even when he'd first fallen in with Vivian had he felt this way. Something about Alicia was different, and he wanted to see if it was everything that it was cracked up to be.

However, he knew there would be hell in his family if things didn't work out between them.

This isn't about me and Alicia. I need a footprint in the city of Atlanta and she can provide that for me, he thought as he smoothed Burt's Bees lip balm across his lips. *Besides, that woman is here to enjoy her reunion, and I'm starting a new business. We're not looking for anything else.*

Alicia couldn't wait for the moment when the dog and pony show was over. She and her friends had shaken hands with the same people who'd said they'd never amount to anything other than be someone's wife or mistress. And while her friends had made the marriage part come true, it seemed as if people had been overlooking her accomplishments as a businesswoman. Alicia grabbed a champagne flute from a passing server and glanced out into the crowd. College had been fun for her only because of her friends and the things that they did together.

"Alicia," a deep voice said from behind her. Whirling around, she stared into the face of the man she'd hoped to avoid for the rest of the night.

"Felix." She took a step back from him, not out of fear but from loathing.

"You look really good." He reached out to touch her elbow and she took another step back from him.

"What do you want?" Her words were terse and low.

"Just wanted to say hi. I was hoping that I'd see you this weekend."

She folded her arms across her chest. "Why?"

"Because I owe you an apology for what happened all of those years ago."

"Apology noted. Excuse me." She took a step and he reached out and grabbed her arm. Alicia gasped. "Please don't touch me."

"Girl, are you still holding on to—"

"Fuck you then and fuck you now," she snapped.

"Maybe that's the problem, we never had a chance to do that." Felix licked his lips. "That night could've happened differently then, and tonight we could—"

"Are you kidding me? Are you seriously kidding me right now?" Alicia gritted her teeth and thought about slapping him, but the last thing she wanted was to cause a scene. That's why she'd never reported the assault in college. Now this bastard wanted to make light of the situation—just like he did when they were in school. *Just breathe,* she thought as she turned to walk away from him.

"Dark skin is in now, so you could definitely get it now without any issues." He winked at her, then gave her a soft pat on the bottom. She turned around and glared at him—her eyes blazing with years of anger.

"If you don't get away from me, you slimy bastard," she muttered as she glanced around the room. Everyone seemed oblivious to the hell she was going through right now.

"I said I was sorry, what more do you want from me?" He ran his index finger down her cheek and Alicia quivered. His touch made her ill; the memory of that night flooded her brain and made her body freeze.

"Alicia," a voice said from behind her and a warm hand on the small of her back brought her to the present. "This dance is mine, right?"

Turning around, she gave Richmond a coy smile. "Of course."

Felix snorted. "Nobody wants this black bitch anyway."

Shaking her head, Alicia was ready to head to the middle of the dance floor with Richmond, but he stopped and squared up with Felix and punched him in the face. Alicia gasped but was relieved to see that bastard fall to the floor.

Then Richmond drew her close. "I believe you said this dance was mine." Sade's soulful voice filled the air as they made it to the middle of the floor and swayed together. His lips brushed against her ear as their bodies merged together. He spun her around and Alicia looked into his eyes and whispered, "Thank you," as the song ended.

He nodded and brought his face close to hers. She could feel the heat of his breath against her lips, and his hands still on her back made her feel comforted.

"Let's get a drink outside on the patio. It's a little hectic in here," he said as he watched two men lead Felix out the back.

"Good idea," she replied, her body trembling slightly as they walked. Richmond took her hand in his and brought it to his lips.

Alicia closed her eyes and let him lead her to the bar.

Richmond knew something wasn't right with Alicia, but he didn't want to add to her discomfort.

Handing her a scotch neat, he smiled. "Scotch always cures what's bothering you."

"Or gives you a hell of a hangover." Alicia took a slow sip. "Have you had a good time so far?"

He shrugged his shoulders. "I'm just getting here. Everything looks nice. Seems as if these colleges and universities are very important in the social structure."

She nodded as they leaned against the bar. Alicia pointed her glass toward a tall man talking to a group of young alumni. "That's city councilman Lawrence Moore. He's one of the most influential men in city government. There's some talk of him launching a mayoral campaign, but the current mayor is really popular with the people."

"What makes him so special?" Richmond gave Alicia a slow once-over. She was acting as if nothing had happened in the ballroom.

"He knows the right people and doesn't abuse his power. Can't ask for anything more than that." She set her glass on the bar. "I'm pretty sure you want to . . ."

Richmond shook his head just as Kandace and Jade walked over to her. "What in the world is going on?" Jade asked.

Kandace looked from Richmond to Alicia, but didn't say a word. Alicia shrugged at her friends and gripped her glass. "I have no idea what you're talking about."

"Then maybe Richmond can tell us why he knocked out a complete stranger tonight," Kandace said.

"Because he was being disrespectful and I snapped.

Did I do something wrong? Had any of you ladies been in the same situation, I would've done the same thing."

Alicia released a tense breath because she knew her friends wouldn't be in the same situation. Seeing Felix unlocked some emotions that she'd kept hidden for several years. Seeing him just made it come back in ways that scared her. She hoped that she wouldn't have to see that son of a bitch again.

Richmond stroked her arm. "What are you ladies doing for dinner, because I know whatever they're going to serve here isn't going to be as good as Busy Bee Café."

Alicia nodded. "That's a good idea. Rubber chicken isn't what I consider a good meal."

"What about our award?" Jade asked.

"I don't have to be here," Alicia said as Richmond took her hand in his. "We'll link up later at the hotel and y'all can tell me all about it."

Kandace and Jade exchanged confused looks. "Can we have a second before you leave?" Kandace asked.

"Not right now," Alicia said. "I can't do this."

"What's going on?" Jade asked.

"Nothing, I'm just over this. See you later." Alicia allowed Richmond to usher her out of the patio area without looking back at her friends.

Once they were alone on the sidewalk, Richmond rocked back on his heels. "What do you feel like eating for dinner?"

"I don't have much of an appetite for real food, but a chili dog from the Varsity would be awesome."

"What's the Varsity?"

Alicia smiled. "You're really going to have to learn more about Atlanta if you want people to take you seriously. The Varsity is like one of the most iconic restaurants in Atlanta. And I have to introduce you to Southern hot dogs."

"What's the difference?"

"You'll see." Alicia sighed and felt her heartbeat calm down. "Richmond, have you started your marketing research yet?"

"Yes. Actually, I have a copy of the report saved in the cloud and . . . We're not doing this tonight. Let's just eat the hot dogs."

"Sounds like a plan. I'd be happy to look over it with you."

"Great idea, because I can admit that I will need some help learning this city. Should we take Uber or walk?"

"We could walk if I weren't wearing these shoes." She held her foot out and showed off her four-inch heels. Looking at her shapely leg, Richmond couldn't help but wonder again what they would feel like wrapped around his waist.

She placed her hand on his wrist. "I'm going to order an Uber."

"Cool," he said.

About fifteen minutes later, a black car came to pick them up. Richmond opened the door for Alicia and she slid into the car. The scent of her perfume filled his nostrils and his want for her rose like yeast.

"What's that scent you're wearing?" he asked as he closed the door.

"Jasmine oil."

"Smells amazing," he said. "Can I ask you a question?"

"You can ask, but I might not answer."

"That guy back there. What was that all about?"

Alicia rolled her eyes. "Just some unresolved college issues. And I don't want to talk about it."

"That's fine. If you ever need my hands again, know that I'm here for you."

She offered him a smirk. "That's good to know. I hope you don't think that I'm some drama queen and this is how I roll in business and life."

"I have no room to judge anyone after all that I've been through. Things happen and you can start over or let it consume you."

"Is that why you're in Atlanta?"

Richmond shrugged. "Being here is more about me blazing a path of my own. I'm sure you've read about it in the papers—my whole life was a lie."

"You don't have to get into it if you don't want to. We're just going to have hot dogs. We can save the commiserating for another day."

"So, that means we're going to see each other again—outside of a business office?"

Alicia's cheeks heated. "I guess we can make that happen."

He wanted to kiss her as much as he wanted to take his next breath. And though he tried to stop himself, Richmond stroked her smooth cheek. "You are so beautiful."

"Richmond, you—"

"Guys, we have made it to the Varsity," the driver said.

Alicia looked into his eyes. "Guess that's our cue to get out."

Richmond exited the car, then held the door for Alicia. "All right, let's see how these iconic hot dogs compare to the dogs from New York."

Chapter 4

It was official, Richmond decided as he pushed his half-eaten hot dog into the middle of the table. Southerners ruined a good dog with that damned coleslaw.

"What's wrong?" Alicia asked before taking a bite of her hot dog.

"Southerners really know how to mess up a hot dog. Sauerkraut, not coleslaw, belongs on hot dogs. Mustard and ketchup and that's it."

She laughed and took another bite of her hot dog, which was filled with cheese, chili, coleslaw, and ketchup. "You, my friend, have been missing out."

"No, you don't know the truth about what a hot dog should taste like. The fries are great, though."

"Maybe you should order a burger. Because if you leave here hungry, then I have failed at my job."

"Then I will get a burger and some more fries."

She nodded and watched him walk up to the counter. Alicia sighed and sipped her milkshake. Being with Richmond over these last few hours had been so calming. She hadn't expected to be so affected by seeing Felix again. His voice and the arrogance of him thinking that she would ever allow him to touch her. What a fucking moron. She slammed her empty glass on the table.

"You're all right?" Richmond asked.

"Yes, I think I need another milkshake. It's been a while since I've had this kind of late dinner."

He nodded, but Richmond wondered if there was more going on. "Vanilla, right?" He set his burger and fries on the table.

"I got this. As a matter of fact, I'll get you one so that you can get the taste of coleslaw out of your mouth," she said as she rose to her feet. Richmond smiled as he watched Alicia sashay to the counter. They stood out like a pair of stylish sore thumbs. Richmond smiled as she crossed the room looking like a model. He figured that she would sell thousands of milkshakes if anyone saw her on a poster holding that milkshake with a smile on her face. Though he knew it was common knowledge that Elliot Crawford was not his biological father, and that Richmond had been arrested in Los Angeles—though the details of his arrest hadn't been exposed, he wanted to talk to Alicia about all of that. He knew he could trust her and he wanted her to feel that comfortable with him.

"Here you go," she said as she set the creamy concoction in front of him. "I had the whipped cream added because everything is better with whipped cream on top."

Richmond's mouth fell open as he imagined whipped cream covering her chocolate breasts. He took a big sip of his milkshake, but the fire that was burning inside him couldn't be extinguished. He wanted Alicia, badly.

"What's that look?" Alicia asked when their eyes locked.

"Just thinking that we must look pretty ridiculous right now." He looked around at the crowd, most of the customers dressed in shorts, tank tops, and sneakers. Richmond noticed the strange looks they'd received. Especially the looks that Alicia got. She was beyond beautiful in that dress. But he knew a place where he'd like to see that frock—on the floor beside his bed.

"Richmond? Did you hear me?"

"I'm sorry, what?"

"Are you ready to go? I just called a car for us."

"I was going to do that."

"Well, I just jumped the gun because I want to see your house. If you don't mind having a little company tonight."

Richmond shrugged. "There's really not much to see there. One room is furnished and . . ."

"You know, in Atlanta, your house is your calling card, and since you're in the hospitality industry, your home has to be magical. I can help you with that. Get your face out there and make people remember your name."

Richmond folded his arms across his chest. "What does my house have to do with the hotels?"

"Because people are going to want to get to know you. And by knowing you, that means getting inside your home. It's an image thing. Think of it like this: If people are going to spend money for your luxurious hotels, they're going to want to see how you're living."

Richmond frowned. "I guess this is the part of building my brand that I didn't consider in the marketing aspect of everything. I've had enough about letting the world into my life."

"That's why you control the narrative and I have a friend who can help. Like get you on the cover of *Atlanta Scene Magazine.*" Alicia rubbed her hands together. "And Dunwoody is the new hip spot in Atlanta, so let me see this house."

"All right, let's do it." They headed outside to wait for the car and Richmond placed his hand on the small of Alicia's back. It seemed as if his hand belonged there, as if holding this woman was what he was meant to do. Even though it felt so right, nothing good could come from this. Not when he needed her to help him take over the city of Atlanta. He'd seen firsthand how mixing business and pleasure blew up in Solomon's face, and he couldn't make that same mistake. Still, it felt so good to have this woman in his arms.

Alicia melted into his embrace, felt the heat coming from his hand as they stood there. She leaned her head on his shoulder. A feeling of calm rushed through her and Alicia was shocked. This made absolutely no sense. She wasn't that weak-willed woman who thought a man with a strong right hook was the cat's meow. She always prided herself on being able to handle herself without the assistance of a man. So, why was Richmond different? Was this a reaction to months without having any interaction with a man? She took a deep breath and tried to shut her mind off.

As the black car pulled up, Richmond crossed over to the passenger side and opened the door for Alicia. "M'lady," he said in a horrible British accent.

"Ooh, don't do that again," she quipped as she slipped into the car. Richmond followed and eased close to her. He stroked her cheek and brought his lips down on top of hers in a slow and gentle kiss.

"As long as I can do that again, I'll stop."

Blinking, she looked up at him and sighed. "We'd better get going."

"Right. But you should answer my question. Will I get to kiss you again?"

She stroked her chin and smiled at him. "All I'm going to say is maybe."

He wrapped his arms around Alicia's shoulders as the car started. She leaned against him and closed her eyes. She was tired, but excited to see what Richmond was working with in the burbs.

As they cruised along, the car hit a pothole, jostling Alicia and Richmond. He wrapped his arms around her and she made no move to break out of his embrace.

The car stopped and Alicia looked up at the colonial house with wide-eyed wonderment. First she was captivated by the ivory columns, then the redbrick porch made her think of the charming Old South, where debutants were photographed with parasols and beaus holding their hands.

"This is beautiful," she said as she stepped out of the car. Though it was dark, she could tell the lawn was manicured, as a great Southern lawn should be.

As she walked up the steps, her shoe slipped from her left foot. Richmond picked up the shoe and smiled.

"I see you, Cinderella," he said as he held the shoe out to her.

"Sorry about that," she said as she took her golden sandal from his hands. "Richmond, this place is magical." Alicia spun around in the empty foyer. "We can get you styled and up and running in no time. How did you find this place?"

He shrugged. "I just wrote a check."

"Must be nice," she said as she walked into the empty living room. Her eyes went straight to the crystal chandelier above her head. "Turn this on."

Richmond flipped the switch and the room was bathed in a golden light that sparkled.

"You're going to have to take your picture in this light."

"I guess I can do that," he said with a smile. Richmond wrapped his arms around her waist and spun her around. "Next you're going to tell me that I should have a party here."

"Oh, you can read my mind now. It's a good idea, though." He dipped her and they locked eyes as if they had heard a song of their own. She felt like a cartoon princess as he held her.

"Well. I guess I should get the full tour," she said as they broke their embrace. "You took ballroom dancing lessons, huh?"

"You know it was a thing for a while. Vivian and I did it because everyone else was. She didn't realize that we were actually going to have to touch each other." Richmond laughed, then took Alicia's hand in his. "All right. I did furnish my bedroom."

"Typical," she quipped as they reached the top of the spiral staircase. "This place is beautiful, though. Can't believe you haven't had it decorated yet."

"I had no idea that I was going to have to share the ins and outs of my house with the city of Atlanta in order to do business."

"You don't have to, but you keep forgetting that you're the Yankee in this situation. A little honey and Southern hospitality never hurt anybody."

"Catching more flies with honey has never been my style," he said. Richmond opened the door to his bedroom. Alicia immediately thought of candles, rose petals, and satin sheets. Then it was as if she felt his hands wrapped around her body, peeling her clothes off and touching her body in all the right places.

"Is it that bad?" Richmond asked, his lips against her ear.

"What?"

"You haven't said a word."

Facing him, she grinned. "Nice room. And this carpet." Alicia took her shoes off. "So soft." Crossing over to the window, she looked out on the velvet-black night. "I bet the sunlight coming through these windows is all the alarm clock you need."

"Nah, I have blackout shades," he said with a smirk.

"What a waste of a view."

Not from where I'm standing, he thought as he gave Alicia a slow once-over. Her silhouette in the moonlight was nothing short of perfection. That was a view he wouldn't mind waking up to every morning. Feeling a bulge in his slacks, Richmond realized that he needed to get his hormones under control.

"I have a bottle of merlot in the wine cellar. Want a glass?"

"That sounds amazing. I'm guessing your wine collection is legendary."

He winked at her. "If I have to toot my own horn, it is. Want to see the wine cellar? The Realtor turned me on to this great wine shop, Perrine's. Gave me a chance to amp up what I brought from New York."

"Sure," she said, then reached for her shoes. Richmond stopped her.

"You don't need them." He stopped himself from scooping her up in his arms. But Richmond wanted to feel her body pressed against his and kiss her again. She'd awakened something in him that had been dormant for too long.

He couldn't even remember if he'd felt that way about Vivian in the early days of their courtship. Actually he could remember—he'd never felt this way about a woman in his life. The yearning, the want, and the need for Alicia Michaels was overwhelming.

"Watch your footing," he said as they walked down to the cellar. "The last thing I need is to have to explain to your girls how you fell down the stairs."

Alicia glanced at her watch. "There's going to be a lot of questions when I get back to the hotel."

"The right answer is always *I don't know.*" He flipped the light on in the cellar. "When I found out this was a part of the house, I knew I had to have it."

"I thought you just wrote a check."

"Yeah, when I found out about the wine cellar." He laughed and took her hand in his. "Now, to find that amazing bottle of merlot."

Alicia glanced around the cellar and nodded as she drank in the brick and oak walls. The soft lights gave the room a warm glow. "If you had some cheese and grapes, you could live down here."

"That's not creepy at all," he quipped. "Ah. Found it, Albertoni merlot. One of my favorite California brands."

Alicia took the bottle from his hands and read the awards. "I'm impressed."

Richmond grabbed two wineglasses and a corkscrew. He led Alicia over to a settee in the corner, then took the bottle from her hands. Richmond made short work of opening the wine and poured a small amount in her glass. She sniffed it, then sipped the wine.

"This is delicious," she moaned.

Richmond filled their glasses with the merlot and smiled. "Here's to the start of a beautiful relationship."

She clanked her glass against his. "*Salut.*"

They sat in the cellar and drank the merlot and cabernet sauvignon. Richmond and Alicia fell into a comfortable conversation about Atlanta, decorating, and his hardwood floors.

Glancing at her watch, Alicia pushed her empty glass aside. "It's getting late."

"You know what they say about time and having fun."

Rising to her feet, Alicia was a bit wobbly and stumbled into Richmond's arms. Their lips were inches apart. "I guess I should go."

"It's late. Maybe you should stay and go back to the hotel in the morning," Richmond said.

Alicia's knees quivered. If she spent another moment with this man, they would wake up with regrets. Pressing her hand against his chest, she sighed. "I'd better go."

"Let me call a car for you. The last thing I need to do is introduce myself to Atlanta with a mug shot. But I'd love to pick you up for brunch tomorrow and we can tour the big peach."

She ran her thumb across his bottom lip. "Just so you know, no one calls Atlanta the big peach."

Richmond leaned in to her mouth and kissed her slow. Deep. Hard. Their tongues tangoed as if there was a symphony playing for their passion. Pulling her closer, Richmond felt their hearts beating in sync and he wanted to slip her out of that gold dress and make love to her right then and there.

Be responsible. This is not the time. He broke the kiss and focused on her kiss-swollen lips. "Yeah, we'd better stop before . . ."

"Things get out of hand," she finished. Alicia pushed out of his embrace, thinking about how good his hardness felt against her thighs and how one more kiss would've melted her dress from her body. "West Egg."

"What?"

"That's where we're going to have brunch. You're going to like it better than slaw on hot dogs."

"You'd better be right," he said with a wink, then headed for the stairs. "If not, I'm not going to share my '86 Malbec, from France."

"Trust me, you're going to want to share," she said with a wink.

Chapter 5

It was after two when Alicia made it back to the hotel, and if she thought she was going to avoid questions from her friends, it was clear that she was wrong when she walked into her suite and they were sitting there.

"Why aren't you people sleeping?" she asked as she kicked her shoes off. "And how did y'all get in here?"

"Where have you been all night?" Jade asked as she glanced at her watch.

"More importantly, who were you with all night?" Serena asked.

"And why did Richmond go all Apollo Creed at the gala?" Kandace asked as she walked over to the coffeemaker and poured herself a cup of coffee.

"It's late and I'd like to go to bed," Alicia said with a sigh. "So, you all can return to your corners and leave me alone. I have a meeting in the morning."

"A meeting?" Serena asked. "With?"

Alicia leaned against the dresser and tilted her head at her friends. "When did I get three mamas?

I know y'all mean well, but the last time I checked, I'm grown."

"Let me say this and then I'm done," Kandace said. "Richmond is freshly divorced, so tread lightly. He's going to spread his wings and see what's out there and—"

"Hold up," Alicia said. "Why are you assuming that Richmond and I have anything more than business going on between us?"

Jade laughed. "Because we all have eyes. Alicia, you lit up when that man walked in the room, and you'd been in a foul mood all night."

"I'm sorry, I didn't want to be there—like I'd told you all in Charlotte."

"But this was our night to thumb our noses at those assholes who underestimated us and thought we were just a bunch of silly girls," Serena said with a smile. "I got quite a thrill when Marvin Roland walked in looking like he ate his former self and the girl he'd cheated on me with."

"I'm not petty like that. I couldn't care less what these people think about me. Didn't give a damn in college and I have lost all the—"

"Then what was that all about with Felix?" Jade asked as she folded her legs underneath her.

"Don't you all have your own rooms to sleep in?" Alicia faked a yawn. "Again, I'm tired."

"Oh no, this is probably one of the last times that we're going to be together and carefree, so slumber party. And that was the fakest yawn ever."

Kandace laughed. "Just like that time she tried to kick us out of her room because Bobby Venton was coming to her room to study."

Alicia chuckled at the memory as well. "He was supposed to be the one," she said as she crossed over to the coffeemaker and poured herself a cup. "We were going to get it in that night, and he saw Serena. I think you took his erection away."

"I don't know why that grown little man was scared of me."

All of the women focused their stare on her. "Really?" Alicia asked. "You made his brother jump out of a window because you chased him with an ice pick."

"He was in my room kissing that girl from Jade's study group. He's lucky the ice pick was the only thing I could get my hands on."

"Why did you have an ice pick in your room anyway?" Alicia asked.

Serena shrugged. "There was a movie that I saw where the lead actress used it to crush ice. It was cute."

Jade shook her head. "And if you ask me, that was the night the Ice Queen was born."

"You ever tell Antonio about that?" Alicia asked, then took a sip of her coffee.

"I didn't, and if anyone in this room tells my husband about my misdeeds as a youth, I will do more than chase you with an ice pick."

"Man, had I threatened you with that a long time ago, I probably could've enlisted your help in stopping Jade's matchmaking," Alicia said.

Jade shook her head. "It was networking!"

"Please," Serena said. "You were really bad at it because your dinner parties were a joke. Even

Antonio knew you were trying to hook Alicia up when we'd get an invite."

"I missed so much while I was in New York," Kandace quipped.

"Every week," Alicia said as she started another pot of coffee. "Every damn week."

Jade rolled her eyes. "So, I'm wrong because I wanted to introduce Alicia to a nice guy? Oh, and I know what happened with punk-ass Tyson Jordan."

Serena nodded. "Yeah, that was a punk move on his part. I can't believe he was married and tried to play you."

"How long have y'all known about that?" Alicia asked. She'd been too embarrassed to tell her best friends about Tyson. But Charlotte wasn't a place where secrets stayed buried for long.

Kandace raised her hand as if she was sitting in a lecture hall. "Who is Tyson Jordan?"

"No one important," Alicia replied with an eye roll. "As a matter of fact, he's all the proof you need that I'm not some vapid broad looking to jump into a relationship with anyone. And that includes Richmond Crawford."

"I hope you're right," Kandace said.

"But what's so wrong with Richmond?" Alicia asked, trying to be nonchalant.

Kandace raised her eyebrow at her friend. "Nothing is really wrong with him, but you would be opening yourself up to so much drama. I really don't think Vivian is going to quietly fade away when she realizes that her name is mud in New York. You know Solomon has put the word out that Vivian isn't a part of the family anymore."

Alicia laughed. "You make it sound as if the Crawfords are some medieval royal family that runs New York."

"No, but they're rich, and that name opens a lot of doors. Trust-me, Kandace Crawford gets a lot more in New York than Kandace Davis. Sometimes to avoid the hoopla, I will make reservations under my maiden name. And with the whole thing following Elliot's death and the scandal in Los Angeles, it's too much."

"Is that why Richmond came to Atlanta? And what happened in LA?"

Kandace nodded. "And I believe he's just hiding out until things die down. Once things blow over, what do you think he's going to do? Head back to New York and get back on his throne. That's why I'm not for you getting involved with him. But, you know Elliot had another family on the West Coast. Adrian, his son, hated everything Crawford. Let's see, he set Richmond up with a hooker."

"What?" Jade exclaimed. "That's what those charges were?"

Kandace nodded. "Then he tried to start some kind of drama with Solomon and his ex, Heather-I-can't-act-my-way-out-of-a-paper bag."

Serena hissed at Kandace. "That's the girl I know and love."

Shooting her friend a cold look, Kandace turned her attention back to Alicia. "I know Richmond is a good guy, but this project has a lot to do with his bruised ego and it's not going to be long before he leaves Atlanta to go back to New York."

"I can handle it," she said. "If I was interested in

more than a friendship with Richmond, then all of this would be important. However, he's the biggest client in my portfolio right now. I'm doing my job."

Kandace, Jade, and Serena exchanged knowing looks. "Sounds like someone may be trying to fool herself," Jade muttered.

"Whatever," Alicia said as she folded her arms across her chest. "I'm not trying to be with Richmond Crawford. But he is giving me some prime office space until I get my own."

"And what are you giving him in return?" Serena asked, then wiggled her eyebrows.

"You're such a jerk," Alicia said. "Richmond and I are going to be working together and I'm going to introduce him around the city. Besides, having him as a client with this huge project coming down the pipe is going to raise my profile as well."

"Whatever you need to tell yourself to pretend you're not getting in deep," Jade said as she raised her arms above her head.

"Since we're going to be up all night, we might as well go to the Waffle House," Kandace said. "I'm hungry and the food at the gala was not good."

"Who's sober enough to drive?" Alicia asked. All eyes turned to Jade.

"Y'all make me sick. Let's go."

Feeling as if they were coeds again, the four women headed out to Jade's car and drove to the restaurant.

Richmond reached for her, wanted to kiss her good morning after the amazing night they'd had together. But he grabbed an armful of pillows and realized that he'd dreamed of making love to Alicia. Glancing at his alarm clock, he realized that he was going to be late for brunch if he kept lying in bed, dreaming about Alicia. He climbed out of bed and hopped in the shower.

After dressing in a pair of dark jeans and T-shirt, Richmond headed to his car and typed in the address for West Egg, the café that Alicia swore he was going to love. Even if the food didn't live up to the hype, he'd enjoy spending the morning with Alicia.

What was it about that woman that made him so excited, and how had he missed this beauty all of these years? Even when things had gone bad with him and Vivian, he tried to honor his vows even though there were rumors that Vivian had lovers all over New York.

Part of him didn't mind, he'd just wanted to keep his life as normal as possible after Elliot's sins came to the surface. If that meant indulging Vivian's affairs, he'd been willing to do that. For a while at least.

But seeing the real love that his brothers had with their wives, Richmond knew he deserved more than the loveless marriage he'd settled for. Vivian made it clear that she wasn't in their marriage for love, and when the news of Richmond's paternity broke, she made it clearer that she wasn't sticking around. There was something about Alicia that made Richmond realize that he could and should take his chance at love. Settling would no longer be a part of his life. And maybe nothing would happen between them, but Richmond was going to have fun exploring the possibilities.

The business side of his brain knew that he needed to focus on getting the construction and marketing for the hotel off the ground. He had to make this venture successful, and Alicia was key to that. He couldn't allow his hormones to mess things up before they'd even gotten started.

When he arrived at the restaurant, Richmond had to drive around for fifteen minutes to find a parking spot. Then when he headed for the entrance of the restaurant, the line was out the door.

"This place must be good," he muttered as he glanced around the sea of humanity, looking for Alicia. When he spotted her sitting on a bench reading the local paper, he smiled and crossed over to her. "I guess it's a good thing that I didn't bet you about how good this place is."

Her head snapped up and she greeted Richmond with a dazzling smile. "Glad you made it." She rose to her feet and gave him a tight hug. He inhaled her sweet scent and didn't want to let her go.

"Parking around here is crazy," he said.

"Sorry, I should've warned you. I put our names on the waiting list for a table." She glanced down at her watch. "We have another twenty minutes to wait."

"Want to take a walk? This area looks really interesting," he said. "I'm all about exploring today."

Alicia nodded. "The neighborhood has changed a lot since I was here. Atlanta should change its slogan to 'the city that keeps growing.'"

"I hope the growth doesn't come to a standstill anytime soon," he said as he reached for her hand.

Richmond didn't know why he had this possessive yearning for Alicia all of a sudden. When her hand locked with his, ripples of want teased his senses. What was really going on right now?

"This farmers market is new," Alicia said, breaking into his wanton thoughts.

"Let's check it out. I've always wanted to check out a real Southern farmers market."

Alicia raised her eyebrow at him. "Are there even farms in New York?"

"Funny. When's the last time you've actually been to New York?"

She shrugged. "When Kiana turned one, I think. I've never been a big-city girl. And since I can't get tickets to the one Broadway show that I want to see, I'm boycotting."

"If you're talking about a musical about a certain founding father . . ."

"Don't tell me that you've seen it!" Alicia exclaimed.

Richmond nodded. "Three times, actually."

Alicia dropped his hand. "And I thought we could be friends," she quipped.

"See, I was going to say that I could get tickets for an upcoming show, but . . ."

"If you did that, you'd be at the top of my most-awesome-person-in-the-world list."

He smiled and eased closer to her. "I can make that list without the tickets."

Alicia took a deep breath and tried to act as if Richmond wasn't making her body throb with desire. The heat of his breath against her ear, the memory of their kisses last night, and the way he held her hand made her painfully aware of how long it had been since she'd been this close to a man, or even wanted to be this close to one.

"Maybe you can." She glanced at a display of muscadine grapes. "Yes! We have to get some of these."

"What are those things?" Richmond gave the strange-looking fruit a side-eye that made Alicia laugh.

"I keep forgetting that I'm with a sheltered Yankee. These are the most delicious grapes that God could've ever graced us with." She ushered him over to the display. Richmond picked up a container of the large grapes.

"They look like eyeballs that you would see in a haunted house on Halloween."

"Whatever. Wait until you taste them. It's like a little piece of heaven in your mouth."

"Is that so?" He opened the package and waved for the attendant.

"Yes, sir?" the petite woman said.

"I was just told that these big old grapes are the closest thing to heaven that I will put in my mouth today. I've never had one, so I was wondering if I could sample it before I tell this lady that she's right or wrong."

"Oh, I can tell you right now, she's right. I'll rinse these off for you," she said as she took the package from his hand.

Richmond winked at Alicia. "I'm going to go on record and say you did say coleslaw on a hot dog was good, and it was not."

"That's because your taste buds are all jacked up. Trust me, if you don't like this, I will find you a year's supply of bagels and lox."

Richmond leaned back and grinned. "What do you know about that?"

She shrugged. "I read about it somewhere. And what is lox anyway?"

He stroked her shoulder and shook his head. "Smoked salmon that makes sesame seed bagels taste delicious."

She frowned and made a gagging sound. "Now, that sounds disgusting. A salmon sandwich on boiled bread? I'll stick with grits and salmon."

"I thought it was all about shrimp and grits down here?"

Alicia sighed. "Oh, you have so much to learn. You're lucky I'm willing to teach you."

"And just what other lessons am I going to learn from you? I'm your dedicated student."

Something about the way he said that made her quiver. There were so many things she could teach him, and if he was willing to learn, they'd both be happy. Glancing at his hands and lips, she wondered what lessons he needed to learn and how much he could teach her.

"Here you go," the woman said as she handed Richmond the grapes. Alicia reached over and took one from the package. He watched her bite into the grape and then followed suit and bit into the succulent fruit.

Alicia was right. The grapes were delicious, but they didn't compare to the taste of her lips.

"Am I right? Isn't this the most delicious thing

you've tasted?" she asked as she swiped another grape.

"It is good, but . . ." He looked up at the attendant and smiled. "It's really good." Richmond paid for the fruit.

"You should try the wine made with these grapes. It's amazing and sweet."

"Is it as sweet as you are?" His lips brushed across her ear as he eased closer to her.

The tingles were back and Alicia turned away from him. "I guess you're going to have to sample it to see."

"I plan to get more than a sample," he replied with a wink.

"Let's get back before we lose our place in line." Alicia turned to the attendant. "Thanks for your help."

"Y'all have a good day. Next weekend, we're going to have some jelly and biscuits."

"That sounds wonderful," Alicia said.

"Sounds like we have another date next weekend," he said.

She smiled, thinking that she was going to enjoy spending time with Richmond. He was funny, and introducing him to the Southern side of life was going to be interesting.

"Think there's a table open for us now?" Richmond asked as he popped a grape into his mouth.

"I hope so or we're going to have these for breakfast," she said as she grabbed a grape of her own.

They walked slowly back to the restaurant and were happy to find that they'd made it back in time for a table in the corner. "Now I don't have to share my new favorite thing," he said with a grin as the hostess led them through the crowded restaurant.

"Remember who introduced you to your new favorite thing," she said, then bumped him with her hip. Richmond wrapped his arm around her waist.

"So, you're saying I have to share?"

She tried to ignore the heat from his touch, but the ripples racing up and down her spine were impossible to shrug off. It had been a long time since she'd allowed herself to have these thoughts about a man. Alicia had been ready to leave all of that love shit to her friends and focus on her business. She wasn't bitter, just realistic. Everyone didn't get a fairy tale, and she was fine watching her girls live their happily-ever-afters.

Looking at Richmond, she actually wondered if this might be her chance. *Too soon and we work together,* she thought as she turned away from him. Too soon to get caught up in these kinds of thoughts.

"Is this all right for you two?" the hostess asked.

"It's great," Alicia said as Richmond held out the chair for her. Easing into the seat, Alicia smiled at Richmond and then began studying the menu.

Richmond glanced at Alicia as he sat down. He wondered if she knew how beautiful she was. A classic beauty with brains, all dipped in chocolate. She was the kind of woman he could see himself spending weekends with, making love to, all night, and touring the city with. Of course, he could hear his brother telling him to enjoy the single life and not to fall for the first woman who smiled at him. But there was something different about Alicia that made him want to get to know her. What drove her, what made her so focused, and what were her hidden desires?

"So, what do you suggest?" he asked, breaking the silence at the table.

"The Westside Pileup is good. I also like the black bean cakes and eggs. And you have to try the grits. If you don't like them, we're going to have to work on your taste buds."

"I love grits," he said with a wink. "Kandace brought some into the city and I've been hooked ever since."

"Good to know. Now, here's the big question—sugar or salt?"

"Huh?"

"On your grits. Sugar or salt?"

"Definitely salt," he said. "There's other places for sugar."

She raised her eyebrow, but didn't respond.

Richmond smiled, liking the shy side of this woman. Just how many layers made up Alicia Michaels?

"Do you think we can go check out your office space later today?" she asked. "Not that I'm trying to be pushy, but I want to set up shop as soon as possible."

Before he could reply, Alicia's cell phone rang. When she looked down at that screen and smiled, he wondered if that was a special guy calling her to put a smile on her face like that.

I'm not sitting up here getting jealous about who this woman talks to on the phone, he thought as he read the contents of the meal Alicia recommended. Maybe he'd been moving too fast in his mind, thinking that he could move forward in a relationship with someone he barely knew. Maybe Solomon was right. He was out of practice and needed to just chill out for a while.

"I have to make a call," Alicia said, breaking into his thoughts. He watched her as she headed outside, and thought about calling Solomon, but he wasn't some teenager needing advice on how to win over a girl. And Alicia was far from a girl. She was all woman, and he couldn't sit there and wonder if she was seeing someone else. It wasn't his place. Not yet, anyway.

When the waiter walked over, Richmond ordered a carafe of orange juice and two cups of coffee and tried to pretend he wasn't feeling some kind of way about Alicia being outside talking to some man.

"All of y'all make me so sick," Alicia said to Serena. "You lazy heifers wanted to sleep in, so I let you."

"Are you with Richmond?" Kandace chimed in.

"Wow, speakerphone, Serena?"

"It was either that or I'd have to retell this story. So, everyone is here. Let us know what's going on and then frick and frack can leave me alone. I'm ready to go back to Charlotte, and they aren't leaving until they get all up in your business."

Alicia sighed. "Yes, I'm having brunch with

Richmond and y'all are being super annoying right now. For the record, we're discussing business."

"Where are you guys eating?" Jade asked. "I mean, we're hungry too."

"West Egg and there are no seats. I'm hanging up now, because this is just rude." Alicia ended the call and turned her ringer off before returning to Richmond. When she saw the coffee and juice on the table, she smiled.

"You're awesome," she said as she sat down. "Sorry about that. My friends think we're still college students."

Richmond nodded. "Maybe they just wanted to make sure you're safe," he said as he filled her glass with orange juice.

Alicia's mind flashed back to last night and her encounter with Felix. Though she'd thought she'd gotten over the assault, seeing him and having him touch her made it all come back as if it had been yesterday. The insecurities, the fear, and the rush of emotions that she'd thought she'd pushed away.

As she looked at Richmond, Felix's words echoed in her ears, past and present ones.

"Alicia?" Richmond said, breaking into her dark thoughts. "Are you all right?"

"Yes," she sputtered. "Just thinking about . . . I don't think you really know what it meant to me last night when you came to my defense." Tears welled up in her eyes and Richmond reached across the table and placed his hand on her wrist.

"You wanted to be left alone and that guy wasn't doing what you asked him to do."

She smiled and blinked back the tears. "I don't really do the damsel in distress thing, you know."

He brought her hand to his lips and gave her a gentle kiss. "I get that, but sometimes even the hero needs an assist."

She exhaled and picked up her juice when he let her hand go. Taking a huge sip, she hoped it would calm her nerves. She wasn't about to share her story with Richmond and sound like somebody holding on to the past, unable to move forward. But if she was honest, that incident in college had colored her life in a way that she had yet to deal with.

"Anyway, enough about that. Did you bring the keys to your office space?"

"I did, but going up to the office is pretty boring for such a beautiful day. Besides, I want to see the Atlanta that isn't in the travel guides," he said with a smirk. "I mean, if you're up for it."

"I'm up for anything," she replied, matching his smirk with a smile of her own.

Richmond took a deep breath and tried not to think about what he'd really love to do today rather than tour the city. If he had his druthers, he'd spend the day exploring every inch of her body with his tongue and fingers. He wanted to put his hands all over that soft ebony skin and find all the spots that made her scream with joy.

"Richmond?"

"I'm sorry, what?"

"I said do you want to ditch the cars and take the train?"

"I think I need to check out this Atlanta traffic

that everyone always complains about. So I'll drive, and you be my GPS."

"Sounds like a plan to me," she replied.

He had plans, but he knew it was too soon to share his desire with her. After finishing their meal and Richmond telling the waiter that this was going to be his new go-to breakfast spot, he and Alicia headed out to his car.

"Where to first?" he asked after they were strapped in.

"Mmm," she said as she stroked her chin. "Let's go to the Shakespeare Tavern."

"What?"

"It's a tavern where you can actually see plays by the Bard and get some craft beer. Think of it as an unpretentious Broadway."

"You cut me to the quick, woman," Richmond said as he started the car. "Sounds like a nice place, though."

"I think you'll like it," she said as she pulled out her phone and typed the address into her Maps app.

"Food and liquor seem to be the way to get things done around here," Richmond joked as the GPS voice began giving him directions.

"It's the South, food is a good way to get you in the door. But no bagels and lox."

He shot her a quick glance. "Have you ever had it?"

"Nope."

"Then expect to be amazed in the morning," he said.

"Excuse me? I hope you don't think I'm spending the night with you, because—"

"Slow down. I was talking about bringing you breakfast to the office. But if you want to stay, I'm all for it." He winked at her, then took the turn the GPS suggested.

Alicia exhaled but didn't say a word. *Open mouth, insert foot.*

Chapter 6

Richmond clapped as the actors took their bows. He had to admit that he wasn't expecting to see such an amazing show at a pub, but the Shakespeare actors did an amazing job with *The Taming of the Shrew.*

"There's no need for Broadway when you have this tavern," Richmond said as he downed his beer.

"Yeah, right," Alicia replied. "I doubt there will be a performance of *Hamilton* here."

"I've seen it already, so I'm good until the next big thing comes along."

She shot him a frown and shook her head. "Spoken like a theater elitist."

Richmond laughed and shrugged off her comment. "Stick with me and I'll make you an elitist too."

"I'm holding you to that," Alicia said as she waved for the bartender. "I can't believe we've been here for two hours. Want a drink? After all, it's five o'clock somewhere."

Smiling, he nodded. "No. I'm guessing our next stop is going to be a coffee shop or something?"

"Have you ever had Dancing Goats coffee? You're going to love it. It's not too far from here," she said. "We can walk if you'd like."

"Sounds good. The best way to get to know a city is to walk the streets," he said with a smile. The truth was, he just wanted a chance to watch her shapely bottom as they walked. "Tell me something," he asked as he settled the bill. "What attracted you to Atlanta when you moved here all those years ago?"

She shrugged. "At first I just wanted to get away from my small hometown and have a new adventure. Atlanta turned out to be the place where I found myself, lost myself, and met the best friends a woman could ever have."

"How did you lose yourself?"

"A story for another day," she said, then looked away from him. "Let's get this coffee."

Richmond wrapped his arm around her small waist. "Let's do this. Dancing Goats, huh?"

"Better than anything you've ever tasted."

He highly doubted that. He glanced at her lips and smiled. Richmond was sure nothing compared to her lips. All day, Richmond had been fighting the urge to kiss her and taste her sweetness again. He couldn't fight it any longer. He drew Alicia into his arms and pressed his lips against hers. Slow and sensual, their tongues danced to the beat of a song their hearts played.

She placed her hand against his chest and pushed back from him. "Whoa," she breathed. "What was that all about?"

"Clearly, it's about me wanting you."

Alicia's cheeks heated and she turned her head away from him. "Richmond, I think . . . ."

"If I crossed the line, I apologize, but I won't say I'm sorry for wanting to kiss you and enjoying it."

"Isn't this happening a little too fast?" she asked, tearing her gaze away from his lips. Those luscious, need inducing, panty-wetting lips. Her mouth may have said things were moving too fast, but her body was yelling *faster, faster!*

"Maybe, maybe not. We should just enjoy the ride." Richmond smiled and took her hand in his. "Let's get this coffee."

Alicia needed to make a decision and quick. How in the hell was she going keep her world from spinning out of control when she couldn't focus on anything but her desire for Richmond Crawford? What if Kandace was right and Richmond was on the rebound from his divorce?

She knew she needed to get her mind wrapped around business and ignore her yearnings to be wrapped around Richmond. Exhaling, she focused on the electric signs above the crosswalk telling them to stop.

"Another thing I will not get used to in the South," Richmond said.

"Trust me, the last thing you want to do is get hit by a speeding driver. We don't really stop around here." As if on cue, a car blew through the intersection as if the driver was qualifying for a NASCAR race.

"And I thought New York had the worst drivers," he quipped.

"Whatever. Most of the crazy drivers around here aren't from Atlanta. There are a lot of transplants in the city."

"Is that so?" he said, then popped his imaginary collar.

Alicia laughed, then looked away from his lips. How was she going to help him make the connections he needed in Atlanta when all she wanted to do was connect her body to his?

Arriving at the coffee shop, Alicia decided that she was going to wrap her mind around business and not wanton thoughts about Richmond's naked body.

"So, what's so great about this coffee?" he asked as they stepped through the door.

"It's one of those things you can only explain with a taste of it. Smooth and strong but not bitter."

Richmond nodded. "The perfect test for a cup of coffee is how it tastes naked."

Alicia inhaled and shivered at the way he said *naked.* "Is that so?"

Before Richmond could respond, a beaming woman with a short haircut excitedly called out Alicia's name.

"Oh, joy," Alicia remarked before plastering a smile on her face. "Dionne, hi."

Dionne, who was focused on Richmond, gave Alicia a sidelong glance. "I was wondering why I didn't see you last night with your crew. I guess I know why now." She extended her hand to Richmond. "Hi, I'm Councilwoman Dionne Ashe. Alicia and I went to college together. And you are?"

"Richmond Crawford," he said as he shook her tiny hand.

"You're not Kandace's husband, are you?" She looked from Alicia then back to Richmond and brought her free hand to her mouth.

"No, I'm her handsome brother-in-law."

Alicia rolled her eyes. "Dionne, Richmond is in Atlanta to open a chain of boutique hotels."

"Really? I've always stayed at a Crawford hotel when I visit New York. Talk about elegant. Where are you looking to build? My district, I hope," she said with a wink. "Maybe we can get together and I can give you a tour of my little part of Atlanta."

Alicia shook her head, forcing herself not to allow herself to give in to the heated jealousy flowing through her body. Dionne had always been known as a flirt, but this was borderline disrespectful. Just because Richmond wasn't married, it didn't mean that he and Alicia weren't together. But Alicia knew she didn't have a right to these feelings. She turned her head away from them.

"That sounds like a good idea," he said. "We're still scouting places for the hotel, and a unique area of the city that would make it a special destination spot would be amazing."

"Oh yes," she replied as Alicia gritted her teeth. "I have some great property in my district that would fit the bill. How can I get in touch with you?"

Richmond reached for his wallet and handed her a business card. "Maybe we can get together on Monday afternoon and take this tour."

Alicia raised her right eyebrow but kept silent.

Who was she to stand in the way of his business dealings? Dionne would definitely be able to help him with zoning and everything he'd need to start construction on the hotels. Still, something was rubbing Alicia the wrong way and she needed to get over it.

"I can pencil you in before the full council meeting on Monday. It might be a good idea for you to come to the meeting as well," she said with a smile. Then Dionne turned to Alicia. "You're welcome to join us as well."

"Monday is a busy day for me," she said. "Moving into my new office space."

"Oh, so you're coming back to Atlanta? I thought you and your girls had set your sights on taking over Charlotte."

"We can take over the entire Southeast if we choose to," Alicia said with a smile. Turning to Richmond, she placed her hand on his shoulder. "I'm going to order my coffee. You two keep chatting."

She didn't look back to see the shocked expression on Dionne's face. If Alicia had to describe her relationship with Dionne, she'd say they were frenemies. Dionne thought she should've been part of the clique with Alicia and her girls back in college, but she was the kind of woman who took a diva attitude to the highest level. Yes, she was smart and beautiful, but she thought that gave her the right to lord it over people who she deemed beneath her. And then she acted as if she was God's gift to mankind, emphasis on *man*.

Good Lord, I hope Richmond doesn't fall for her act, she thought as she studied the menu.

Richmond hid his grin as he watched Alicia coolly storm off. Dionne, though, seemed unfazed.

"So, Richmond, why did you choose my city for your expansion?" She ran her tongue across her bottom lip seductively.

"Atlanta seemed ripe for the picking."

"Is that so? Just keep in mind, there are a lot of *ripe* things around here that you could have your pick of. A man like yourself will have no problem getting your share of the cream of the crop." She offered a smile, as if he was a lamb being led to the slaughter. Richmond recognized her game. A beautiful woman with power could be dangerous, but there was no need to make an enemy in the political arena too quickly.

"That's good to know," he replied with a smile. "Listen, it was a pleasure meeting you and I can't wait to see your district tomorrow."

"Not that it matters, but will we be alone, or is Alicia joining us?"

"That's going to be up to her. Alicia and I are working together on the marketing for the hotels, but I doubt she needs to see a city she already knows."

"That's true. So, you two are just working together? I wouldn't want my friend to think I was making a move on her man." She brushed her fingers across his forearm.

Richmond glanced at her hand and took a step

back. "See you Monday," he said. Dionne nodded and sauntered over to the counter. Before he could join Alicia at the coffee bar, his cell phone rang.

"This is Richmond."

"How's Atlanta, bro?" Solomon asked. "And by Atlanta, I mean Alicia."

"I have no idea what you're talking about."

"Bullshit. My wife just spent an hour on the phone telling me what a bad idea whatever you two are doing is."

"Being that we aren't doing anything, tell Kandace to calm down, all right?"

"Don't lose focus, Rich. If these hotels aren't successful, we're going to lose a lot of money."

"I know that, and I don't need you looking over my shoulder when I clearly know what I'm doing."

"Never said that, but let's keep a few things in mind here: This is your first big solo project and I'm not trying to—"

"Solomon, I've overseen new hotel construction for years—"

"With Dad's guidance."

Richmond gritted his teeth and counted to ten.

"Rich, I'm sorry," Solomon said contritely. "I—this is important to you and I'm rooting for your success."

"Then show me a little more trust."

"It's not the business that I'm concerned about. Alicia is smart and practically family."

"What does that have to do with anything? I'm taking care of business and what I don't need right now is a micromanager."

Solomon broke out laughing. "I'm tripping. Rich, I'm sorry that I'm acting like an ass."

"What you mean is you're acting like I was when you opened the Sugar Mountain location." Thinking back to that time in their relationship, Richmond shuddered inwardly. He'd been willing to watch the resort fail just so he could prove to his parents that he should've been running the company and Solomon just should've been run out. Richmond thought running the hotel chain would give him the respect he so desperately wanted from his *father.*

"Truth is, you taught me everything I know and I'm a fool for thinking that you're going to make a business decision based on who you're dating."

"We're not dating," Richmond said, silently adding, *not yet anyway.* Glancing in Alicia's direction, Richmond wondered why everyone seemed to be so against the two of them getting together.

"When and if that glorious day does happen, you better make sure you're ready to give her everything she needs. I really believe Kandace will kill you if you hurt her."

"Again, you and Kandace can stop worrying about me and Alicia. We barely know each other and we're going to work together to make sure the Crawford boutique hotels are the hottest thing to hit Atlanta since Sherman dropped the match."

"That was the corniest thing I've heard all day. And don't say that to anyone from Atlanta," Solomon said with a laugh. "I got your report on what you need down there. Whitney and Kyle from human resources are going to come down there next week to help you get your staff together. The labor laws in Georgia are much different than New York. We should move all of our hotels to Atlanta. No unions."

"There may not be unions, but the rules of social engagement are worse. And y'all want to take my translator of the South? Besides, it was Kandace's idea for Alicia and I to work together in the first place."

"So, it's safe to tell my wife that you're not going to make her friend your rebound from divorce?"

Richmond laughed. "That's what she thinks? I'm not looking for a rebound or anything else. Alicia is a smart woman who's offered to help me navigate these Atlanta streets. I wouldn't do anything to hurt her or mess things up."

"You better mean it."

"I don't play basketball, so I'm not about that rebound life. I'm going to order my coffee and I'll give you an update on Tuesday."

"Got it."

After hanging up with Solomon, Richmond walked over to Alicia. "What did you decide on?"

"Oh, you remembered I was here," she quipped.

"Actually, you're the one who walked away from me. I think my feelings are hurt."

"I'm sure Dionne will rub them for you."

"I thought you guys were friends."

Alicia pointed to a dark chocolate item on the menu. "This is one of the best lattes ever," she said. "You should try it."

"Nope. I have to try this coffee naked first, to make sure it lives up to the hype."

She nodded. "The single-origin blends are over there. I'm going for decadence."

"You definitely have that covered," he replied with a smile. Leaning in, Richmond gave Alicia a quick peck on the cheek. "Thanks for an amazing day. I get the feeling that we're going to make a lot of magic together."

Chapter 7

Alicia could think of several ways she could make magic with Richmond. But they needed to focus on business, not magic, not passion, and not the sizzling heat between them. She needed to focus on getting her business together and lining up more clients that would pay the bills. The last thing she needed to put her mind on was whether or not Dionne and Richmond were flirting. But, he did seem to be enjoying whatever was going on between them.

"Are you okay?" he asked, breaking into her thoughts.

"I'm fine. I guess my night is catching up with me." Alicia faked a yawn, then smiled.

"It's wrong to yawn in a coffee shop, though."

"Anyway, what are you and Dionne planning?"

"She's going to show me around her district and help me scout out some sites that might be good for building the hotels. I'd like to start construction as soon as possible."

"You should introduce yourself to Atlanta first;

that way you won't be depending on one politician to get you what you need." She pulled out her cell phone and smiled. "One call and I can get you the cover of *Atlanta Scene.* The editor and I graduated from college together."

Richmond shrugged. He knew it would be a great marketing tool to get his face out there, but any decent journalist would do a Google search and find everything that he was trying to leave in New York, the scandal with his family, his arrest in Los Angeles, and his divorce.

"Give me a couple of days to think about it," he said.

"What's there to think about?"

"A lot. I know you're fully aware of everything that's been going on in my life lately. The last thing I want is to bring that baggage into this situation."

Alicia nodded, trying to understand what he'd been going through, but didn't he understand that this story could be about the biggest comeback in his life?

"It's different when you have control over the narrative. Think of it as you setting the record straight."

"I'm not trying to set any record straight," Richmond said. "If I have to do some dog and pony show to get my hotels built, I'm not doing it."

Alicia sighed. "No one is asking you to do a dog and pony show. How about this, what if we get all of the questions first and tell the reporter what's off limits?"

"This may be the South, but reporters are the same. Your friend is going to dig up all the dirt possible to make this story sell. The only thing that sells more than sex is drama."

"You're way too cynical for your own good. It's my job to make sure the story doesn't go in the direction you don't want it to go in."

"And after it's printed or online, you can't do anything about it. Alicia, I'm not ready for all of that."

She folded her arms across her chest. "So, you're just going to sidle up to politicians and hope that you can get things done that way? You've said yourself that your name doesn't open the doors down here that it does in New York and you want to do things differently. I'm trying to make that happen for you."

"Maybe we just need to find another way."

She raised her right eyebrow. "Whatever you want to do, I'm sure you're going to do it."

"Listen, I'll consider it, but I don't want a media storm around this construction. I want it to be about—"

"I got it." Alicia took a deep breath as the air between her and Richmond seemed to chill like a winter's night. She didn't understand why he was so against doing a story that would help build his brand. Glancing at him, Alicia wondered what he was so afraid of.

"This coffee is good," he said, breaking the silence between them.

"Yeah. Told you."

Richmond smirked. "You're right about a lot of this, huh?"

"That's right."

"So, you think this story with *Atlanta Scene* is going to help?"

"I know it will, but—"

"Let's do it, then. If you're going to be my marketing guru, then I guess there will be moments when you push me out of my comfort zone, right?"

She nodded and lifted her coffee cup to him. "I'll make the call, and let the reporter know what questions are off limits too."

"Sounds good," he said, then glanced at his watch. "Well, I've taken up your entire day."

Alicia smiled. "And you still haven't shown me the office space."

"Thought we agreed that we weren't going to do any work today."

"Well, that went out the window when you made a date with the city council lady," she quipped. "Besides, I need to know where I'm going to be laying my work hat."

"All right. Let's go." Truth be told, Richmond wasn't in a hurry to leave Alicia, and if she wanted to see the office space, he was just fine with getting more time with her.

They walked back to the car in silence, Alicia's mind still thinking about whether Dionne's involvement with Richmond's project would help or hurt him. And would she try to use her political influence to weasel her way into his bed?

Why am I worried about who this man sleeps with? It's not my business and I have no control over what or who he does.

* * *

Once they reached the car, Richmond smiled at Alicia. Though he didn't want the day to end, he really couldn't monopolize all of her time today. But all he wanted to do was wrap her in his arms until the sun set and rose again.

"What's that look all about?"

"What look?"

Alicia elbowed him in the shoulder and smiled. "Whatever. You're looking like you're up to something."

"Me? I think you're just judging me because I'm from New York."

"That's why you're going to need that *Atlanta Scene* article. You're the new kid in town and people are going to want to know everything about you." She winked at him. "Aren't you lucky to have me?"

Having Alicia was something he'd been struggling with all day. Being with this woman awakened sensations inside him that had been dormant for years.

"That's one way to look at it," he finally said. "Come on, let's head to the office—or, as we'll be calling it soon, our second home."

Vivian Crawford sat at a posh New York restaurant feeling as if she had been sucker punched in the stomach. Shaking her head, she looked at the waitress and smiled. "Surely, my credit card is not declined."

"Ma'am, we ran it through twice and the result was the same. Do you have another card or cash?"

Vivian reached for her purse. "Vivvy," her friend

Gisselle said. "Don't worry about it. I'll take care of the check."

"Don't be silly. I invited you to lunch, so I'm paying," Vivian said, then handed the waitress another credit card. "This must be some kind of mistake."

Inside, Vivian seethed, thinking that Richmond had some nerve to cut her off. Who did he think he was? It was bad enough that she'd lost her table at her favorite restaurant, and now this? He was trying to embarrass her because she chose to end their marriage. A marriage that had been a joke. And he had the nerve to make her look bad now. Who in the hell did he think he was dealing with?

"Vivian, is everything all right?" Gisselle asked. "I know you and Richmond divorced, but the settlement couldn't—"

She held her hand up. "Everything is fine. I guess he's flexing his power now with the credit cards. I thought we had an understanding. Obviously, my ex isn't the man I thought he was. But there's nothing to worry about . . ."

The waitress returned to the table with a frown on her face. "I'm sorry, ma'am, but this card was declined as well. Do you have another method of payment? Perhaps cash?"

Vivian rolled her eyes and Gisselle handed the waitress a card. "Just take care of it with this. You know no one in New York carries cash these days. And it would be nice if you didn't make a scene."

"And it would be nice if one of these cards went through."

Vivian gasped. "Who do you think you're talking to?"

The waitress turned on her heels and muttered, "Obviously a broke bitch."

Vivian closed her eyes and counted to ten. This was not her life. And she knew Gisselle was eating up every minute of it.

"I hope that Damien doesn't act like this once our divorce is final," Gisselle said with a sigh. "I know they give you a settlement or alimony, but these men know what kind of lifestyle we're used to."

"Well, I'm sure Damien and his new wife aren't going to want the publicity that you would create if he did this nonsense." Vivian fingered her hair and shook her head. "It's so freeing though, not having to deal with Richmond and his insecurities about his place in the family. Ugh. Just give me my piece of the pie and move on."

"But men don't think like that. They want to make us suffer for moving on." Gisselle shook her head. "Richmond should be happy you stayed with him as long as you did."

Vivian nodded. "I'm going to get to the bottom of this," she said as she rose to her feet. "And I will get everything I deserve for being the good wife all of these years." Stalking out of the restaurant, Vivian wondered if she should call Page Six and drop a nugget about Richmond cutting her off. She'd even spice it up and say he was losing money because no one wanted to deal with a fake Crawford. Granted, she'd received a handsome divorce settlement and the monthly alimony had been nice, for a while. But Vivian thought she could still live off her last name. She'd blow through the ten thousand dollars in a week. Yes, she'd been living above her means, but she'd been spoiled by being able to do whatever she wanted to do. Richmond was going to pay, or she would make him regret it. Who did he think she was? Marla Maples? She'd been quiet about all of his scandals of late, but if the money didn't start rolling in again, Vivian wouldn't be above selling stories—even if she had to make them up.

"I'm going to hold on to that until he gives me my money," she groaned as she pulled out her cell phone and dialed Richmond's number.

Looking down at his cell phone as he unlocked the office suite, Richmond groaned. "I'm not dealing with this right now," he muttered as Alicia crossed over to him.

"You can't open the door?" she quipped. "Don't let me find out you really don't have a lease here."

"I don't have a lease," he said as he unlocked the door. "I own it."

Alicia took a step back. "What?"

He winked at her, then held the door open. "And I thought you were easing into the market," Alicia said as she pinched his arm. "Look at you with prime real estate."

"This was too sweet of a deal to pass on. I didn't even have to do much talking to get Solomon to agree with me."

"Do you know how many businesses will want to have this address on their letterhead? Well played."

"And I just need my first tenant to excitedly tell the world how much she loves it here."

Alicia raised her right eyebrow. "Then your first

tenant better have a beautiful place to do business. I don't just give away five-star reviews."

Richmond walked over to the suite and opened the door. "I think we're going to earn every star."

Alicia walked in behind him and viewed the suite with wide-eyed wonderment. "This is amazing," she said as she stood in the middle of the space. The oak floors shone like polished diamonds and the view of the city was amazing. Alicia stood in the middle of the suite and spun around, thinking about the artwork she'd hang on the walls, where her desk would sit, and how she would put an Afghan rug in the middle of the floor to protect her shiny oak.

"This is beautiful," she said as she faced Richmond. "Ten stars."

Richmond crossed over to Alicia and was about to draw her into his arms when his cell phone rang again.

"Somebody wants you," she said as Richmond looked at his phone, groaning when he saw it was Vivian again.

He knew he wasn't going to get a moment of peace until he found out what Vivian wanted, but she could wait. The way Alicia's hips were calling out to his hands made everything else outside of that building a non-factor. He wanted nothing more than to pull her into his arms, kiss her again and taste her essence. Crossing over to her, Richmond was about to reach out and touch her, but the phone rang again. Sounded louder than before. Part of him thought this was a fitting turn of events.

He wanted to move forward and his past wanted to interrupt it.

"That could be your new favorite politician."

"I'm trying to be inappropriate with my new favorite tenant. That phone can ring all night." Richmond crossed over to her and pulled Alicia against his chest.

"What are we doing?" she breathed. "We're about to start working together and—"

He silenced her with a kiss, pressing her body against his and cupping her bottom as their tongues danced.

"We haven't started working yet. And you know what they say about all work and no play," he said after breaking the kiss.

"Can we be serious for a minute?" she said, though her knees quivered at the thought of playing more with Richmond. This wasn't supposed to be happening, and she didn't know if she could stop it. Easing back from him, Alicia took a deep breath. "Today was fun, but we have to seriously get down to business," she said.

Richmond nodded, though he wasn't feeling anything she was saying. This was his business and he wanted more than just one fun day.

"It's not Monday yet," he said with a wink.

Alicia shook her head. "You're too much. We have a lot of work to do and this is going to be a distraction that we don't need."

"Is that what you think, or what you feel like you're supposed to say?"

Alicia sighed, not wanting to answer the question.

No matter what she said, it would feel like a lie. She looked away from him and tried to come up with a logical reason for him to stop trying to seduce her.

"Business and pleasure never mix," she said, aware that her cliché statement was the furthest thing from the truth. She saw the results of this mixture every time she looked at Jade and James. Richmond's cell phone rang again. He took the phone from his pocket and tossed it across the room.

"Someone wants you pretty badly."

"And that sums up how I feel about you." Richmond closed the space between them. Part of him wanted to grip her hips while he kissed her senseless. But she wanted things to be on the business level with them. He wasn't sure if he could play by those rules.

Hell, what had playing by the rules gotten him anyway? He drew her into his arms. "But you have to be honest and tell me you feel the same way for this to work."

She eased out of his embrace. "I tell you what, we're going to table this discussion. It's getting late and Monday is going to be here before we know it."

Her legs were weak as they headed for the exit. Alicia knew one thing for sure: She needed to get her head together. Maybe she needed another talk with Kandace to remind her what a bad idea it would be to get involved with Richmond.

Then she stole a glance at him and realized that it was going to take more than a stern talk from her friend to quell her growing desire for Richmond Crawford.

"Maybe . . ." Alicia's voice trailed off as she glanced at his hands. "I should find another space to set up shop?"

"Why would you do that when you have prime real estate here?" He winked at her. "I'll keep it together while we're here. But we won't be here twenty-four seven," he said with a smile.

"And that means what?"

"You'll see." Richmond led her out of the building.

The ride back to the West Egg Café might have been silent, but the air between them sizzled. As much as she tried to focus on the road, Alicia couldn't help but steal glances at her sexy driver. His heat wrapped around her and wouldn't let go. Arriving at the café, the scene was a lot different than it was that morning. Parking was a breeze and the streets were practically empty.

"Breakfast in the morning?" Richmond asked. "I can introduce you to the joy of bagels and lox."

"And I'll bring eggs and biscuits just in case this experiment of yours doesn't work out."

"Trust me, it will be better than coleslaw on a hot dog." His deep laugh vibrated through her body, making her quiver with want.

"Such a Yankee," she joked as he pulled up next to her car. Richmond stroked her cheek, then leaned in and gave her a gentle peck on the lips.

"See you in the morning. Unless you want to join me tonight for a nightcap."

"I'd better pass," she said. "I have some things I

need to take care of before I get started in the morning."

"And I thought I was a workaholic." He shook his head. "Thanks for showing me around today, and I look forward to our partnership."

Alicia smiled at his uber-professional tone. "Goodbye, Richmond."

Chapter 8

Richmond hadn't wanted to leave Alicia, but there was only so much he could do in the face of her objections. As soon as he got into his car, the phone rang again. As much as he wanted to continue to ignore Vivian, he knew the calls would continue until he found out what she wanted.

"Yeah?"

"Really, Richmond?" Vivian snapped.

"What are you babbling about?"

"It's bad enough that you have people at my favorite restaurant treating me like a pariah, but now you've cut off my credit cards?"

"Did you read the divorce agreement or not? My support of you is done—including continuing to pay for your credit cards. And the alimony was only good for a year. Remember that prenup you signed? Maybe you should get a job."

"What the . . . You have some nerve. Now that you've moved across the country, you think that you can ignore your responsibilities?"

"Sweetheart, you're no longer my headache."

Richmond ended the call and tossed the phone in the passenger seat. He knew Solomon was behind Vivian's social woes, but she had to be crazy to think that he was going to support her after the hell she'd put him through. Being rid of her had clearly taken years of pain out of his life.

Richmond stayed in his marriage longer than he should have because he thought it had been his place to combat Solomon's playboy image. And after watching his parents' relationship, Richmond knew marriages weren't all about love. Then Solomon and Kandace showed him how wrong he was. Seeing Solomon change his ways to win the woman he loved and become a faithful husband, made him realize he deserved more in his marriage. Of course, Vivian hadn't been on board. She'd enjoyed separate bedrooms and a marriage that was valid on paper and nothing else. The once-in-a-while intimacy that had become their marriage had been fine with her.

So, when he started talking about a real marriage, Vivian had been disgusted. She'd married Richmond for his name, for the status that being a Crawford in New York brought her. Vivian never waited for tickets to the hottest Broadway shows, never missed the openings at the best and newest restaurants. When she'd told him that, Richmond had no other recourse than to divorce her. He wanted real love and she wasn't going to give it to him.

Richmond walked into his empty house and wished Alicia had come home with him. Business be damned. Sure, he needed her skill and knowledge of the city, but he wanted that woman. Needed to feel her lips against his as much as he needed to breathe. Something about Alicia sparked him in a way that made him feel like he'd never felt before. Vivian's years of rejection had taken a toll on his psyche for a while, but things had changed when he realized that life was too damned short to worry about a false image.

Finding out that Elliot Crawford wasn't his real father made him realize that everything he'd tried to do to please his father had been an effort in futility. When he was growing up, Richmond wanted his father's approval more than anything. That was why he'd tried to distance himself from Solomon. Richmond lived and breathed Crawford Hotels, while his younger brother tried to separate himself from the family business.

Maybe that was why it had been so easy for the two men to be pitted against each other when they were younger. Richmond had wanted to be the one running Crawford Hotels, and Elliot had dangled that carrot in front of him for the longest time. But when Solomon decided that he wanted to be in the family business after his first engagement blew up in his face, Elliot snatched that carrot away.

Richmond spent so many years trying to prove to his father that he was the one who should've been running the family business. That meant that he'd turned himself into Elliot's puppet. All his father had to do was say *jump*, and Richmond asked *how high?*

But those days were over.

Richmond had decided to take his life back and

be his own man for once. No more meaningless battles with Solomon over bullshit and scrabbles created by Elliot. Adrian, Elliot's other son, had also shown him how freeing it was to live by his own rules—even though they had a rocky start to their relationship.

Picking up his phone, he called Solomon. Maybe his brother would be able to help him understand what to do about his Alicia problem.

Alicia poured herself a huge glass of wine as soon as she walked into her hotel room. Ignoring the notes from her friends, she plopped on the bed and downed her chardonnay. Why had Richmond Crawford gotten under her skin? What if she would've listened to Kandace and stayed away from the newly divorced Richmond?

Setting her glass on the nightstand, she sighed and thought about that kiss. The heat, the tenderness, and the passion. She couldn't remember the last time she'd been kissed so senseless. But was she setting herself up for another heartbreak? Perhaps he wanted to test the waters as a single man; Dionne certainly wanted to test the waters. And it bothered her to no end.

"Like you have any reason to be jealous?" Alicia took another sip of wine and forced herself to think about something else. A place to live, not next to Richmond's gorgeous house and not in the horny councilwoman's district either.

Alicia polished off her wine, then decided that she needed to talk to Jade.

"Well, well, look who remembers she has friends," Jade said when she answered the phone.

"Don't do that. My friends made me want to forget them because they wanted to get all up in my business," Alicia said with a laugh.

"So, there is something going on with you and Mr. Crawford?"

Alicia sighed. "That's why I called you. Jade, there's something about Richmond that has me all out of sorts. I'm feeling things that I haven't felt in a long time."

"Forbidden fruit is always the most tempting. I'm all for you being happy, but this guy has a lot of baggage and—"

"Like James didn't? Like we all don't?"

"In defense of my husband, his baggage didn't play out in the media."

"True. But we're a long way away from New York," Alicia said.

"Okay. That may be true, but what happens if things go left and you still have to see him when we get together with Kandace?"

"Oh, so I can't have my happily-ever-after?"

"That's not what I'm saying. But," Jade said, "you have to take this into consideration."

"And I thought you would be the one telling me to go for it," Alicia said with a chuckle. She rose to her feet and poured herself another glass of wine. "I mean, how many months have you spent trying to set me up with every single man your husband knows?"

"I didn't . . . Listen, if Richmond is really what you want, then you don't need my encouragement.

You will do your thing and be done with it. But if you're calling me for advice, I guess it is pretty deep."

Alicia took a sip of wine and realized two things: Jade could be smug at times, and her friend was right. "Fine," she said. "I just don't want to be a rebound fling."

"I get it," Jade said. "But that's the risk you take when you deal with a newly single man. Kandace was right. Richmond spent years in a loveless marriage and now he's in Atlanta."

"Tell me about it." Alicia then recounted her interaction with Dionne and how she flirted with Richmond as if Alicia wasn't even there. When Alicia heard her friend chuckling, she was livid.

"Really, Jade?" Alicia snapped.

"Yes. I haven't seen you this riled up about a dude . . . ever. Damn. Maybe Richmond is the one."

"I'm hanging up this phone, and do me a favor, keep this between us," she said.

"Of course," Jade said. "But if you want him, then you better make it clear, because if Dionne is still the tramp she was in college, she's going to let him know."

"Maybe I should just let it go. After all, it's not as if—"

"Nope! Don't you start with that. One thing I know about you is that if you want something, you can't be stopped. If that happens to be Richmond Crawford, then go for it. And save that man from Dionne, please. How in the hell did she get elected to anything?"

It was Alicia's turn to laugh now. "I know good and well that you aren't still holding a grudge."

"I don't hold grudges, but if I don't like you, that's for life. Besides, she broke all sorts of girl code back in the day, showing that she wasn't trustworthy at all."

"Well, obviously the city of Atlanta disagrees with you. But that's neither here nor there."

"Kandace is going to kill him if he hurts you, though."

"Jade, I'm not playing with you. Don't you say a word to Kandace until I figure all of this out."

"Might be a good idea. But don't feel like you have to hide your feelings from him, even if you are hiding them from Kandace."

Alicia laughed and took a sip of wine. "I should've taken him up on his offer."

"Wait. What?"

"I got to go," Alicia said, then ended the call. Taking another sip of her drink, she decided to call Richmond. But what in the hell was she going to say?

Richmond moved his phone from his ear as his brother laughed loudly. "I should've known you would fall for the first woman you met."

"I haven't fallen for anyone," Richmond said. "Alicia and I are starting a business relationship and I just happened to notice how smart and beautiful she is. All right, the woman is amazing and I'm possibly falling hard for her."

"You'd better be sure," Solomon said with a sigh. "Because if you're just playing the field, which you should do, Kandace is going to kill you."

"This has nothing to do with Kandace, and I'm probably not going to get the chance to be anything more than her business associate. This is a woman who doesn't have a problem focusing on business, or my seduction skills are weak."

"Probably the latter," Solomon quipped. "What you need to do is weigh the pros and cons about being more than a business associate of this woman. Alicia is a beautiful woman, but are you sure she wants to settle down? Hell, are you trying to settle down again?"

"Did I say I wanted to marry the woman? Shit. Vivian is still trying to play the wife role. She had the nerve to call me because a credit card was declined."

Solomon chuckled. "Vivian is feeling really average right about now. Since all of y'all were in Atlanta this week and I didn't have anything to do between Kiana's naps, I might have gotten your ex blackballed."

"Aww, hell," Richmond groaned. On the one hand, he was happy that Solomon had put Vivian in her place, but that meant he was going to have to deal with the fallout. And he was sure that meant more calls from his ex as their financial ties were severed completely. Richmond tried to do right by Vivian, if for no other reason than to keep her mouth shut.

Now that Solomon had blackballed her in social circles, that would probably be a lot harder than he'd thought. But Richmond wasn't going to let her use his goodwill against him.

"So that's what that call was about," Richmond

said. "While I can appreciate what you've done, do me a favor and stay out of this. Vivian can be trouble."

"How so?" Solomon asked. "She was living off our name and she can't keep that going, especially with you starting over in Atlanta."

"And now that I'm starting this new chapter here, the last thing I need is Vivian dredging up the past. Just let the sleeping dog lie."

"I'm going to go on record and say this: Even when I didn't like you much, I liked that lying bitch even less. I'll respect what you want me to do when it comes to her, but I'm not sad that she's not in the family anymore."

"Neither am I. Maybe I should've done it sooner," Richmond said.

"Maybe?"

"Anyway! Alicia wants me to do some cover story with this local magazine, and the last thing I need or want is a reporter reaching out to my bitter ex."

"But the South is different. A handsome face and a compelling story will make people forget about scandals."

Richmond released a frustrated sigh. While Solomon had weathered his own publicity scandals in the past, these days he was a media darling. A happy family man who didn't seem bothered by his father's seedy past. But for Richmond, it wasn't that simple. He couldn't deal with the fact that his mother hadn't been the perfect woman he'd crafted her to be. It was pretty obvious that she and Elliot had been cut from the same cloth. Richmond thought about finding his real father, but what would that change for him? Did he really want to open that can of worms? It wasn't as if he had a clue as to who the man was. And after all these years, did it really matter? The past was the past. But the future was where he needed to focus. And he wondered if Alicia was going to be a part of that future.

She was all class and beauty. The woman of his dreams, even when he was wide awake. She had to know that she was irresistible. Richmond couldn't help but wonder how many broken hearts she'd left in Charlotte when she decided to move to Atlanta.

"Why did you get all quiet on me?" Solomon asked, breaking into Richmond's thoughts.

"Just thinking that I've never had the chance to fall in love. If Alicia could be my chance at love, I'm taking it."

"So, you're serious about this thing?"

"Hell, yes. One thing I can say I've learned from you and Adrian is that when chances are given to you, you have to take them."

"Then you'd better do it, big brother," Solomon said. "Alicia isn't the typical chick that you can impress with your name and business acumen."

"I got a strategy."

"Dude, this isn't a business arrangement. You—"

"I got this."

"I hear you, my brother. Hopefully, you won't mess this up."

"Like I said, I have a plan and I'm about to work it." Richmond's phone beeped in his ear and he was surprised to see Alicia's name flash across his screen. "Let me call you back."

"Make it tomorrow. My wife just walked in the room and we're about to be busy."

Richmond laughed and clicked over. Silence greeted him after he said hello. Pulling the phone from his ear, he pressed the screen to call her back.

Alicia allowed the phone to ring once before ending the call. What would she say to Richmond if he'd answered the phone? *This is insane,* she thought as she tossed her phone on the bed. *No more wine or talks with Jade at night. I'm losing my mind.*

Rising to her feet, Alicia whispered a prayer that things wouldn't be awkward when she saw Richmond in the morning. Maybe he hadn't even noticed her call.

When her phone rang, she knew he'd seen it.

"Shit." She grabbed the phone. "Hi."

"I see I missed your call. What's going on?" Richmond's voice was like velvet. She closed her eyes and imagined his arms wrapped around her waist, his lips pressed against her ear as he talked.

"I—uh—misdialed. Hope I didn't disturb you."

"Not at all. I was hoping you were calling because you wanted to stop by for a nightcap."

He laughed and Alicia's knees went weak. She was going to blame it on the alcohol. She wasn't a college coed anymore, there was no need for her to act like a lovesick fool. Hell, she hadn't even acted like this when she was in college.

"We have work in the morning and I've taken up enough of your time today."

"But you were thinking about me, huh?"

"Get over yourself, Crawford," she teased.

"You know, you could come over and . . . Well, according to your rules, it's too close to Monday for pleasure."

"Don't forget breakfast in the morning," Alicia said, then ended the call with a smile on her face. This was going to be the most interesting Monday morning she'd had in a long time.

Chapter 9

Monday morning, Richmond was more excited about going to work than a kid on Christmas Day. Even if Alicia didn't like his classic New York City breakfast, he would at least get the chance to spend the morning with her. But he was going to have to play it cool when he saw her. The last thing he wanted was to come off as if he was some lame stalker. Packing up the bagels and lox, he wondered if she would like it. It was important to him to make sure Alicia was satisfied. Sure, he was starting with food now, but when he got the chance, he was going to satisfy her in every way.

But this morning was about work and breakfast. Maybe by lunchtime he'd be able to push forward on other ways to satisfy her. Since this was the first time he'd driven in Atlanta rush-hour traffic, Richmond finally understood why everyone complained about the traffic all the time.

When he arrived at the office, Richmond was surprised to see that Alicia was there already. He got out of the car and crossed over to her. "What's your secret?" Richmond asked.

"What do you mean?" Alicia smiled and leaned against her car.

"Somehow you avoided the traffic hell that was a part of my commute this morning." Richmond gave her a slow once-over, drinking in her delicious image wrapped in an emerald green dress and golden sandals that were professional and sexy at the same time. Richmond's mouth watered as he glanced at her frosted pink toes. Sweet strawberries came to mind.

"Richmond?" she asked.

"Yes. So, your secret?"

"I know the back way to get here without heading down I-285. Stick with me and I can show you a whole new world of avoiding traffic backups and interstate traffic. But first, I want this amazing NYC breakfast you promised me." She smiled and Richmond knew that no woman other than Alicia should wear cherry-red lipstick.

"Breakfast is in the car, let me grab it and we can eat."

"I hope you have some coffee as well," Alicia called out. "But if you don't, I got us two lattes."

"You thought of everything, huh?" Richmond said as he turned back to his car. He decided that today would begin his strategic seduction of Alicia Michaels. This woman would be his, and their future would be amazing. But he would have to find a way to convince her that she belonged with him.

* * *

Alicia took a deep breath when Richmond walked away from her. That man had made her early morning trip to the office worth it by just getting out of the car and smiling at her. If someone had told her two weeks ago that she would be acting like a lovesick child for Richmond Crawford, Alicia would've laughed and called the men in white coats to come and get that person. But somehow, this man had gotten under her skin and made her believe that he was a different breed.

Calm down, she thought as she watched him grab two bags from the car. *Today begins the day of business. I need to make sure we're on the same page and that I'm not making a fool of myself. Richmond's a single man who can do whatever he wants to do, and I'm not going to stand around and pretend that a single rich man in Atlanta won't have his choice of women. We're working together and nothing more.*

All Alicia had to do was convince herself that she could actually believe all the lies she'd just told herself. She took the coffee cups out of the car and followed Richmond into the building.

"You ready for this?" he asked as he unlocked the door to his office suite.

"Ready for?"

"The best breakfast you've ever had in your life."

His smile disarmed her and made her think about the erotic dreams she'd had about this man, all night. "You'd better hope it lives up to all of your hype."

Richmond set the bagels and lox on the desk and held his hand out to Alicia. "Let's dig in."

She set the lattes on the desk and grabbed one of the sesame-seed bagels. Richmond opened packages of lox and cream cheese, then took Alicia's bagel from her soft hand. "You're about to skip out on the best part." She watched as he smoothed the cream cheese across the bread and then dropped the thin pink salmon on top of it.

"Enjoy," Richmond said with a wink.

Alicia's mind wandered to all of the enjoyment she could get from his hands, lips, and fingertips. Shaking her head, she took a bite of the bagel and it was delicious. "Oh, this is good."

"Stick with me, kid, and I'll show you a lot of good things." He took a sip of the coffee she'd brought in for them. "Dancing Goats?"

Alicia nodded as she took another bite of the bagel. "We're going to do this every morning."

"Sounds like a great plan to me."

Alicia glanced at her watch. "But I have to cut this short, my first meeting is in about twenty minutes. Thanks for breakfast," she said as she turned and headed for her office suite. Alicia knew she had plenty of time to meet with her client, but she had to get away from Richmond and those lips. All she could think about was kissing him, when she'd told herself that today was about business.

Richmond seemed to be in line with keeping things business professional in the office. Not that she was expecting a kiss or a hug this morning, but it would've been nice. "You can't have it both ways," she muttered as she walked into her office. Looking around at the empty space, she pulled out her cell phone to check and see when her furniture delivery would be ready.

Just as she was about to make the call, Richmond knocked on the door. She waved him inside. "What's up?"

"You have a delivery, and I was wondering if I could get a slot on your calendar later. I have some ideas I want to go over with you about the expansion of the Crawford hotels."

"Sure, around four thirty?"

He nodded as his cell phone rang. "Excuse me," he said, then walked away.

"Vivian, what the hell do you want?" Richmond growled into the phone.

"You and Solomon are really cute with the way you talk to me," she snapped.

"I really don't have time for this. When I wanted to talk to you, you couldn't be bothered. So please tell me what is so important now?"

She sighed into the phone. "You really think that I'm just going to fade into the background and live like some common bitch from Queens because you've run away from the city?"

Richmond snorted and stopped himself from telling her that she was a common bitch from Maryland. He wasn't trying to argue with this woman today. He had too much to get done today, and dealing with Vivvy's rantings wasn't high on his list of priorities. "I don't have, nor will I make time for your bull today."

"Is that so? How do you think your business

venture in the South would go when people find out that you like hookers?"

Richmond laughed. "You're resorting to blackmail now? You know, you could've had the life you wanted and still be spending my money as if it grew on trees, but you filed for divorce and wanted to walk away. When are you going to be gone? I don't owe you a damned thing. And I'm not going to give you shit. Do me a favor and don't call me again. Try this, get a job." Richmond ended the call and shoved his phone in his pocket. The last thing he needed today was to be distracted by his ex-wife's threats. He and Dionne were going on a tour of the city, and he was going to scout locations for the hotel. She'd already texted him and told him how much she was looking forward to showing him *her* Atlanta.

But if Richmond had his way, he'd spend all day watching Alicia simply breathe. But that wasn't the plan. He needed to get his life together because Adrian and Solomon would be expecting a report at the end of the week about locations for the hotel and a marketing report on Tuesday.

Richmond had a few ideas about where he wanted to build the hotel, but he needed the place to stand out. The hotel in the mountains stood out because it captured the winter wonderland experience. He knew he needed to capture the glamour and excitement of Atlanta in this hotel. But how did you capture that and be original? Glancing toward Alicia's suite, he realized that she was going to be key to his success. Somehow he would make her see that their business could be mixed with pleasure.

But business was what he needed to focus on right now. Opening his laptop, Richmond started reading résumés for all of the positions that he needed to fill. First on his list was going to be an assistant.

He couldn't wait for the human resources help from New York to get there. Richmond had sifted through fifty résumés before he was ready to poke his eyeballs out.

Three hours later, he had scheduled four interviews and hired a headhunter to fill his key positions. He made it clear that he'd hire his assistant on his own.

Alone in her office, Alicia dialed Serena's number because she needed the dose of realism that only her good friend could deliver.

When the voicemail picked up, she was disappointed, but figured that she needed to focus on her work and not spend the morning talking about Richmond Crawford. They were working together and had agreed to keep things strictly business. She had to focus on that and not the fact that she wanted to kiss him with all of the passion inside her.

Alicia was about to leave the office and let the delivery guys have access to set up her new furniture and equipment, when her cell phone rang.

"This is Alicia Michaels."

"We need to talk."

Shivers ran down her spine as she recognized Felix's voice. "What the hell do you want?"

"Alicia, what was all of that about at the reunion? You had your man punch me because of a misunderstanding in college?"

"How did you get my number? You know what, don't even answer that. Just lose it."

He laughed, and her mind floated back to that day he told her no one would believe that he would assault her. But Alicia had to remind herself that she wasn't a college student anymore and he had no power over her. "Go to hell, Felix. Just watching you get that smug face of yours bashed in was the best part of the reunion."

"You've always been a stupid black bitch. This isn't college anymore, and if you start bringing up the past, the only person who will be hurt is going to be you. I stayed in Atlanta and built a great reputation. What you won't do is ruin that."

It was Alicia's turn to laugh now. "If that's the case, then why have you worked so hard to find me? You working with kids now or something? Did you trick the world into believing that you're a good person?"

"Don't bring up the past unless you're willing to get burned as well. I can tell stories too," Felix said.

"About what? Felix, I'm not now, nor have I ever been, afraid of you." Alicia placed her hand on the wall. She might not be scared, but she was affected. The last thing she needed was for her past to impact her future. Sure, she'd come to Atlanta to start over, but she'd never thought that she'd run into this clown. Part of her hoped that he would be locked away. She knew she hadn't been his only victim. But no one ever turned him in because he'd been such a big star. Alicia prayed that she hadn't made a mistake and allowed him to get off the hook. But she wasn't going to allow him to continue to play on that night. Maybe his guilt was showing since he'd seen her.

"You stay out of my way and we'll be fine. But I swear, you don't want to start a war with me." The line went dead and she shoved her phone in her purse. Heading out of the suite, she ran chest first into Richmond.

"Where's the fire?" he asked when they collided. "Everything all right?"

She nodded. "Just running a little behind. Excuse me." Pushing past Richmond, she headed outside and got into her car. Alicia hadn't realized that she was shaking. Had Richmond noticed that? The last thing she wanted Richmond to think was that she was some damsel in distress. She never wanted anyone to think that about her. Alicia had been taking care of herself for a long time, and she didn't want anyone to believe that she couldn't handle herself.

Starting the car, she headed to her hotel. She needed a moment to calm down and then continue with her day.

Arriving at the hotel, Alicia dashed to her room and Googled Felix. When she saw that he was a high school principal at a charter school in the city, she felt ill. What if he was molesting young students at his school, or worse? Taking a deep breath, Alicia shut down her computer and wondered if she should expose the kind of monster that Felix was. One thing she knew for sure, people like him didn't change.

Richmond was confused about Alicia's behavior before she left. He could tell something was wrong by the way she rushed out of the building. Part of him wondered if it had anything to do with the scene at her reunion.

"She said she was fine," he muttered as he returned to his office. He knew she was lying and he couldn't help but wonder what that guy had actually done to her. Alicia didn't seem like the kind of woman who scared easily.

He hadn't asked her any details about the guy he'd punched at the gala, but he knew that she had been shaken that night. He wondered if that had anything to do with how she looked today when she left. He wanted to follow her and make sure she was all right, but Richmond knew there was something deeper going on and he wanted Alicia to be comfortable coming to him with any issues that she might have.

Somehow he knew that wasn't something she felt comfortable doing. He watched her as she tore out of the parking lot and wanted to follow her. What had happened to cause her to rush out like that?

He was about to shoot her a text when his phone rang. "Richmond Crawford."

"I hope you haven't forgotten about me and our outing today," Dionne cooed in his ear.

"How could I forget that?" he replied with a chuckle.

"I have a tiny favor to ask," she said. "This afternoon, I'm cutting the ribbon at a new restaurant and I'd love for you to come with me. The food will be on me. And then we can go on the tour. This will be a great way for you to meet some other tastemakers in the city."

"Sounds like a good plan. What time is this ribbon cutting?"

"Oh, in about an hour. Does that give you enough time to get ready?"

Richmond glanced at his watch. "Barely, but I'll make it work."

"I knew you were awesome. I'll stop by and pick you up. Text me the address where you're going to be," she said. "Oh, and tell Alicia hi. But please don't invite her. I just want us to take this time and get to know each other, and you can see everything my district has to offer."

Richmond shook his head after hanging up the phone. Maybe Dionne had something more than business on her mind, but he wasn't even checking for the overtly sexy politician. He had eyes for one woman.

Chapter 10

Alicia headed to the Varsity for a hot dog with coleslaw. Despite what Richmond thought, there was no other way to eat a hot dog. And after the morning she'd had, she deserved the hot dog and the thick shake she was about to devour.

After getting over that call from Felix, Alicia turned back to business. But it seemed as if she was the only person looking to do some work today. Her client never showed up for their meeting, and when she returned to the office, the deliverymen had dropped off her new furniture without putting a piece of it together, even though she'd paid extra for it. Since she was alone in the office, she had stripped out of her shirt and put her desk and chair together. By the time she'd finished, Alicia was a hot, sweaty mess. Part of her wondered where Richmond had gotten off to. "I can't believe my slum landlord isn't here," she quipped as she wrote him a note and left it on his door.

Going to have the best lunch ever. A hot dog with chili, coleslaw, and loads of mustard. You're missing out.

Sitting at a booth in the Varsity, Alicia released a sigh. Things could only get better from here. After all, it was just Monday. She pulled out her phone and called Jade.

"What's going on, Ms. Lady?" Jade asked. "You've been busy today."

"Do you have cameras in my office or something?" Alicia joked.

"No," Jade replied. "But I did see Richmond on CNN today at the opening of that Wounded Warriors restaurant."

"Huh?"

"Come on, now, I know your work, and that was a great way to get some buzz going about the future boutique hotels and his partnership with the Atlanta University Center. It's as if you guys have hit the ground running. How are you going to celebrate later?"

Alicia sighed. Whatever got Richmond on TV today, she didn't have anything to do with it. "That's odd," she began. "Richmond told me that he wasn't ready to get in front of the media. Do you know how hard it was to convince him to let me set up an interview with *Atlanta Scene*?"

"I wonder what changed his mind?" Jade asked. "He looked really comfortable on screen though. Dionne was standing by his side, looking as if she'd found her next meal. I figured that you'd come up with—"

"Wait, he was with Dionne? That's just stupid! I told him we can't depend on one sex-crazed politician to make this project work. I hate it when people don't listen to me."

"Oh. Kay. What's really going on?"

Alicia groaned. "While I'm sitting up here having the worst day of my career, Richmond is on CNN. That's crazy to me and . . . Forget it. I just have to get some other clients who will actually show up for meetings and follow my advice. I have to go." When she hung up the phone, Alicia downed her milkshake and decided that she was going to confront Richmond about his little media appearance.

But not until she finished her hot dog.

Richmond was livid. He was beyond pissed at Dionne and himself. First of all, she didn't tell him that the restaurant opening was going to be covered by so many media outlets. Then there was the reporter from CNN who used to work in New York, who recognized Richmond. Savannah Idina wasn't a fan of Solomon, because he'd slept with her once and never called back. Then, when he married Kandace and Savannah brought a camera to the wedding after Solomon had banned media, she had a vendetta against the Crawfords. Richmond was surprised that she had been fair with him and asked about why he was in Atlanta.

Still, after the cameras were gone, he'd turned to Dionne with anger in his eyes. "What the hell was that all about?"

"It was supposed to be about the restaurant. I wasn't aware of your own celebrity. I hope you plan to put one of these restaurants in your hotel." Her smile reminded him of a snake.

"That's why you wanted me here?"

"No, I wanted . . . Look, you got a lot of free publicity and you could thank me."

Richmond folded his arms across his chest. "I don't even have a location for my hotel and you have me on TV talking about it as if it is a done deal."

She'd smiled and folded her arms across her breasts. "It can be if you decide to build in my district. I can make things so simple for you, or I can make things a little tough. Let me know how you want to go with this."

Richmond shook his head and smirked. "You're slick, just like every other politician I've ever met. Good job for getting me out here to bring more attention to this restaurant."

"Honey, I don't need you. You need me. That girl, Savannah, doesn't like you or anything you do that doesn't jive with Atlanta's qualities. She is going to fry you like crispy chicken."

"And, of course, you're going to be her source? What's your game plan?"

She smiled, looking sweet, but Richmond knew better. "I want your hotels in my district. It's going to lead to a lot of other developments that will make me look like a great woman to be the next mayor of Atlanta."

"A quid pro quo? Being that I haven't found a site for my hotel, you had a chance to get everything you wanted. But I don't take to blackmail."

"You're not going to get anywhere without my help."

Richmond winked at her. "We'll see. Enjoy talking to your people. I'm going back to my office."

She stepped closer to him and brought her lips to his ear. "You don't want to make an enemy of me. I'm the honey you can use to catch all the flies you need to get everything put together to build your hotel."

Turning to her, Richmond ran his index finger down her cheek. "I'd rather eat fifteen hot dogs with coleslaw than deal with you on any level. Have a good day, Councilwoman." He turned away from her and hit the Uber app on his phone so that he could get back to his office building.

When Richmond arrived at his office, his anger had subsided somewhat. But he wasn't going to forget Dionne's betrayal. Maybe he should've listened to Alicia about Dionne. Richmond knew it wouldn't be long before Savannah started digging around into the real reason he was in Atlanta. She'd be too happy to cover all of the controversy surrounding his family, from his messy divorce to his paternity.

What if she wasn't over her hate for the Crawfords and was just setting him up to be humiliated later? He knew that Vivian would be happy to share all the negative stories she could come up with to anyone who would listen. Savannah would be happy to lend an ear.

How in the hell was he going to fix this issue?

"Well, well," Alicia said as Richmond walked into the office complex. "I guess you changed your mind about the media attention. Would've been nice to know what you had planned today."

"I didn't have anything planned today except a tour with Dionne. She set me up," he said as he unlocked his office door. Richmond noticed the note Alicia had left for him. "Coleslaw, huh?"

"That's not important. We have to talk about this CNN buzz and the fact that you haven't started any construction on the hotel. Why didn't you let Dionne do her thing and just smile like a pretty boy?" She folded her arms across her chest. "How am I going to help you market what you're doing if I don't know what you're doing? I thought this was one of the reasons that you needed me to work with you."

"Calm down. I made a mistake, but I won't do that again."

"And how does Dionne feel about that?"

"Want a drink?" He reached into his desk drawer and pulled out a bottle of scotch. "This has been a hell of a Monday."

"I told you to watch her, but most men don't listen when it comes to a big butt and a smile."

He pushed a shot glass of scotch toward Alicia. She glanced at the glass but didn't pick it up immediately. "The whole damn world saw you. What do you think Solomon is going to think?"

Richmond downed his shot of scotch. "Who cares? This is my project. And maybe I started a buzz that we can ride." Why did he say *ride*? Giving Alicia a slow once-over, he wondered how it would feel to have Alicia riding him and making him call out her name. Those thighs wrapped around him would give him pleasure beyond belief. Would he ever be about to find out?

"Hello?" she snapped.

"What?"

"I said, we should start a social media campaign to capitalize on what you've started today. We can create an Instagram account to show *the city guy* in Atlanta. And we can chronicle the building of the hotel."

"That sounds like a great idea. I just want to make sure that we're not going to get a lot of comments on pictures that don't have anything to do with the hotel and—"

"You can't control what people post on social media. But we have to make sure that people are interactive with what we post and are ready to come and see as well as stay in our hotel." Alicia picked up her glass of scotch and took a sip.

"You said *our* hotel."

"Well, if I'm working in marketing with you, it is ours. And this scotch is amazingly smooth."

"I keep good liquor for situations just like this," he said, then offered her a seat. "How did your day go?"

"Let's just say that the best thing that happened to me today was having lox and bagels for breakfast."

"Then we should have a great dinner to make up for the day we've had."

Alicia smiled and nodded. "I know the perfect place. We can—"

"Go to my place. I don't want to see another person for at least eighteen hours."

She nodded. "That sounds like a great plan. How about we raid your wine cellar too?"

"I still have a bottle of merlot that we need to share. Just no coleslaw."

Vivian gritted her teeth as she watched Richmond grinning on the TV screen. Who in the hell did he think he was? *I guess he's in Atlanta trying to pretend that he's important. And that must be his new woman. Who does he think he is—Solomon?*

She shut the TV off and decided that she wasn't going to let this stand. If he thought he was going to be this new and improved man while she struggled in New York, he had another think coming. Pulling out her iPad, she opened her airline app and booked a flight to Atlanta. She needed to let Richmond know that she wasn't going to sit by while he made a new life and left her penniless.

Granted, Vivian could've lived comfortably off her divorce settlement. But what about the trips and all the shopping that she had grown accustomed to? Maybe Gisselle was right, she should've given Richmond that baby that he'd always whined about.

She couldn't imagine being a mother. Especially a mother to Richmond's child, and he probably would've fought her on the divorce and tried to make them work things out. That last night she'd been with Richmond, Vivian knew that she couldn't live the lie of being his wife anymore.

She'd married him because when they met in college, he was from an elite family. While Vivian was smart, she was lazy and didn't want to work for riches. She was too short to be a supermodel and couldn't sing to save her life. When her mother had told her not to leave college without her MRS, she'd taken that statement to heart.

And Richmond had been a boring but rich man she knew she could hook with a baby story. Her plan had worked, but she had no idea that she'd waste so much of her life as a fake Crawford wife. The moment she met Solomon and saw how much he and Richmond didn't get along, she'd hoped to have an affair with her brother-in-law and use it to hold over Solomon's head. But Solomon hadn't liked her from the first day that they'd met. For a while, that worked in her favor because Richmond and Solomon didn't get along. But after the truth about Elliot and his other son came out, Richmond acted as if he wanted a real marriage—something they never had. Vivian figured that he had a little something on the side, as she did.

How could he love her when she hadn't shown him any love since they were college students? Vivian found out that Richmond was crazy enough to believe that they could revive a marriage that was never real, and have a future.

She wanted a check. Not a husband. And if Richmond wanted to be a hot shot in Atlanta, he would give her the money she wanted so that she could walk away.

Monday was starting to turn around for Alicia. She had two new clients call her before the end of the day to sign on to her company. It was a win for her, and just as she was about to get up and do her happy dance, there was a knock at her door.

"Come in," she said.

Richmond walked in with a smile on his face. "Are you ready to put a period on this day and get out of here?"

She glanced at her watch. "You might want to wait about forty-five minutes before you leave. Traffic is going to be hell right now."

Richmond looked around her office suite. "It looks nice in here," he said.

"It should. I worked hard to make this happen."

"Those guys didn't put your furniture together?"

Alicia shook her head. "It's a good thing that I'm handy with a screwdriver."

"Had I been here, I would've been happy to help you. There's no way that you should've worked in here with just a screwdriver."

Alicia rose to her feet and crossed over to the refrigerator in the corner. Pulling out two bottles of water, she passed one to Richmond. "You know what they say, if you want something done, you have to do it yourself."

"Is that so?" he asked as he closed the space between them and wrapped his arms around her waist. "There's something I want to do."

Before she could ask what, Richmond captured her mouth in a slow kiss. Her body melted against his and he hardened instantly. In that moment, he'd never wanted anyone more than he wanted Alicia Michaels. He wanted to bury himself deep inside her and let the world disappear.

She pressed her hand against his chest, breaking their kiss. "I-I thought we had an understanding."

"I thought that was only during office hours."

"Richmond," she breathed.

He pulled her closer. "What?"

"We're playing with fire and I don't like to get burned."

He nodded. "Trust me, we're not going to get burned and it's going to be a lot of fun."

"I'm not trying to mix business and pleasure," she said as she took a step back. "You made it pretty obvious today that you don't pay attention to my suggestions."

"Let me make it up to you," he said, then scooped her up in his arms. He set her on the edge of her desk, then lifted the hem of her dress up to her waist. She didn't get a chance to protest or tell him that they should be focused on business. In a quick motion, he was down on his knees with his face buried between her thighs. The heat of his breath against the crotch of her panties made her weak.

Pulling her panties to the side, Richmond licked her wetness as if it was the most delectable treat he'd ever tasted. Alicia's moans filled the air like the notes of Miles Davis's trumpet. Loud. Passionate. Thrilling. She urged him to go deeper as she arched her hips into his lips.

Her desire poured down on him like rain as he licked, sucked and kissed her most sensitive spot. "Yes," she cried as his tongue dove deeper into her wetness. "Richmond! Richmond!"

As her body began to shake, he pulled back and

admired the look of bliss on her face. "Delicious," he said, then licked his lips.

Alicia shook her head as she sat up. "We really shouldn't have done that."

He placed a finger to her lips. "Don't do that. We enjoyed what just happened and recognize that you needed it." She raised her right eyebrow at him. Richmond continued. "Oh, yeah, and I needed to know that you're just as sweet as I dreamed that you were." Removing his finger from her lips, he gave her a slow kiss.

Alicia wrapped her arms around his neck, pulling him closer. Richmond felt good, and had made her feel even better with his magical mouth. She was glad that she had put her desk together properly, because the way he had her bucking and dancing could've toppled the ebony desk.

"What happens next?" she asked when they broke the kiss. "We still have to—"

"Have dinner, though I know what I'd like to eat more of," he said with a saucy wink.

She shook her head as she adjusted her clothes. "Let's get out of here."

Chapter 11

Following Richmond to his house, all Alicia could think about were the waves of pleasure that had rippled through her body while he'd been buried between her legs. How was she going to sit in his house, eat dinner, and keep her thighs together?

I got this, she thought as they pulled into the driveway. Getting out of the car, she looked up at the house and smiled.

"This traffic is something else, morning and afternoon," Richmond said as they headed up the front steps.

"You'll get used to it, eventually."

"Or I will start taking MARTA."

She folded her arms across her chest. "Did you take public transportation in New York?"

"Nope, but I had a driver."

"So spoiled. How are you ever going to survive down here without a driver?"

"As long as I got you around, I guess I will survive.

What do you have a taste for?" Richmond unlocked the door and ushered Alicia inside.

Giving him a slow once-over, she had so many ideas. She wanted his hands all over her body as she tasted his lips again. Wanted him deep inside her, thrusting back and forth until she screamed his name.

"Alicia?" he asked.

"What were you planning on ordering?"

He snorted and shook his head. "We're cooking. I mean, you own a restaurant, you have to be amazing in the kitchen."

Alicia laughed, nearly buckling over. "Absolutely not. Now, I can probably help with some prep work. None of us can cook. That's why we had Devon in our lives for so long. As much as we wanted to hate him because of what he did to Kandace, the brother could cook. And she even forgave him over a slice of chocolate cake."

"I wonder if Solomon knows the way to his wife's heart is chocolate cake? What's your must-have meal?"

She shrugged. "I just like savory things. Which is why the lox was delicious to me this morning. But let's see what you do with this dinner tonight before I answer that."

"Don't expect any hot dogs and coleslaw."

"Good thing I had that for lunch." Alicia was surprised to see that Richmond had gotten furniture in the house. "That was quick."

"Well, I couldn't just hang out in the bedroom. And someone told me I needed to get ready to show off my home in a magazine."

Alicia sucked her teeth. "Well, you've already shown off on TV."

Richmond groaned as he walked into the kitchen. "Your girl set me up. Dionne's a slick politician who wants a bigger stage."

"And I thought she was just a . . ." Alicia let her crude comment drop. "So, what happened?"

Richmond told her how Dionne had called him and asked him to go to the ribbon cutting for the restaurant. He had no idea that it was part of her plan to let the media know that she was working with Crawford Hotels to revive her district.

"And to make things even worse, the CNN reporter who was there doesn't really like my family too much, so I get the feeling that there's going to be some fallout from this that won't look good for me."

"That snake," Alicia said. "She would try to use someone else's good deeds to make herself look better. I thought she would've outgrown that by now. Don't worry about her, I have another friend who can help you with zoning and property in the city of Atlanta and Fulton County. Dionne knows better."

"But she did make a good point. Those wounded warrior restaurants would be great in the hotel."

"Does the menu fit with the theme of what you're trying to do?"

"We'll make it work. One of the things that my parents—mother—always wanted our hotels to do was reach back and help others. It wasn't until things started breaking down with her and Elliot that a lot of the philanthropic work that we'd done got put on the back burner."

"Let me ask you a question," Alicia began as she watched Richmond pull out the ingredients for dinner.

He looked up at her as he set a package of chicken breasts on the counter. "Yeah?"

"Are you trying to rebuild your mother's legacy?"

"Subconsciously, I think I am. You know, my mother was a beautiful and strong-willed person. But after everything that went down with my father and her own demons, I feel like Cynthia Crawford is only a footnote in something that she created."

"Why don't you name the first boutique hotel after her? Make it look like all of the things you love about your mother."

"I don't know if Adrian and Solomon would be behind that. As much as I want to honor my mother, she did some cruel shit."

Alicia threw her hands up. "I don't know the entire situation, but maybe your mom was trying to protect her family and she acted out of anger."

"It was morc of a pot calling the kettle black. Neither of them were faithful, and there's evidence on both sides, in the form of me and Adrian. And as much as I would love to honor my mother by building a hotel monument to her, what would that do to Adrian? How would he feel about coming to the *Cynthia*? My mother was horrible to his mother."

"Maybe it's time for y'all to bury the past?"

"How about we table this discussion and you help me chop some onions?"

She nodded and crossed over to the counter where Richmond had dropped the knife. Alicia chopped onions and mushrooms and he prepared the chicken breasts for the cast-iron skillet. Alicia smiled as he poured a bit of oil in the pan.

"I haven't seen one of those since my grandmother passed."

"Everything old is new again," he said. "And you don't get a better sear on chicken breasts than in a cast-iron skillet."

"You sound like a real cook over there."

"Let's just say that when you're married to someone who doesn't even walk through the kitchen to pour water, you have to learn how to do a lot of things for yourself. There's only so many times you want to go out to eat."

"That's because there isn't a Hometown Delights near you."

"Maybe you're right," he said with a wink. "Since Charlotte isn't that far away, you're going to have to show me what's so great about your place."

Alicia wanted to show him her place and everything she had to offer, but she had to remember that they were still business associates—no matter how good his tongue felt between her thighs. Had they crossed a line that would make it harder for them to work together?

"I think we're good with the onions," he said. "What's next?"

"Can you boil water? I have some jasmine rice I'm going to put on."

"Boiling water, I can handle," she said as she grabbed a pot and filled it with water.

About an hour later, Richmond was opening a bottle of merlot to go with their dinner of pan-fried chicken breasts, rice, and grilled asparagus with garlic sauce.

"I should've gotten something for dessert," he said. "Well, for you at least. I've already had my dessert." Richmond poured the wine, then sat down across from Alicia.

"You're a bad man, Mr. Crawford." She raised her glass to him. "Here's to a great dinner."

He clanked his glass against hers.

Richmond could barely eat his food because watching Alicia's reaction to the food was damn near erotic.

From the way she chewed the tender chicken breast to the way she bit into the spear of asparagus, her lips were like works of art and he couldn't wait to feel them against his again. But from the way she took that chicken in her mouth, there were other parts of his body that yearned to be kissed.

"You might have a future in this," she said as she polished off her chicken. "This meal was delicious."

"Thanks. But it was nothing."

"Didn't taste like nothing, but what do I know?" she quipped.

Richmond rose to his feet and cleared the dishes. When Alicia got up to help him, he knew that he'd been right about her all along. "You don't have to help," he said.

"I know," she said as she playfully bumped her hip into his. "But you can't feed me an amazing meal and think I'm just going to sit here and watch you wash the dishes."

"You mean load the dishwasher." Watching her rinse the plates and silverware they'd used, Richmond couldn't help but wonder what it would be like to spend every night like this for the rest of his life.

"Richmond?"

"Huh?" He tore his eyes away from her and shook his mind free of his fantasy life with Alicia.

"Do you want to go over the media plan for getting you out of this mess with Dionne?"

He shook his head. "It's way after business hours and there is still half a bottle of expensive merlot on the table. Let's have a drink and maybe watch a movie and R-E-L-A-X."

"Relax? What is that?"

"Let me show you." He wrapped his arms around her waist and led her into the living room where he now had a plush sofa, a fifty-inch TV, and a Blu-ray DVD player. "Have a seat, kick off your shoes, and tell me, who's your favorite James Bond?"

"Roger Moore, of course."

Richmond crossed over to the TV and popped in *A View to a Kill.* "Grace Jones makes this movie for me. She is one sexy woman."

"And a badass to boot," Alicia said. "There is a video of her doing the hula hoop while performing one of my favorite songs ever."

"'Pull Up to the Bumper'?"

Alicia snorted and shook her head. "You're nasty!

Of course that would be your favorite song. But it was 'Slave to the Rhythm,' and she did it in heels and a silver mask. If I'm still that dope in my sixties, then my life will be something special."

He gave her a slow glance and decided that no matter what, he was going to be around to see that happen. "So, when is this going to happen? I want to see you do everything the lovely Miss Jones can do."

"Play the movie," she quipped.

Richmond sat on the sofa and took Alicia's feet into his hands, then began to massage them.

"You have found my weakness."

"Really?" Richmond said. "And they are such a pretty weakness. I bet every inch of you is beautiful."

"Stop," she moaned, and slipped her foot from underneath his hand. "I should probably go. I have a big day tomorrow and—"

Richmond brought his lips down on top of hers and silenced her doubts. She melted in his arms for a moment, then she pushed back from him. "I-I have to go," she said. Alicia reached down and grabbed her shoes.

"Why are you . . ." Richmond stopped, his mind flashing back to the scene at the gala. As much as he wanted her to stay, there was no way he could pressure her. "All right, we can watch the movie or I can walk you out to your car so that you can get ready for tomorrow."

She exhaled. "Yeah, I'm going to go. See you in the morning."

He nodded and kissed her on the forehead. "Lox and bagels?"

"You're pretty awesome. I'll bring the Dancing Goats."

"Alicia . . ."

She stroked his cheek. "Thanks for dinner." As Alicia dashed out of the room with her shoes in her hand, Richmond wished she would've stayed the night with him. Waking up with Alicia in his arms would've been the best part of the morning, but she wasn't comfortable, and no matter how hard he wanted to talk her into staying, it wasn't the time for it.

Richmond walked her outside after she put her shoes on. "Thank you again for dinner," she said.

"We can do it again tomorrow, if you would like."

"Sounds like a plan." Alicia placed her hand on the door handle of her car. "I had a really good time tonight."

"Anytime I spend with you is always good."

Alicia hopped into her car and sped down the road. She knew one thing for sure, she needed a long, cold shower. Her desire for Richmond was driving her crazy. As soon as she got to the hotel she stripped out of her clothes and headed straight for the bathroom. Standing underneath the cold spray, she thought about dinner, how sweet he was, how he made her feel. So what was she so afraid of? Clearly, she'd already mixed business and pleasure after that interlude in her office earlier.

But being with him on the sofa and in his home just felt so right and so comfortable. It scared her because there had to be something on the back end that would make this go left. Kandace told her that he was freshly divorced. What if he wasn't over his ex? People get divorced and get back together all the time. She hadn't wanted to be his rebound chick and end up with her heart broken. Maybe he just wanted a fling? She could deal with that if he was honest about what he really wanted.

When her cell phone rang, Alicia almost jumped out of her skin. Shutting the water off, she wrapped up in a towel and padded across the room. "Hello?"

"I just wanted to make sure that you made it home safely," Richmond said. "And something about watching Grace Jones parachute off the Eiffel Tower made me think of you."

"Interesting. Why did that make you think of me?"

"A big badass move like that, I could totally see you doing that. I'd be willing to take you to Paris to see if you'd do it."

"I'll take that trip to Paris, but I'm not jumping off anything." She laughed.

"So, when do you want to go?"

"Go where?"

"To Paris. And if it would make you feel better, we could call it a business trip. Go and visit some of the chic hotels in the city and add some Atlanta to it when I build here. I've actually been planning a trip to Paris to check out the hotels over there. Think about it, when people visit Paris, they don't come back complaining about the accommodations."

"Must be nice to decide you can just up and go to Paris for research."

"What can I say? I'm the boss. Would next week be good for you?"

Alicia cleared her throat. There was no way this . . . "Are you serious?"

"Yeah, I'll pull together a plan and we can get going. I'll have it ready in the morning."

"Okay," she said, still in disbelief.

"Sweet dreams, beautiful."

"See you in the morning," she said.

Chapter 12

Three weeks later, Alicia was sitting in Hartsfield-Jackson International Airport waiting to board a flight to Paris. She was beyond excited and impressed. First-class tickets and reservations at some of the best hotels in Paris. She'd reached out to Devon and Marie Harris so that they could get together for dinner. One that Devon would cook, of course. Richmond walked over to her and handed her a large cup of coffee.

"This is what I hate about international flights—the delays," he said.

She laughed. "I'm surprised there isn't a Crawford corporate jet."

"It's in Queens."

"How are you going to get along without all of your devices down here in the South?"

"As long I have you on my side, who needs a private jet?" He held up his coffee cup to hers. "Cheers to a lovely trip."

"Cheers." Alicia smiled and took a big sip of

coffee. "You've gotten a lot done in these past few weeks."

Richmond nodded. "I've been focused because you've been working your butt off on the marketing side. I love how you've built a buzz about the hotel before we've broken ground."

She nodded. "That's why we have to make sure it lives up to the hype." Alicia didn't say anything about how he'd fought her in the beginning of the social media campaign. He glanced at her as she took another sip of her coffee.

"You're not going to say it?"

"Say what?"

"That you told me so?"

Alicia laughed. "It's too early to be smug, and you already know."

"Let me be the first to admit it, I was wrong."

"And if this is how you correct your wrongs, you'll never hear me complain."

Richmond wrapped his arm around her shoulder. "This trip is going to change everything," he whispered against her ear.

Who knew what this trip was going to change between them? She already knew that it was going to be more than business going on in the City of Lights.

The question was, could she handle it?

Richmond watched Alicia nap as they waited to board the plane. Did she realize how beautiful she was—awake or sleeping? He ran his index finger down her smooth cheek. This trip to Paris was totally unnecessary, and he didn't care. He wanted to have uninterrupted time with the woman he was falling for.

There was just something special about Alicia Michaels that made him happy to be a man. She shifted in her seat and he drew her into his arms, letting anyone who passed by know that she belonged to him.

"Attention Air France travelers, flight 8945 with nonstop service to Paris, will begin boarding momentarily. We apologize for the delay and thank you for your patience. We hope you will enjoy your flight with Air France today."

"Yeah, if we ever get in the air," Richmond muttered.

"That wasn't nice," Alicia said as her eyes fluttered open. "We're going to get there. It's not as if you have a schedule to stick to. You're the boss, remember?"

"Cute. But you're right. It could be worse and we could've had a layover in Boston or something."

"See," she said as she reached up and stroked his cheek. "There is always a silver lining. But next time we take a flight, let's get a later one."

"So, there will be a next time, huh?"

Alicia's cheeks heated with embarrassment from her slip. She didn't want him to know during her brief nap that she had been dreaming about a future with him and a trip to Lagos and holding hands while walking down Ibeno Beach.

"We'll have to see how this trip goes first," she

replied with a grin. "You might be a horrible flight mate."

"There are other ways to get around. You know, I actually suggested Crawford Cruises once."

"And what happened to that idea?"

"An oversaturated market, overhead that was beyond ridiculous, and the fact that Solomon and I were still at each other's throats all the time. It would've never worked. I think I just suggested it because I wanted to get away from everything. Family, a failing marriage, and New York."

Alicia paused and wondered if his Atlanta relocation was an extension of him wanting to get away from everything.

He caught the question in her eyes and smiled. "Things are a lot different now," he replied. "Atlanta is going to be my new home, where I plan to make new memories and find the new and improved Richmond."

"And learn to love coleslaw?"

"That's the one thing that is not going to happen." *Unless you cover yourself in coleslaw and I have to eat it off to save your life.*

"I bet I could change your mind," she said with a smile. "We just have to get you some coleslaw with the right pairing. Biscuits and chicken, maybe."

"Definitely not on a hot dog, ever again. But we can deal with that after Paris. I get to taste the famous food of Devon Harris."

"Who makes some amazing coleslaw, by the way."

Richmond took her face into his hands. "You know what tastes better than coleslaw? Your lips."

Leaning in, he captured her lips with a slow and deep kiss. Alicia moaned as his tongue danced against hers. His body wanted to melt with hers, wanted to make love to her as if no one else was around. But he knew he had to pull back before he lost all of his self-control. "Delicious."

"You can't keep kissing me like that," she breathed.

"Why not? It was amazing. And you kissed me back, so obviously, you like it." He brushed his nose against hers. "Let me tell you this. I plan to kiss you several times when we get to Paris. Be prepared."

"And if I don't want you to kiss me?"

"Then I won't, but you will want it."

Before she could respond, the gate agent began to announce that first-class passengers could begin boarding. "Time to go," Richmond said. As they walked to the boarding gate, he kept his hand on the small of her back. He couldn't remember the last time he took a trip where his partner didn't complain about every little thing, from things that they could control to the size of the leather seats in first class. Alicia, while annoyed by the delay as anyone would be, was still polite and a pleasure to be around. The last time he'd taken a trip with Vivian, she'd been a monster—berating the ticket agent, complaining about the wine choices on the flight and the fact that she had to sit beside her husband. Richmond knew he could've taken the corporate jet, but he'd flown commercial just to piss off his wife. It worked, but he was tired of being petty and going tit for tat with Vivian.

After his arrest in Los Angeles, he knew his marriage was over; it was just a matter of how much it would cost him. Solomon had told his brother to stick to the prenup. But Richmond thought if he gave her what she wanted that she'd disappear and live the life she wanted. One without him. But Vivian was greedier than he'd thought and Solomon wasn't very helpful by blackballing her, even if it was what she deserved.

Alicia stroked the back of his hand as they settled in their seats on the plane. "You're all right over there?"

Richmond nodded. "My coffee's wearing off, which is a good thing because I need a nap."

"And I need to brush up on my French. So, I guess my coffee is just kicking in." She pulled her iPod out of her carry-on bag. "I downloaded one of those language programs a while back."

"*C'est une bonne idée, mademoiselle.*" His fluency in French almost made Alicia's knees go weak. She was thankful that she was sitting down.

"Well, well, aren't you full of surprises?" she said with a smile.

Richmond winked at her. "I aim to please."

"So, where was this guy when Kandace and Solomon first moved to New York? I really thought you were the model for Oscar the Grouch."

Richmond laughed. "Back then I was, and I didn't think Solomon's wife liked me."

"Do you think you gave Kandace or anyone else a reason to like you?"

He shrugged. "Aren't you glad that you were wrong about me, though?"

"I haven't decided yet. I'm just glad you and your brother worked out your kinks and we all got a chance to get along. Because if Kandace hadn't given you her seal of approval, I wouldn't have given you the time of day," Alicia said.

"And that would've been a loss for all of us." Richmond took her carry-on bag and placed it in the overhead compartment then returned to his seat.

"You're right about that," she said. Richmond got comfortable for his nap. The plush leather felt almost as good as Alicia's arms. He glanced at her as she prepared for the flight, pulling out her tablet, headphones, and a magazine. Yeah, she was organized as hell, but this woman needed to relax. He recognized the behavior and he knew it masked a lot of things. He wondered if Alicia would feel comfortable enough to talk to him about it.

"What?" she asked when she caught his stare.

"One of the best things about a long flight is the fact that you can relax."

"This is me relaxing," she said. "I just like to have everything in its place."

Before he could respond, the captain began making flight announcements. He leaned over and kissed her on the cheek before fastening his seat belt. "I still say, you need to relax."

"Welcome to Atlanta, Georgia. We do hope you enjoy your stay in our beautiful city. Today's weather is seventy-five degrees with a thirty percent chance of rain."

Vivian gritted her teeth as the other passengers began to deplane. She hated flying commercial, but sitting in coach had to be the biggest nightmare of her life. When she found Richmond, she was definitely going to make him upgrade her ticket. The sooner she got out of the South, the better.

Before getting to Atlanta, Vivian looked up Richmond's new girlfriend and found out that she was a city councilwoman. She figured since she was a public figure, she'd be easier to find than Richmond. Solomon wouldn't take her calls anymore, and Vivian was tired of being ignored. It had been nearly a month! She was going to get cash or a pound of flesh. Either way, she was leaving Atlanta with what she wanted or the Crawford crew was going to find their business spread across every rag in the nation by the time she was done.

Finally, she was off the plane. As she slapped her oversized sunglasses on her face, she moved through the busy concourse like a woman possessed. Knowing Richmond, he was probably in this woman's face, buying her anything she wanted to keep her interested. He was a boring man who'd be nothing without his money. So, he'd lost weight and got a makeover—he was still the same boring and needy man she'd married. At least, that was what Vivian thought. She'd failed to see the other changes in her ex, because all that mattered to her had been the money she had access to. Vivian had never loved Richmond, and after faking her pregnancy to get a ring from him, she saw that the Crawfords were about projecting an image—no matter what was happening behind the scenes. She'd watch her in-laws argue and cut each other down on a daily basis. She'd actually admired Cynthia Crawford's ruthlessness and figured that she'd handle Richmond the same way. She had no idea that Elliot and Cynthia's relationship had been wrapped in layers of infidelity and years of fighting. Finding out the truth had only given her more ammunition to use in order to keep her ex-husband in line. Now he wanted to act like she didn't have the power to ruin their lives, even his new one in Atlanta. "He's going to regret trying to play me," she muttered as she headed to the taxi stand to get a ride to a hotel.

Paris, France

"Paris has always been one of my favorite cities," Richmond said as they stepped off the plane. "Always loved the art and the food." What he didn't say was that he'd never had a chance to experience it with someone that he cared about. Glancing over at Alicia, he knew that this would be a different type of trip and he was going to make sure that they both had a great time.

"This is only my second time here," she replied. "First time I came was when Devon and Marie had their little girl. We all came to celebrate her birth. We didn't really have time to do a lot of sightseeing, but we did eat a lot." Alicia smiled. "I don't understand how the French stay so thin with all the bread they eat. I would probably be four hundred pounds if I lived here."

Richmond smiled. "And you'd still be the most beautiful woman in the world."

Alicia turned away from him, hiding her smile. "So where are we off to first?" she asked.

"Well, I figured we could get checked into the hotel. I've reserved a couple of suites at one of Paris's newest boutique hotels just to see what it looks like. My plan is to take the best of what they're doing and add it to our Atlanta location. I'm sure we'll get guests who are used to styling and things like this at our hotel, so I want to make sure that we're ahead of the curve, not trying to keep up with the Europeans later."

"Sounds like a good idea," Alicia said. "But I hope we're going to get some rest first."

Alicia needed to get some sleep because while she was on the plane, she couldn't sleep. Every time she closed her eyes all she could think about was joining the mile-high club with him. Her attraction to Richmond was growing every day, and she just wondered if she'd be able to keep herself under control in Paris, the most romantic city in the world, with the man who was doing nothing but turning her on with his butterfly touches and smiles.

After getting into the black car that was waiting for them, Alicia found herself transfixed by the man sitting beside her. There was something about Richmond that just kept a smile on her face. Maybe it was his laid-back nature and the fact that he was different from all of the blind dates that her friends had tried to set her up on. He was someone she could see herself growing with. Someone who wanted more out of life than just arm candy, and at the same time made her feel like both—the brains and the beauty.

"You're not sleeping already, are you?" Richmond asked when he noticed Alicia's silence.

"Almost," she said. "But I'm definitely going to have to eat something before I go to sleep."

"I thought we could try the hotel's restaurant. One thing I always do is judge the place I'm staying at by the food they serve me."

"Well, I've come to believe that if you have a bad meal in Paris, it's your own fault."

"We're just going to have to see about that, now, aren't we?"

She sucked her teeth. "Mr. Picky."

For the rest of the ride, a comfortable silence enveloped them. Richmond drew Alicia into his arms as they rode. She nestled against him and suddenly, Alicia started to believe that her happily-ever-after might happen.

Vivian sat in Dionne's office waiting for the woman to show up. Patience was never Vivian's strong suit, and this Dionne woman was testing the hell out of her patience. The door finally opened and Dionne walked in. "About time," Vivian muttered.

"Hello," Dionne said as she extended her hand to Vivian. "How can I help you today, miss?"

"Crawford. Vivian Crawford. I saw you on CNN with my husband a few weeks back."

"Your husband?"

"Richmond Crawford. Look, I'm not here to cause a scene or fight over him. If that's what you want, have at it. I just want to make sure that I'm getting what's due me. I spent too many years playing the dutiful wife to get locked out because he wants to start a new life in Atlanta."

"First of all, Mrs. Crawford, your husband and I don't have anything more than business going on."

"Is that so?"

"And if you're still married to him, then I'm not the woman you need to be worried about. From what I've seen, it's Alicia Michaels who's riding his jock like a pony."

Vivian leaned back in her chair. "What do you mean?"

Dionne smiled, then pressed the button for her assistant.

"Yes, Ms. Ashe?" he asked.

"Hold all my calls for an hour or so. Thanks." Turning to Vivian, Dionne began to unload about Alicia and her friends from college.

Chapter 13

Paris, France

Richmond sipped the best champagne he'd tasted in his life. It was almost good enough to wash down the burnt taste of the sole meunière out of his mouth. Two things he'd been sure of, before today, had been that chefs couldn't mess up chicken and fish. He'd sent the dish back twice and when it came out burnt again, he figured he would try it. Big. Mistake.

Alicia shook her head as she looked down at her meal. "I guess I was wrong," she said.

"About?"

"Never getting a bad meal in Paris." She pushed her plate away.

He poured her another glass of champagne. "This helps, a lot."

She accepted the glass and took a big swig. "They have a great marketing ploy. The food is so bad, you don't even think about the cost of the liquor."

"That's a technique we won't be taking home with

us." He downed another glass. "I want people to have fond memories of our restaurant, like they have of the Busy Bee Café."

"Good idea," she replied through her yawn. "Do you think they got our room situation straightened out yet?"

Richmond shrugged, though secretly he hoped that the room situation wasn't taken care of. Somehow, the reservation for the second suite had been canceled. Richmond did the gentlemanly thing and told Alicia she could take the suite and he'd wait for another room. She'd said that she wasn't going to take his room, since he'd booked the trip. The front-desk clerk had done Richmond's job by suggesting that they could share the suite, since it was big enough for at least four people.

"We could always share. I'm sure they're going to get us a second room in the morning."

"As tired as I am, I think we should. I need a nap before we call Devon and Marie."

Richmond waved for the waiter so that he could pay the bill. If Alicia wanted to rest, then he'd make that happen. Besides, he needed to call Solomon and let him know what was going on. Though he'd said this was a business trip, he was paying for this trip himself. This was a part of his plan to win Alicia, and he couldn't charge the company for it. Even though Solomon had used a whole hotel to win his wife.

"You take your nap and I'll make some phone calls while we wait for the other room."

She leaned over to him and gave him a kiss on

the cheek. "You're awesome. I'm sitting here fighting sleep like a toddler."

Richmond paid the bill and then helped Alicia to her feet. "Let's go, my dear," he said. Once they got on the elevator, Richmond took Alicia into his arms and brushed his lips against hers. "Remember when I told you that I planned to kiss you a lot when we got to Paris?"

"I think I heard you say something like that."

He captured her lips in a slow, sweet kiss. "That's because you're tired," he said once the elevator stopped and they broke the kiss.

"You need to stop."

"I'm just getting started. But I'm going to let you rest first." He winked at her, then stepped off the elevator. Once they entered the suite, Richmond was finally impressed. The suite looked like a studio apartment in midtown Manhattan.

The bedroom was spacious, the seating area had a desk, sofa, and a fireplace that he wanted to light and make love to Alicia in front of. The sofa and love seat looked as if they were ready to seat guests. This was a home away from home. When Alicia walked into the bedroom, all Richmond could think about was Alicia stripping down to her underwear and crawling into bed. He wanted nothing more than to join her, make love to her, and feel the bite of her nails against his skin. But right now, she needed rest, and he'd give that to her. Because when they made love, he wanted Alicia to be at full strength.

"Richmond," she called out. "You probably need some rest too. You can join me in bed."

He walked into the bedroom and crossed over to the bed, where Alicia was already covered up. "I thought you wanted rest."

"Oh, I do. And you need some as well. We were on the same flight. I'm not that selfish where I'm going to take this comfortable bed just for myself."

Richmond leaned in and kissed her on the cheek. "You know, you're sweet and I could use a nap. But I've got to make a few calls, and I might snore."

"Whatever."

"It's good to know that you share, though." He winked at her. "Sweet dreams."

Richmond sat on the sofa with every intention of calling Solomon, but within seconds, he was knocked out.

Atlanta, Georgia

Alicia Michaels was Richmond's mystery woman. The thought of it all made Vivian laugh. Seemed as if he hadn't been Mr. Loyalty, as he wanted everyone to believe. Since Alicia was one of Solomon's wife's friends, she and Richmond could've been carrying on for years. He'd played her, and she was going to get her revenge. Not only the money, but every ounce of his happiness. She had to thank Dionne Ashe for being petty enough to hold on to a college grudge against Alicia and her crew. In another world, Dionne and Vivian would be besties, but right now all Vivian wanted was her pound of flesh from her ex. She Googled Alicia and found the website for her business and the phone number. She'd hoped there would be an address as well, but this was a start.

Vivian dialed her number, hoping the trick would answer the phone so that she could tell her to leave her husband alone. Voicemail.

"She can't be that busy," Vivian muttered as she looked at her watch, then decided to call Richmond. He needed to know that she was in town and they should talk. She got his voicemail too and realized that the two were probably together. How she wished this was happening on her turf back in New York. Richmond was so predictable that she'd know exactly where he'd take Alicia. Some little café on the Upper East Side near the Whitney Museum so that the little country bumpkin could be impressed by the bright lights of the big city.

Then they'd go walk in Central Park. Boring. But at least she'd know where to look. Atlanta was big, busy and had too many damned one-way streets. She had been lucky to find her way to a hotel after leaving Dionne's office. Vivian hated to do this, but she was going to give them a day before she pounced and got what she wanted.

Paris, France

Soft lips brushed across hers as fingers danced across her thighs. Alicia moaned as she felt his tongue touch hers. His hands pushed her thighs apart and stroked her wetness until she cried out in delight. "Alicia."

"Yes."

"Alicia."

"Oh, please don't stop."

"Wake up, sweetheart."

Alicia's eyes fluttered open and embarrassment flooded her body when she looked into Richmond's eyes. Had she been dreaming out loud? Did he hear her? "What's going on?"

He stroked her cheek and grinned. "I thought you were having a nightmare, at first. Then I heard my name."

Alicia turned away from him and sat up in the bed. She was happy she hadn't stripped down to her underwear as the blanket fell off her shoulder. "It still could've been a nightmare," she quipped. "What time is it?"

"It's either eight o'clock East Coast time or two a.m.," Richmond said with a shrug. "When I woke up, I realized that I was starving and needed something to eat."

Alicia nodded. "I could definitely eat something. But it's so late and we've already seen what the hotel's kitchen can do."

"That's why we're going to Chez Denise. It comes highly recommended on the Internet. Want to get dressed and go?"

She nodded because what she really wanted was to watch him take off all his clothes and make her sexy dreams come true. "Give me about five minutes."

Richmond left the room and Alicia hopped out of the bed to get dressed. A few minutes later, the duo headed downstairs to the car that was waiting for them.

Richmond watched Alicia's backside as she climbed into the town car. *Delicious*, he thought as he got in behind her.

"What's so great about this place?" Alicia asked as they rode.

"Google says good food and lots of fun," he said as he wrapped his arm around Alicia's shoulders. "I'm going to try the steak tartare."

"That's raw steak, isn't it?"

He nodded. "A classic meal that I've never had the guts to taste."

"You won't have to worry about me taking food off your plate today." Alicia grinned as she snuggled against his chest. "I guess we start working tomorrow?"

"Yeah, because we're not getting started at this time of night. Woman, do you ever take a break?"

"That's what I did when I took my nap," she said.

"A nap is not a break, it's a recharge. And, your sleep didn't sound too restful."

She rolled her eyes and pinched him on the forearm. "You don't know what you heard."

"You saying my name over and over again. It was a really sweet sound. Tell me, were we going over spreadsheets or marketing plans?"

"Funny. I guess that's for me to know and for you

to try and figure out," she said as the car came to a stop.

"Looks like we're here," he said. When the driver opened the door, Richmond hopped out, then held his hand out to Alicia. Both of them were surprised to see the café was packed with patrons at this hour. "Lots of hungry people in Paris tonight."

"I see." Alicia was hungry as well, but her hunger was deeper than food. She wanted the man beside her. Turning away from him, Alicia decided that she'd keep her hormones under control and enjoy some classic French food. Then Richmond placed his hand on the small of her back and it felt as if nuclear bombs of desire exploded inside her body. She decided that it was time to listen to the voice telling her to go for it. He was sweet, tender, and sexy. Every kiss broke down a piece of the wall she'd built to protect her heart. It was time to take a chance.

"Richmond," she whispered.

"Yes?"

"Can we take this food to go? I really want to be alone with you."

Richmond's smile spread from ear to ear. "Baby girl, you haven't said anything but a word. As a matter of fact, food is overrated."

"Oh, no," she said, pointing her finger at his chest. "We're going to need to eat something, first."

He leaned into Alicia and brought his lips to her ear. "I plan to eat all night long or until you're satisfied."

"Less talk, more action," she said.

Chapter 14

Alicia and Richmond ate their entrées in the car as they rode back to the hotel. His steak tartare and fries were an interesting starter for what he now had a serious craving for. "Sure you don't want a taste?" he asked as he dipped a fry in the steak tartare.

"Yeah, no," she said as she turned her head to the side. "I'm sticking with the coq au vin."

By the time they made it back to the hotel, their food was gone and Richmond could hardly wait to take his woman upstairs. Glancing at her, he realized that Alicia was his. His present, his future, his everything. She'd changed his life in ways that he hadn't expected and he couldn't wait to see what the future would hold for them. Richmond hadn't expected to fall for Alicia, or any woman, after his divorce. But Alicia's warmth and brilliance opened his eyes to a chance at real love. The kind of love he'd watched his brothers enjoy with their wives. He knew Alicia would challenge him, she would encourage him and make him a better man.

The car stopped and Richmond didn't wait for

the driver to open the door. With one hand, he helped Alicia out of the back seat and with the other, he gave the driver a hefty tip.

"Let's go," he said, then scooped Alicia into his arms. She wrapped her arms around his neck and brushed her nose against him. "Umm. Alicia, we're not going to make it to the suite if you keep doing that."

"You mean this?" she asked, then ran her tongue up and down the side of his neck. "Or this?" She kissed his neck, slow and deep. Richmond's knees almost buckled.

"Woman," he moaned. "You and your mouth are asking for trouble."

"Bring it on," she replied as he pressed the up button on the elevator. Once they stepped on the elevator, Richmond pressed Alicia against the wall and kissed her with a hot passion. She moaned as their tongues danced. She was so happy that she'd worn a skirt to dinner. Richmond's hot hands on her thighs made her cream with desire. Then he slipped his finger inside her lace panties. "Umm," she moaned.

"This is what I call payback," he said as he stroked her throbbing bud. "And this is only a preview of what's to come."

"I-I think I'm about to . . ." Alicia cried out as she felt the waves of an orgasm wash over her.

"That was too easy. Now I know there hasn't been someone cherishing everything about you. That changes now," he said as the doors to the elevator opened. Though he wanted to rush inside the suite,

Richmond knew tonight was going to be about going slow and making pleasure last.

Opening the door to the suite, Richmond took Alicia straight to the bedroom and laid her across the bed. Her ebony skin against the white sheets made him think of chocolate. His mouth watered as he slowly peeled her clothes off. Alicia's skin felt like satin underneath his fingertips.

Her naked body was the purest beauty he'd ever seen. She belonged in an art gallery; then again, this was a sight for his eyes only. Richmond ran his index finger between her thighs, seeking her hot wetness. Alicia moaned when he found it. Throwing her head back, she pressed her body into his finger. "Richmond," she cried as he pressed deeper and deeper.

"It's time for my dessert," he said, then dove between her thighs. Richmond lapped her sweetness as she squirmed under his tongue lashing. Suck. Lick. Kiss.

"Yes, yes, yes," she cried as he deepened his kiss. Alicia's thighs quivered as she met her release.

Richmond met her gaze as he took her to the brink of pleasure. The look in her eyes urged him on to give her more pleasure and make her feel sensations that she'd been denied way too long.

"Need. You. Inside!" Alicia cried. "Please. Don't stop."

One more lick, one more suck, and then he pulled back from her. Richmond stripped out of his clothes and joined Alicia in the bed. Pulling her against his chest, he captured her mouth in a hot kiss. Skin to skin with Alicia felt better than anything he'd ever dreamed of. Better than every fantasy he had of the lovely Alicia. Then she wrapped her thighs around his waist as their tongues danced and Richmond nearly lost it. She was hot and ready. He nearly pressed into her unprotected, but had the sense to reach for his discarded slacks and grab a condom.

"Protection," he said when he broke the kiss. Alicia nodded and watched as he slipped the sheath in place. He pulled her into his arms again, her thighs parted as he slid his hands up and down her sides. Richmond dove inside her, pumping and thrusting deep and fast. Alicia matched him stroke for stroke. Her hips filled his hands as they slowed things down. Richmond wanted to savor everything about this moment. The way she felt, the way she tasted and the sounds she made when she was satisfied.

"Look at me, babe," he whispered. "Look at me."

She locked eyes with his, her face comely with bliss as he thrust deeper. "Yes!" Alicia cried out. "Yes."

"You like that? Damn, you feel good."

She threw her head back and cried out in delight as she reached her climax. Richmond tried to hold off his own orgasm until he was sure that Alicia was satisfied. But when she tightened her sugar walls against him, he was powerless to hold back. Collapsing against each other, they drifted off to sleep.

Alicia woke up with a start. The warm arms around her waist were not a dream, Richmond was holding her. She closed her eyes again and released a satisfied sigh.

Richmond stroked her flat belly. "Morning," he whispered in her ear.

"Morning."

"How are you feeling?" He brushed his lips against the back of her neck.

"Better than I have in a while. You know last night was amazing."

"It was, and I'm looking forward to more nights and days like that with you."

Alicia turned over and faced him. "Richmond, we're in Paris and everything is . . ."

"Going to be the same when we get back to Atlanta. I'm too old for flings and things like that. And I'm too old to pretend that you're not the best thing that's happened to me."

Alicia's breath caught in her chest. Was he serious? Could she believe that what they shared was the beginning of her happily-ever-after?

"Richmond," she moaned.

"Let's get dressed and go take in the sights of Paris," he said. "Want to join me in the shower? We can save the world and start our morning making love."

"I like the way you think," she said with a wink.

Richmond turned the water on as he drank in the beauty of Alicia's naked body. Smooth, chocolate, and dark. Now that he'd gotten another taste, he was officially addicted to this woman.

She crossed over to him and ran her hand across his chest. "You're a beautiful man, you know that?" Alicia cooed.

"And you're the most stunning woman I've seen

in my life," he replied, then captured her lips in a hot kiss that was almost as steamy as the shower. He lifted her in his arms and carried her into the shower. As the water beat down on them, Richmond deepened the kiss, making her quiver with delight. Alicia grabbed a bar of soap and ran it across his chest and down to his erection.

Richmond moaned as she took his penis in her hand. When she dropped to her knees and took the length of him into her mouth, Richmond gasped with pleasure. Lick. Suck. Lick. Her lips felt like heaven, and when she took him deeper inside her mouth, he nearly exploded.

"Oh my God!" he cried as he took a step back.

She smiled and winked at him. "And you taste as good as you look." Rising to her feet, she wrapped her arms around Richmond and he pressed into her awaiting body. Their reckless interlude felt good. Skin to skin, hot passion that seemed to raise the temperature in the bathroom. Just as Richmond was about to meet his release, he tried to pull out and protect them as much as he could. But Alicia's heat was too good to let go of, and when she moaned in pleasure, then tightened herself around him, all he could do was explode.

"To hell with coffee," he whispered as he shut the water off. "Being with you is the best part of waking up."

Atlanta, Georgia

Vivian was beyond pissed as she called Alicia again. No answer, no address for her office. The only conclusion she could draw was that Alicia had no class. Then there was Richmond. She had no idea where to find him, and Solomon Crawford had told her in not so gracious terms to go and love herself.

"You should hope that I find Richmond before I find a reporter," Vivian had threatened.

"No one cares what you have to say. If someone did, you'd stop threatening to go to the press and just do it. Don't call my phone again," Solomon had said coolly before hanging up.

Maybe Solomon was right about her threatening to go to the press, but her end game was bigger than headlines. But if this was the game he wanted to play, then maybe her next call would be to a reporter.

I tried to be fair, but Solomon's arrogance is going to cost them dearly. He has just as much to lose as Richmond does if things go left in Atlanta. She pulled out her phone and called Dionne. Maybe she knew where Richmond's office was. Vivian knew she'd wait there for him today, because it was time for everyone to know that she was serious.

Chapter 15

Richmond finally believed the hype about Devon Harris. He'd never been a huge fan of desserts, but this chocolate cake was almost as delicious as the chocolate woman he'd had the pleasure of eating this morning.

"Wow," Richmond said as he took the final bite of the decadent cake. "That's one of the best things I've had in my mouth since I've been in Paris."

"I'm going to take the compliment and not ask any questions," Devon said with a laugh. "So, y'all just decided to get up one day and come to Paris. I want to be like you guys when I grow up."

"We're here on business," Alicia said as she swiped some icing from Richmond's plate. "Crawford Hotels is expanding in Atlanta, and Richmond had the brilliant idea to see how he could make his boutique hotels stand out."

Marie walked into the TV studio where the trio had been eating. Devon and Marie had moved to Paris about four years ago after the famed chef had been tapped to lead a restaurant and popular cooking show. Before he left, Devon surprised Marie with a wedding at Hometown Delights because he wanted to take his wife to France with him.

"*Bonjour, mes amis!*" She crossed over to Alicia and gave her a kiss on the cheek, then looked at Richmond. "And who is this?"

Richmond extended his hand to Marie. "Richmond Crawford."

She gave him a quizzical look and furrowed her eyebrows. "Solomon Crawford's brother? Wow, you've changed. Nothing like the pictures on your hotel website."

"That's my wife, always speaking her mind," Devon said as he crossed over to Marie and kissed her on the cheek. "Where is my baby girl?"

"Sleeping in your office with her nanny. She's living the dream, eat, sleep, poop, and let someone else clean it all up. Why did we ever become adults?"

"Because there was no alternative," Alicia said. "I bet that little beauty has everyone on the production crew wrapped around her finger."

Marie nodded with pride. "No one more than that man right there," she said as she nodded toward Devon. "She looks at him and it's as if he's hypnotized. Couldn't say no to her if he wanted to."

"Sounds like she's just like her mama," Alicia quipped. "When are you guys coming stateside again?"

"Soon," Devon said. "After I wrap up this season of the show, I'm doing a program on the Food Network with Bobby Flay, and I was hoping to use Hometown Delights as the backdrop."

"That is a great idea," Alicia replied excitedly.

"And if there is a live taping, I want to be there. I have got to meet Bobby Flay."

"Why?" Devon and Richmond asked in concert. Alicia and Marie laughed.

"Because, he's my second favorite chef," Alicia replied. "Why are you two acting like I can't have another favorite out here?"

Richmond inched closer to her and brought his lips to her ear. "My feelings are hurt, because I thought I was your favorite chef."

Turning to him, she kissed his cheek. "You know when it comes to you and Bobby there's no competition."

Marie and Devon exchanged knowing looks, then turned back to the couple. "So, how much of this trip is business?" Marie asked as she grabbed a bottle of water from Devon's hand. "Because it looks like we're going to be attending a wedding before my husband meets up with Bobby Flay."

"It's not like that," Alicia said.

"Yet, anyway," Richmond added. "Alicia and I are here on business, but no one works twenty-four seven."

Devon smiled and nodded. "This is good. I knew you seemed happier than I've seen you in a while," he said. "Rich, my man, you already know these ladies are a handful, so you better do right by this one."

Richmond took Alicia's hand in his and brought it to his lips. "I'm not worried about doing her wrong. When the right thing walks into your life, you do everything to keep it."

Devon gave Marie a quick kiss. "Don't I know it.

So, what do you two have planned for tonight? I'm having a little dinner party at my new restaurant and I'd love for you guys to join us."

"You don't have to ask me twice," Richmond said, then told Devon about their experience at the hotel restaurant.

"That's what you get for not allowing me to feed you immediately. Alicia knows better," Devon quipped. "But I have this new Southern fusion menu that I'm debuting tonight. So, you get a small taste of home with a French accent."

"Sounds delicious," Alicia said. "Any chance of you sharing these recipes?"

"Not until after the show with Flay."

"Alicia," Marie said. "You have to take some pictures with me tonight for my blog. And that sounds like an excuse for us to go shopping."

Devon rolled his eyes. "The sun shines and my wife sees it as a reason to go shopping."

"You knew who I was when you brought me to Paris, so hush," Marie quipped.

Alicia turned to Richmond. "Do you mind?" she asked.

"Not at all. Your shopping trip will give me some time to pick Devon's brain about some things, especially making sure our hotel restaurant will be on point."

"Cool," Marie said. "We should be back in about two hours or so. There is this great boutique that has some of the best clothes, and everything is pretty much one of a kind."

As she and Alicia walked out the door, Devon eyed Richmond. "All right, brother, what's the deal?"

"What do you mean?" Richmond asked.

"How long have you been in love with Alicia?"

"Probably since the day I laid eyes on her in Atlanta. She's intense, though."

Devon nodded. "Alicia has always been the one who's about her business. She doesn't play games, and if you can't handle that, you're in trouble."

"I can handle it, I just need her to know that I'm for real."

"Just be real, then. And I'll be happy to bake the wedding cake."

"We're definitely going to want the *gateau d'amoureux* at the wedding, if it ever gets that far."

Devon folded his arms across his chest. "Tell that to someone else. I know two things for sure: Men don't bring women to Paris they don't want a future with, and baking with coconut milk is not a good idea."

Marie Charles-Harris knew one thing, and that was how to shop, Alicia decided after they'd hit three boutiques in thirty minutes and the shopkeepers had everything waiting for her. They knew her name and were happy to see her when she walked in the door. A few of them had a close enough relationship with Marie to ask her about her daughter.

Marie spoke perfect French when she told them that her friend needed a killer dress for a dinner party and to make her man drool.

"He's technically not my man," Alicia said.

"Please, the way you looked at him, he's clearly yours. Anyway, you could've done worse."

"Is that so?"

"Look, honey, I lived in Charlotte for a number of years and I've seen what's out there. Richmond Crawford is a catch."

"We're not in Charlotte, though. I moved to Atlanta because I wanted a bigger challenge. You and the girls make it so easy to market Hometown Delights. And honestly, if Jade tried to set me up on another blind date, I was going to lose my mind."

"So, how did you and Richmond get together?" Marie asked as she handed Alicia an ivory dress.

Alicia shook her head. "That color isn't going to work on me," she said.

"Why not? This is going to be beautiful. Just try it on and see."

Alicia looked down at the dress and wondered if she should take the fashion risk. She normally stuck to dark and muted colors. Plain and simple.

"Girl, what are you waiting for?" Marie asked. "Try it on."

Alicia took the dress and headed for the fitting room. When she put the ivory dress on, she felt as if she was glowing.

"So, let's see it," Marie said. Alicia walked out of the fitting room with a smile on her face.

"What do you think?"

"You look good. I totally missed my calling." Marie turned to the shopkeeper. "I could be a professional shopper."

"I thought you already were," Alicia quipped. "I'm going to change."

After the ladies finished shopping, Alicia was happy to be back in Richmond's arms again in the hotel. Richmond stroked her hair as they cuddled in silence. They'd both had a busy day. He'd gotten a lot of research done on boutique hotels and what makes them successful. He knew that with Devon's recipes and the tips he'd gotten from a couple of managers from two popular hotels, he was in a great position for success.

"How much longer do we get to stay on our pretend business trip?" she asked.

"I wish I could say as long as we want, but we'd better get our heads back in the game. I'm sure Solomon and Adrian are waiting for reports on what's going on in Atlanta."

"Atlanta," she said. "Not really missing that place right now."

"It's hard to miss Atlanta when you're in Paris. But there is work to do. Now that I have an idea of what I want the hotel to look and feel like, I'm ready to get busy on my vision."

"So, things go back to normal tomorrow?"

Richmond nodded. "Afraid so. But at least we have tonight and an eight-hour flight."

"Then back to the grindstone," she said. "I guess I should check in on my other clients and line up some meetings and—"

"Not today. Today is all about me and you. And I know what I want to do right now."

"And what would that be?" she asked, though she felt his growing desire.

After making slow love, Alicia and Richmond showered and dressed for Devon's dinner party.

When she walked into the sitting room in her new ivory dress, Richmond let out a low whistle.

"We're not going anywhere. Damn, you look amazing. I don't want to share you with the rest of the world."

"You really don't have a choice, because shopping with Marie Charles is an Olympic sport and I'm showing off my find. This dress is my gold medal."

"I know another place where I can't wait to see that dress," he said as he drew her into his arms.

"Where would that be?"

"On the floor or the foot of the bed. Let's go before that happens sooner, rather than later."

Alicia had no problem leaving, because she wasn't above being talked into another dance between the sheets. They hopped into the black car waiting for them downstairs and rode to Marie and Devon's event. Alicia stroked Richmond's cheek and smiled. "I see why so many people are in love with Paris," she said. "It's such a magical city."

"It's only as magic as the person you're sharing the trip with. So, being here with you has been something more than magical."

"Is that so?"

"There's not a word to describe it. I can't wait to see what the future has in store for us."

"So, we're an *us* now?"

Richmond shook his head. "We're beyond an *us*. You're mine, Alicia."

"Richmond, this is happening really fast and right now—in Paris—everything is so . . ."

"Everything is leading toward our future together. We're not going to forget what this trip meant to us and what we mean to each other when we return to Atlanta. I've never met a woman like you before in my life. And I know one thing for sure, you're not the kind of woman a man places on a shelf. You made me feel things that I'd given up on feeling for years. So, going back to Atlanta means that we're going to be mixing business with pleasure and a lot more. Are you ready for that?"

She nodded, unable to form the words to tell him how she felt. About her fears, her hopes and desires. Alicia didn't want to be hurt again and she didn't want to believe that she'd fallen for a trip romance that would make her forget that she said she would never put herself out there to fall in love again. While she didn't love him right now, in five minutes she couldn't say that wouldn't be the case.

"I guess I better get used to this," she said. "A man of his word."

"That's right. I'm all yours, Alicia. All yours."

"I'm going to hold you to that, because I don't share."

He leaned in and kissed her on the cheek as the car pulled up to the restaurant. "We got this."

Alicia should've known that Devon's dinner party wasn't going to be a low-key event. But she hadn't expected a red carpet, camera crews, and microphones. "This has Marie written all over it," she whispered to Richmond as they walked the carpet.

"She's a force of nature. Reminds me of you," he said.

Alicia laughed. "That's a first. Marie is the life of the party; I'm the person working on the spreadsheet behind the scenes."

"I used to be that guy," Richmond said. "You got to do more relaxing."

"That's the main thing I've gotten out of this trip, that relaxing with you can be a lot of fun."

"You haven't seen anything yet. Wait until you see what we can do in the wine cellar. And I have to get a couple of bottles to add to the collection," he said.

"I can't wait to raid your wine collection," she quipped.

"That comes with a price," he said with a wink.

"We'll start with dinner and move from there." Alicia squeezed his hand. They started for the entrance and a photographer touched Alicia's elbow.

"Kiara Kabukuru? You look amazing," the photographer said with a smile.

"I'm sorry?" Alicia said.

"Aren't you Kiara Kabukuru?"

She shook her head as Richmond ushered her inside. "That was weird," she said.

"Who is Kiara Kabukuru?"

Alicia pulled out her cell phone and Googled the woman's name. Alicia was floored. "She's a supermodel." She turned the phone around and showed it to Richmond.

"She has nothing on you, though. She's all right, but you're amazing. With more curves." He kissed her on the forehead.

"Hey!" Marie said when she spotted Richmond and Alicia. "Glad to see you made it." She hugged

Richmond, then gave Alicia a kiss on the cheek. "I knew that dress was going to look amazing on you. Beautiful."

"Thanks," she said, and spun around.

"Well, come on. You two have a seat with me at the chef's table, and these appetizers are amazing."

"I bet they are," Richmond said. "I wish I'd had a chance to taste more of Devon's recipes."

"Then you better stick with Alicia, because she and her friends can't cook and my husband keeps them fed," Marie said with a smile.

"That he does," Alicia said. She glanced at Devon as he worked the room, making sure his guests enjoyed the food. Alicia couldn't help but think about how an event like this would be amazing for the restaurant or for one of the hotel openings.

"You're thinking about work, aren't you?" Richmond asked as he held a mushroom cap out to her.

Alicia took the cap from his fingers. "How did you know?"

"I can read your mind. Nah, I was thinking that an event like this would go over well in Atlanta."

"Great minds," she said with a smile.

"We can talk about this when we get to Atlanta. Tonight we're just going to enjoy the party and the Paris night." He reached out and wiped a spot of cheese from her bottom lip. "All we need to discuss tonight is slipping that dress off your gorgeous body."

Shivers of desire ran up and down her spine. "Would it be rude if we left right now?"

"Umm, yes!" Marie said, reminding them that she

was still within earshot. "But I do understand. Just tell Devon hello and goodbye before you leave."

Alicia bumped her hip into Richmond's. "We can stay a little while longer," she said. "Trust me, it will be worth the wait."

He kissed her cheek. "I know that. But how long do I have to wait?"

Chapter 16

Richmond knew one thing for certain as he danced with Alicia: If he ever got married again, she would be the woman that he married.

He needed this woman like his lungs needed air. Even if he wasn't in love at this moment, he was falling faster than a snowball melting in July. Spinning her around, Richmond closed his eyes and saw them doing these moves at their wedding reception. *Slow down,* he thought as they swayed back and forth.

"You have some moves, Crawford," she said as the song ended.

"Remember, I took ballroom dance lessons."

Alicia nodded and leaned in closer to him. "Yeah, I remember you told me that. Your instructor should be proud."

Richmond nodded. "It was fun for a while, then I realized I needed a real partner. If you're game, we can take it up again back in Atlanta. It's a great stress reliever."

"There are just so many layers to you," she said as they headed back to the table.

"And that's a good thing, right?"

She smiled. "Of course."

"When are you going to let me see everything that makes up Alicia?" He reached out and stroked her cheek.

Alicia turned her head away and grew silent for a moment.

"We should get some wine," she said.

"What was that pivot all about?" he asked, taking her chin between his index finger and thumb. "Alicia . . ."

"Richmond," she said. "Let's get the wine and go."

"Are you all right?"

She nodded. But what she didn't say was that he might not like what was underneath. She didn't want to think about how this romance wasn't going to last. She patted the back of his hand and smiled. *We'll always have Paris,* she thought, then leaned in and kissed him on the cheek.

"Red or white?" he asked.

"Surprise me."

As Richmond walked over to the bar, Marie crossed over to Alicia. "I'm going to be expecting my wedding invitation soon," she said as she took the seat that Richmond had vacated.

"You're getting way ahead of yourself."

Marie rolled her eyes. "I've seen the way he looks at you and how you look back at him."

"It's just because we're in the most romantic city

in the world. I'm not trying to get too caught up in these moments."

"Stop being so damn practical. Girl, let go and let that man love you. Then you can love him back."

Alicia looked at the bar and caught Richmond's glance. She smiled, thinking about what Marie said. Maybe it was time for her to let go and allow herself to fall for him. He wasn't Felix and she wasn't a naïve college student anymore. It was time for her to fall in love.

"I'm going to go and talk my husband into leaving," Marie said as she rose to her feet. "If you need help planning that bachelorette party, you know I'm still your girl."

Alicia stood up and gave her friend a hug. "You're too much, still," she said.

"I try," Marie replied, then sauntered away.

Richmond returned to the table with two glasses of merlot. "I'm definitely going to have to get a bottle of this for the collection."

Alicia took her glass and sipped the wine slowly. "This is good."

"Let's see." Richmond set his glass aside, then leaned into Alicia. In a quick motion, he captured her lips in a hot kiss. The sweetness of her mouth mixed with the bite of the wine sent his hormones into overdrive. Realizing that another moment of kissing her would probably lead to him ripping her clothes off at the table, Richmond broke the kiss. "Very good."

"You're a hot mess. But the merlot tastes good on you too."

"Why don't we get out of here and have a nightcap?"

She rose to her feet and extended her hand to him. "Let's go."

Richmond took her hand in his and kissed it. "I can't wait to see that dress on the floor," he whispered as they headed for the exit.

Atlanta, Georgia

Vivian was hot and tired. But more than anything she was pissed off. How had Richmond disappeared in a city like Atlanta? She'd found his office building, but not him. It had been three days and nothing. Alicia was just as much of a ghost. She hadn't returned any of Vivian's messages, and that made her wonder what kind of businesswoman she really was.

"They have to be together," she muttered as she walked into the W hotel bar. Taking a seat, she waved for a bartender. When no one came immediately, she was pissed. Then she remembered, she wasn't in New York and these country bumpkins had no idea who she was.

"Hello, what can I get for you?" the bartender asked when she finally crossed over to Vivian.

"A Manhattan and a menu."

"All right, I'll bring you your drink and a menu. Our special today is roasted shrimp and grits."

Vivian rolled her eyes. She wasn't interested in eating anything, she just wanted to punch Richmond in his face until she got the money she wanted. Glancing at her watch, she wondered if she would be able to get Richmond to give her what she wanted with the threat of blackmail, or if she would actually have to follow through on her threats.

Pulling her phone out, she started to dial Richmond again. Then a man walked over to her and sat down as if he'd been invited.

"If he's not here, he's not worth your time," the man said. Vivian looked up at him, a Boris Kodjoe look-alike with a sexy gleam in his eye. A man like this in New York was probably an actor with no money; in Atlanta, he probably owned a business.

"He's my ex-husband and we have business," she said.

"I'm sorry to hear that he's keeping you waiting, but glad to know you're waiting for an ex. I'm Felix Thompson." He took Vivian's hand in his and kissed it.

She was impressed. Southern hospitality had its charm, and Felix was fine. "Vivian," she said.

"Would you like to join me for lunch? I'm celebrating the last day of school, and I can't think of a better way to do that than dining with a beautiful woman."

"You guys sure lay it on thick here in the South." Vivian looked at this man and realized two things: She was either going to have a good lunch or good afternoon delight. His lips, his eyes, and his hands seemed to be calling out to her body.

"That's what makes the South so special," Felix said. "So let me guess, you're new to the city and you're looking for something adventurous?"

"I'm just trying to take care of my business and get back to New York. I'm not a big fan of being in the South. I'm sorry. Atlanta's nice, but I love New York—as cliché as that may sound."

"Bet I could change your mind," Felix said.

"That's a bet that you will lose," Vivian replied. "And I'm not willing to go there with you right now, but please tell me there's something other than grits that Atlanta has to offer, because I haven't had a good meal since I've been here."

"What do you have against grits?" Felix asked with a smile. "One of the delicacies of the South."

"You all can have that. Just give me some jasmine rice and veggies."

"It's that simple?" Felix asked. "I know the perfect thing we can have for lunch. Even the New Yorker will enjoy it."

"I hear you talking." Vivian smiled as the bartender brought over her drink.

The woman turned to Felix and smiled. "Can I get you something?" she asked.

"I'll have what she's having," he said, then squeezed Vivian's knee.

The bartender nodded and started making the drink.

Felix turned to Vivian as she sipped her drink. "What are you having?" he asked.

"A Manhattan."

"You're so New York. Whatever did your ex do to get you to come down South?"

"Well," she said as she set her drink aside. "He pretty much came down here and forgot that he had responsibilities in New York. Then I get here and it's as if he's disappeared. It's frustrating."

"Who is this guy?"

Vivian rolled her eyes and picked up her glass. "I doubt you know him. He's new to the city."

"Try me. I keep my finger on the pulse of what goes on in Atlanta."

"Richmond Crawford," she said, then took a big swig of her drink.

Felix shook his head. "See, I do know him, and seeing you confirms what I think of him."

She raised her eyebrow as she took another sip of her drink. "And that is?"

"He's not as smart as he wants everyone to think he is. How could he let you become his ex?"

"It was for the best," she said. "Trust me."

"Well, he hasn't rebounded well. I've seen his so-called replacement."

"Alicia Michaels, right?" Vivian shook her head and downed the rest of her drink. "It's funny because they probably have been having an affair for years. That's why he needs to pay. I'm not going to be made a fool of."

"Sounds like you're not the kind of woman someone wants to cross."

Vivian nodded. "That's right. I'm from New York and we don't play that shit."

"Maybe I can help you out."

"And why would you do that? Don't tell me it's because it's the Southern thing to do."

"How about, I met your ex and I don't like him. It's just that simple."

Before Vivian could respond, the bartender returned with Felix's drink.

"So, what did Richmond do to draw your ire?"

Felix took a sip of his cocktail. "Let's just say I don't like to be played for a fool, and your ex tried me."

Vivian rolled her eyes. "Sounds like him. These days he thinks he's the second coming of his annoying brother. Someone should take him down a peg or two."

"Who's his brother?"

"Solomon Crawford."

"I guess the more things change, the more they stay the same. Alicia is still getting by because of her friends. I guess that's how she and Richmond became so close."

"How close are we talking?"

"Let's say this, if you needed to prove he's been having a long-term affair with her, I could help you with that. Kind of makes sense as to why he'd leave the big city to come here right around the same time that she returns to Atlanta."

"Your use of logic is mind-blowing, and I think I should let my attorney know what's going on," Vivian said. "And what do you get out of all of this?"

"We can work that out, I'm sure."

She placed her hand on top of his. "We sure can."

Chapter 17

Paris, France

Richmond unlocked the door to the suite and ushered Alicia inside. Closing the door, he pressed her against the wall. First, he went after her neck. Kissing and licking her, Richmond could feel her body melting against his. Her neck was definitely one of her erogenous zones. Slowly, he moved down to her regal shoulders. His tongue danced across her skin. She reminded him of a salted caramel brownie, sweet and spicy.

Next, he slipped the straps of her dress down her arms, happily exposing her perky breasts. He ran his fingertips across her diamond-hard nipples. She moaned as his fingers danced down her sides.

"You feel so good," he said.

"Mmm," she moaned as he slipped his hand between her thighs. Richmond's fingers sought out her throbbing bud and when he found it, Alicia let out a yelp.

"She likes that," he said as he stroked her again.

This time she leaned into him and bit him on the neck as she screamed.

Richmond lifted her into his arms and her dress fluttered to the floor. Carrying her to bed, he laid her against the spread and smiled at her naked body. "You're beautiful."

She reached up and stroked his cheek. "Make love to me."

"I plan to, all night long," he said as he leaned in and kissed her slow and deep.

Alicia unbuttoned his shirt as they kissed, running her hands across his chest. He pulled back from her and stripped out of his clothes. She watched him with a gleam in her eyes. He was beautiful, he was spectacular, and Alicia realized that she wanted him for more than just a trip fling or just for a short fling. She realized that Richmond could be the one.

Reaching for a condom, Richmond ripped the package open and slid it in place. Easing toward him, she wrapped her arms around his neck and pulled him in bed with her. She wrapped her legs around his waist as they faced each other in silence for a moment. She didn't know what to say or how to tell him that she was falling for him. He brushed his lips across hers.

"Alicia," he whispered. "You're so damned beautiful."

"Richmond, you . . . this has been really special. Thank you." She kissed him slow and deep, their bodies melting against each other. He plunged inside her and they rocked back and forth slowly.

He cupped her cheek as they matched each other stroke for slow stroke. She moaned with delight as the waves of an orgasm began to wash over her.

"Oh, Richmond, Richmond," she called out.

"Yes, come for me, baby. Let me come with you." He dove in deeper and Alicia screamed out in delight. Feeling her release, Richmond allowed himself to explode along with her. Holding each other, they drifted off to sleep, thinking how much better things would be once they returned to Atlanta.

Atlanta, Georgia—

Vivian woke up in Felix's king-size bed wrapped in a satin sheet. She didn't remember much about how she ended up here, but there had been a lot of alcohol involved. And he'd given her a lot of information about Alicia Michaels.

And from what she'd learned, Vivian knew how she could take care of her. If Alicia was as self-conscious as Felix said she was, then using that would be the key to getting what she wanted from Richmond.

"Morning, beautiful," Felix said as he walked into the bedroom with two glasses of water.

"Morning," she said. "I can't believe I spent the night here."

"I'm glad you did. Made the start of my summer just amazing," he said as he handed her a glass.

"Too bad I don't remember such a good time,"

she replied as she stepped out of bed and searched for her clothes.

"What are you trying to say? You didn't have a good time? I can show you the video." He winked at her and Vivian shivered in disgust.

"Video?"

"You know, these days you have to protect yourself and keep receipts. I learned that with my situation from college. Besides, if Richmond is going to give you all of the money that you're looking for, it's only fair that I get a cut. The video just makes sure that you don't go back on your word."

"You slimy bastard."

"And you're a gold-digging bitch, so we're perfect for each other."

Vivian narrowed her eyes at Felix as she snatched her clothes on. "I don't believe this. You lured me here so that you could set me up?"

He shrugged, then nodded. "That's the crux of it," Felix said as he leaned against the wall and sipped his water. "You want me to call you an Uber, or can you hop on the MARTA to get back to your hotel?"

"I'll get back without your help, thank you very much."

"Just remember that I'm due ten percent of what you're getting or I'll have to make my own money. And this video would give me a grip. You've made quite a name for yourself. There are plenty of tabloids that will pay for this."

"And you're willing to risk your career for a small payday?"

"Do you really think my face is visible in your sex

tape?" Felix laughed. "Make sure you call me after your meeting."

Vivian stormed out of his house feeling like a fool. Richmond and Felix were going to pay for this.

Paris, France

Alicia settled into her seat on the plane, wishing for another twenty-four hours in the City of Lights. Richmond slid into his seat and gave her a kiss on the cheek. "Back to reality."

"Do we have to?"

"It's going to be pretty hard to take over Atlanta while making love in Paris," he replied.

"Guess you're right," she said with a sigh. "But this was a great trip."

"We'll have to make it an annual thing."

She glanced out of the window to hide the huge smile on her face. Alicia was glad that he saw a future with her. Because she really spent part of the night dreaming about an intercontinental future with Richmond Crawford.

"You're not sleeping over there already, are you?"

"Not yet. But soon I will be." Turning to face him, Alicia leaned her head against his shoulder. "We're supposed to be this happy, right?"

"No one deserves this more than us," he said, then captured her lips in a hot, passionate kiss. Alicia figured she was seconds away from joining the mile-high club, until she heard, "Sir, we're about to take off. You're going to need to buckle your seat belt."

Richmond broke the kiss and turned to the flight attendant. "And I thought we were already flying."

The woman smiled. "You and your wife must have had a great honeymoon. Let me see if I can get you some complimentary champagne."

"But we're not—"

Richmond placed his finger against her lips. "Thank you very much," he said. "She's still getting used to being my lady."

Alicia laughed and licked his finger.

"Woman, you're lucky I'm strapped into this seat belt."

"You're too much. How miserable were you in your previous life to keep this man hidden?"

"You don't know the half of it. Thank God for small miracles. The worst thing you can ever do to yourself is marry the wrong person and try to make it work."

Alicia chewed her bottom lip, silently wondering if Richmond was actually over his ex. What would he do if she tried to come back into his life? Would be remember how happy they were together and try again?

"Why didn't things work with you two?" she asked, though she really didn't want to know.

"Because I married a woman I wanted to love and have a family with. She married a name and a bank account. When I realized that, I felt as if I couldn't divorce her because I had a reputation to uphold. Solomon was doing his thing with the tabloid headlines and I was the good son." He laughed sardonically. "As it turned out, everything that we believed was damn lie."

"Have you thought about finding your . . ." Alicia's voice trailed off. She wasn't even sure that she should ask Richmond that. How would she feel if she found out the family she thought was hers wasn't. And in image-conscious New York, she could only imagine how hard things had been for Richmond. "Never mind."

"I know what you're thinking, and yes. I thought about my real father and finding him. But what's the point? I'm a grown man who was raised by an asshole who had his own secrets." He shrugged. "It's better to not know and blaze my own path."

"I can understand that," she said.

"I'm glad you can, because I can't."

She stroked his cheek. "When you're ready, I'm going to be right here beside you."

Richmond took her hand in his and kissed it. "What did I do to deserve you?"

"You moved to Atlanta at the right time, I guess."

"It's more than that. You showed me something I never thought I'd see in my life."

Alicia tilted her head to the side. "And what's that?"

He stroked her cheek. "Real love can exist in my life too. So, I should be thanking you."

"We sound so corny right now," she said with a laugh.

"Maybe, but if I'm going to be corny with someone, then it's going to be you."

The flight attendant returned with two glasses of champagne. "Congrats on the wedding," she said as she handed them the glasses. "You're going to have a beautiful marriage."

"Thanks," Alicia said as she and Richmond clanked their glasses together. After they drank their champagne, Alicia leaned on Richmond's shoulder and closed her eyes. She actually couldn't wait to get back to Atlanta and spend more time with her man.

And somehow, she was going to have to break the news to Kandace that she had fallen for her brother-in-law.

Chapter 18

After an uneventful flight, Alicia and Richmond were back in Atlanta. All she wanted to do was go to sleep. But the businesswoman inside her knew she should stop at her office and check her messages. Alicia had purposely left her cell phone, because she didn't have an international plan and she wanted to enjoy Paris. She'd given her two clients the heads-up that she'd be out of the country so they wouldn't be looking for her. Now, she had to check in.

"We really should just go back to my place," he said. "We could use a nap."

"Just let me check in on my clients and then I'd be happy to go to your place and sleep for a week."

Alicia walked into her office and sat down for a few moments before she booted her computer. Then she checked her voicemail. She paused when she heard Vivian's message. "I understand that you're seeing my husband. We should really talk about that. By the way, I'm Vivian Crawford. I'll be in Atlanta for a couple of days and we should meet."

Alicia pulled the phone away from her ear. *Wife? Richmond clearly said he was divorced. Maybe she's just trying to throw her weight around.* But Alicia had to wonder what brought the former Mrs. Crawford to Atlanta and if she was still around. Before she could replay the message and take down the number that it came from, Richmond walked in her office.

"Ready?"

"No, I have some things I really need to take care of before I can leave here."

"I can wait for you, if you'd like."

Alicia smiled and shook her head. "No, I don't want you to miss out on your nap."

"I've gotten spoiled with having you in the bed beside me. I'll wait."

She sighed, wondering if she should share the voicemail message with him or ask him about his relationship with his wife. It was back to reality, and she had to get to the bottom of what was going on. "All right, Richmond. I got a call from your wife while we were gone."

"My what?"

"Your. Wife. So, tell me something. Are you divorced, or did I spend the last few days in Paris sleeping with a married man?"

"I'm not married," he said. "And whatever game Vivian is trying to play, we're not going to let her win. Why would she call you and what's her game?"

"Listen to her message," Alicia said as she replayed the message and pressed the speaker button.

Richmond had never wanted to choke someone as much as he wanted to choke the breath out of Vivian as he listened to the message that she'd left

Alicia. *That bitch never wanted to be known as my wife when we were married, but now she's playing the matrimony card?*

"We're not married, and I have a framed divorce decree to prove it. Now, I don't know what kind of game she's playing, or if she's trying to just get money out of me to make her disappear, but I'm not going to allow her to intrude on my future when she wanted nothing but to be a footnote in my past."

"So, what's changed? Why would she be in Atlanta looking for you all of a sudden?"

Richmond shrugged. "Because now that we're divorced and I'm not the Crawford she thought I was, New York is a cruel place."

"Yeah, but she's in Atlanta trying to be messy. I don't have time for the drama."

Richmond folded his arms across his chest and shook his head. "There's not going to be any drama because Vivian knows our marriage and our business is done." He pulled his cell phone out and Alicia started to ask him why he was going to call her.

"Solomon," Richmond said. "I got an issue."

Alicia rose to her feet and headed out of her office. She needed a minute to wrap her mind around all of this. She was about to walk out of the office when the door opened and a woman walked in.

"Is Richmond Crawford here?"

"Who are you?" Alicia asked as she looked at the woman. Medium height, caramel complexion and a killer weave. She had a shape that would stop traffic, but Alicia couldn't tell if it was the blessing of genes or a surgeon's scalpel that gave her those dangerous curves.

"It doesn't matter who I am, I'm not here to see you," she snapped. "Unless you're his secretary and he has you screening his visitors."

Alicia rolled her eyes, sure she was talking to Richmond's ex. It occurred to her that in the entire time Kandace and Solomon had been married, she'd never met Vivian Crawford. And if this raging bitch was Vivian, Alicia was glad not to have met her.

"Are you the same Vivian Crawford who was looking for me a few days ago?" Alicia asked.

"Oh, you're Alicia. Enjoying life with my husband?" She smiled coldly and Alicia wanted to wrap her hand around her throat and toss her across the room as if she were a wrestler. But Alicia remained calm. Her issue wasn't with Vivian. She needed to know from Richmond if his marriage was officially over.

"You should've put your foot down with that bitch a long time ago. How did she find you?" Solomon asked.

"Fool, I'm not in the witness protection program and I was on CNN. This makes no sense as to why she'd want to come down here and start shit."

"So, you went to Paris and fell in love with Alicia? Nah, but you were probably in love with her before you left because no one takes a woman on a fake business trip for no reason."

"There was some work done, and you're jumping the gun with this love talk."

"Whatever. I know how these things turn out." Solomon laughed. "But if you want to live in a state of denial, knock yourself out."

"I'm not in denial. Maybe I should just say, yet. Being with Alicia makes me feel like I've found the one."

"Is that so? And you're sure about this because she deserves all of you. Not some rebound, not a man who doesn't know what he wants."

"I wouldn't do that to Alicia, and if I had any doubts about where I want to see this thing go, I wouldn't have taken her to Paris."

"I knew it. Don't even try to put the cost of that trip into the Atlanta project."

"Listen, this is about more than money."

Solomon laughed. "I know. But I wouldn't be me if I didn't give you shit about this," he said. "And I hope you're ready to be peppered by my wife with a lot of questions about your intentions with her friend because . . ."

Richmond shushed his brother when he heard raised voices outside in the lobby. "Something's going on out here, let me call you back." After hanging up the phone, he rushed out of the office and stood between Alicia and Vivian. "What in the hell is going on? Vivian, why are you here?"

"Not happy to see me, darling?" Vivian asked as she crossed over to him.

Richmond stepped back from her and folded his arms across his chest. "What do you want?"

"We need to talk, and your little guard dog here," she said, nodding toward Alicia, "thinks that she can stop that."

"Who do you think you're talking to?" Alicia barked.

"Touchy. I thought I was talking to an employee. Please don't tell me he has you believing that you're more than that."

Vivian laughed and Alicia clenched her teeth. She said a silent prayer that she wouldn't punch this woman in the face. Then she wondered if her anger was being focused on the wrong person. Richmond was acting pretty relaxed right now.

This isn't happening again, she thought. "I'm going to let you two handle whatever this is. I have things to do."

Alicia dashed out of the office and headed for her car. She was glad that she'd left her phone at the office when they'd gone to Paris. Now she could escape without having to wait for Richmond and listen to his excuses for why this woman had strolled into the building as if she had a right to be there.

Bitch, she thought. When her phone rang, Alicia ignored it because she didn't want to talk to anyone. She was halfway down Peachtree Street when her phone rang again. Sucking her teeth, she pressed the talk button on her steering wheel.

"What?"

"Who pissed in your cornflakes?" Kandace asked. "First you go off to Paris with Richmond and don't say a word, then you come back and I still don't get a call. What's going on, chica?"

Alicia sighed. "Richmond's wife is in Atlanta."

"What?"

"Umm-huh. Right now, she's in his office batting her eyelashes at him and calling me a fucking employee. I thought he was divorced."

"From what I understand, he is. But why would Vivian be in Atlanta? She never wanted that man when they were in New York. I can't even say that I'd seen them together more than once."

"She's a piece of work, and if I could beat her with a bat and not end up in jail, I'd do it."

"What has Richmond said?"

"Who cares what he has to say? I'm not going through this again."

"You can't judge him by what Tyson did. I know Richmond, and he's not a jackass. But don't you think that you should be focused on business and—"

"Don't start with me right now. I keep making the same—"

"Wait," Kandace said. "I'm not saying you're wrong about falling for Richmond. I saw it coming, but he better be ready to do right by you. And if that divorce isn't real, I'm going to hurt him for bringing you into a jacked situation. I'll beat him with a giraffe."

"A what?"

"Long story, but before I get into that, tell me what happened."

Alicia sighed and told Kandace how wonderful everything was in Paris. How she and Richmond hung out with Devon and Marie and made love.

"Pause. You and Richmond . . ."

"Yes," she said with a sigh. "And it was amazing! I haven't felt that way in years."

"And you're willing to give that all up without hearing him out?" Kandace asked. "Personally, I think Vivian is trying to cause trouble and if you let her, she will. She'd a hardcore bitch from what Solomon has always said about her."

"I've noticed."

"And I don't see Richmond as the kind of man who would try to keep two relationships going at once. Especially after all that he and Solomon have been through this year with secrets."

Alicia knew her friend was right, but she needed a little while to think. "I still need a little time to myself right now."

"Don't take too much time, because I know how you roll. You'll make up a scenario in your mind and won't talk to Richmond again."

"It's not like I have a choice here," she said. "We work in the same building, a building that he owns, and he's a client." Alicia slowed down and shook her head. "This is why I don't mix business with pleasure. Why did I ever listen to Jade?"

"Jade? What does she have to do with any of this? According to her, she was against you and Richmond too. I knew she couldn't help herself."

"But she made perfect sense. When I was hanging out with him and showing him the city, I saw another side of Richmond, and it struck me. I liked it. Liked him. I didn't want to fall for him but it happened. Now . . ."

"If you feel that way, then you need to fight for

him. Don't let his messy ex come to your place and ruin your future."

"Really?"

"Yes, really. I want you and Richmond to be happy, and if you two make each other happy, then damn it, fight for it."

"Wow. I—"

"Didn't expect me to be on your side? Girl, do I need to come to Atlanta and relive some of our undergrad days, because I will."

"I can handle this one. And I'm sure Solomon doesn't want his wife to come down South and pretend she's gangsta. You know we used to throw rocks and hide our hands."

Kandace laughed. "True. But, just know that you can take the girl out of the AUC, but you can't take the AUC out of the girl."

"And I'm hanging up with you now," Alicia said. Feeling a little better about Richmond's situation with his ex-wife, she decided to hit a U-turn and head back to the office.

Richmond glared at Vivian. "I don't know what your game is, but it needs to stop!"

"What? I don't have a game. You can make me go away with a cool million dollars and the payment of some of my expenses for the rest of my life. I don't want much, just what I've earned."

Richmond snorted. "That doesn't sound as if I'm getting rid of you, that's me having to deal with you as if we're still married. Till death do us part doesn't last past divorce."

"I won't be an outcast in my own city. I will not allow my friends to pay for my dinners because you want to flex and pretend you're a big man now. You think you can be the new Solomon?" Vivian laughed. "I know the truth about you and your sordid little history. Do you think people down here are going to take you seriously when they learn that you aren't even a real member of the family? And then there is the arrest in Los Angeles that you all covered up. You're in the Bible Belt, and when the people of good old Atlanta find out that you like hookers, no one is going to want to deal with you."

Richmond snorted. "You keep singing the same song and doing nothing. If you want to play your trump card, then do it."

"I'm not the one who's going to suffer, so don't force me to show my hand."

"You can do what you want to do, because I'm not going to let you blackmail me."

"Want to play this game? You're going to lose."

"The only loser standing here is you. Why don't you get on your broom and fly back to New York?"

"Just give me the money and you won't hear from me again."

Richmond folded his arms across his chest. "That is, until you need more money or you can't get a seat at your favorite restaurant."

"What are you saying?"

"Do your worst. I'm done with your bullshit. You walked away from our marriage, and by doing that, you walked away from my money and everything else you got as a benefit of being my wife."

"So that's what this is all about? You got my attention. Want to get remarried?"

Before Richmond could tell Vivian to get on the highway straight to hell, Alicia walked in. Vivian turned to her and smiled. "Did you get all of that, sweetheart? Richmond wants me back and I'm going to give him what he wants." She crossed over to him and kissed him slowly.

Richmond pushed her away. "Don't do this."

Alicia looked from Vivian to Richmond and didn't know what to make of the scene she saw unfold in front of her. "Have I interrupted the reunion?" she asked.

"There is no reunion, and Vivian was just leaving."

"Doesn't look that way to me," Alicia said. "What's going on with the two of you?"

Vivian smiled. "I don't think I can make it any clearer. I'm here to get my husband back."

Richmond rolled his eyes. "Get out."

"Is that true? She's back for her husband?" Alicia asked, focusing her stare on Richmond. "Because I don't want to stand in the way of a good love story."

Richmond crossed over to Alicia. "You're joking, right? Do you think I would've spent these last few days with you if I had bumped my head and decided I wanted this vile woman back? She wants money and will do anything to get it."

Vivian shook her head. "If it's a battle you want, you got it. And I didn't come to this humid hellhole to lose." She headed for the door and Alicia stepped aside. As she watched Vivian leave, she couldn't help but wonder what Richmond ever saw in her. She might be pretty on the outside, but Alicia could see her insides were uglier than a wicked witch.

Once she was gone, Alicia focused her stare on Richmond. "If you and your ex have some unfinished business, don't let me stand in the way . . ."

Richmond drew Alicia into his arms. "You're not in the way at all." He brought his lips down on top of hers. She gave him a quick peck, then turned away from him.

"What?" he asked.

"I need to know the truth. Are you and your ex done?"

"Like an overcooked steak."

She elbowed him in the stomach. "Be serious. I don't want to walk in here and you decide one day that you're in a New York state of mind and want to give your marriage another chance."

"I tried to give my marriage a chance for years, and now that I'm moving on to better things, she's missing what we had. And by what we had, I'm talking about access to my money."

"And she's not missing you?"

Richmond stroked Alicia's cheek. "She didn't miss me when I was sleeping in the same bed with her. Vivian wants a million dollars and she's been threatening to go to the media with stories about my family if I don't give it to her."

"Is that why you've been so reluctant to do the interview with *Atlanta Scene*? You know what," Alicia said with a smile. "That's why you need to control the narrative. Tell your story the way you want to and don't give her a chance to use her ammo to hurt you."

"I'm not sure I want to talk about all of that. But it makes sense. If I tell my story, my way, no one else has the power to hold it over me."

"So, we can beat her at her nasty little game before she gets a chance to know what hit her."

"All right, let's do it. But before we do that, I need to know that we're good."

Alicia nodded. "We're good." He took her face into his hands and rubbed his nose against hers. Alicia smiled. "Richmond."

"I just have to check. Because you owe me a week in my bed," he said. "I'm ready to get it started."

Chapter 19

Vivian walked around her hotel room wondering if Richmond would give her the money she needed to get Felix off her back and go back to New York and live the life she was accustomed to living.

More than anything, she had to make sure that sex tape didn't get out. It would be so hard to keep the moral high road if something as damning as a romp she couldn't even remember got out. Something didn't feel right about that time she spent with Felix. She wasn't one to hop in bed with a stranger who couldn't do something for her. And on a principal's salary in the South, there wasn't much that Felix could do for her.

"Maybe I can get back into his place and delete the video. Then when I get my money from Richmond, I won't have to share a dime with anyone." Vivian paused mid-stride. Now, she just needed to make her way back to Felix's place. Pulling out her phone, she called Felix.

"I was wondering when I'd hear from you again," he said in lieu of hello.

"I'm sure it was worth the wait. I have your cut. Let's get together at your place and celebrate."

"I can meet you at your hotel."

"No, because I want to see you delete that damned video. This is not a game."

"Neither is my money," Felix said. "But I'm a man of my word. I get my money and the video goes away."

"I don't know you like that to blindly trust you. Look what happened the last time I tried that."

"You loved every minute of it," he said. "Every single minute. Would you like to watch it?"

"You're a slick bastard," she said.

"I've been called worse. What time should I meet you to get my money? And, by the way, how many zeroes should I expect?"

"Let me call you back," she said, then ended the call. This was going to be harder than she thought.

Richmond opened the door to his house and ushered Alicia inside. "I'm going to order us something to eat, and you relax on the couch," he said as he nodded toward his sofa.

"Don't you think we should get started on our media plan?"

"No, I think we need to relax. Merlot or a crisp white?" He winked at her, then started for the wine cellar. Alicia slipped her shoes off and reached for the remote control. Part of her wondered if Vivian had tucked her tail between her legs and headed back to New York. That would've made things a lot easier. *But when has life ever been easy?*

Flipping through the channels, Alicia stopped when she came across a James Bond movie. At least they could finally watch their movie together. Alicia hated feeling like an insecure teenager after she and Richmond had shared such a special time in Paris. But something about Vivian's appearance didn't sit well with her.

"I got the merlot," Richmond said as he walked into the living room. Holding up the bottle and two glasses, he smiled when he saw the Bond movie on TV. "And we're not doing anything until this movie is over."

"You can't multitask?"

He nodded as he set the glasses on the table and went to work opening the bottle of wine. "I can, I just choose a different task." After pouring the wine, Richmond handed Alicia her glass and took a seat beside her.

"We have something serious to take care of," she said. "You need—"

"To relax. It's *The Spy Who Loved Me.* One of the best Bond movies ever."

Alicia took a sip of wine and nodded. "Okay, fine," she said. "I'm going to relax and watch this movie with you." She set her glass on the table and cozied up to Richmond. He kissed her forehead before setting his glass down. Drawing her against his chest, Richmond stroked her hair and smiled. "Remember I said I could multitask as long as I get to pick the task?"

"Yeah, I remember that."

"Here's the task I'm about to do," he said, then captured her lips in a swift motion. Their tongues danced a slow tango and Richmond's hands inched underneath her shirt, reveling in the smoothness of her skin.

Alicia moaned and arched her body into his touch. She wrapped her legs around his waist and immediately felt his arousal.

"Mmm," she moaned as he ground against her. "You're teasing me."

"Yes, I am." He leaned forward and kissed her collarbone. "But I'm teasing myself even more. I feel how wet you are." Richmond reached for the waistband of her slacks and pulled them down. In a swift motion, he pushed the crotch of her panties aside, buried his face between her legs and lapped the sweetness of her juices until she screamed his name.

"Damn, you taste so good," he said as he tore his mouth away from her. "I need some more." Richmond licked her slow, sucked her tender bud until she exploded in his mouth. Her body shook with satisfaction as James Bond knocked out a bad guy.

"Ooh," she moaned. "I like the way you multitask."

Richmond unbuttoned her shirt and ran his index finger down the center of her chest. "Wait until you see my next trick," he said as he pushed her shirt off her shoulders. He kissed each piece of skin he exposed. Alicia moaned, wanting nothing more than to rip his clothes off and make love to him until the sun rose again. But Richmond was in no rush. He unsnapped her bra and feasted on her hard nipples. Alicia stroked the back of his head as he took her pebble between his teeth. Intense waves of pleasure washed over her body as he slipped his hand between her thighs and stroked her wetness.

"Richmond," she moaned.

"Come for me, baby, come for me."

"No, I want to come with you. Take your clothes off and make love to me," she moaned. Richmond pulled back and stripped his clothes off. Alicia's mouth watered as she drank in the image of Richmond's naked body. Inching toward the edge of the sofa, she reached for his erection, stroking him until his knees went weak.

"I pride myself on giving as good as I get." Alicia captured his erection with her lips. She licked the head of his cock and Richmond groaned in delight. But when she took him deep down her throat, Richmond tossed his head back in delight and he nearly exploded.

Their eyes locked as she gave him one last lick. "Damn," he muttered. "You are amazing."

"And you talk too much. I need you inside, now."

She didn't need to ask him twice as he scooped her up into his arms. Richmond carried her to the stairs and dashed into his bedroom. Falling back on the bed with Alicia in his arms, Richmond was ready to melt with her, but Alicia mounted him. She kissed his neck, using her tongue to traverse his body. Goose bumps dotted his body as she continued her tour. Unable to take another minute of her sensual torture, Richmond grabbed her hips. "Let me in."

She spread her thighs and Richmond dove inside. They rocked back and forth, grinding slowly against each other. He pulled her against his chest as he thrust forward. Alicia matched Richmond stroke for stroke. She felt herself getting wetter and wetter. When he ran his fingers up and down her spine, Alicia couldn't fight the explosion growing inside her. She collapsed against his chest as sweat poured from their bodies.

"I can't move," Richmond said.

"Good, because neither can I. How long can we stay here like this?"

"I want to say forever, but knowing you, you want to get some work done at some point."

She ran her index finger down his bicep. "What's work?"

Laughing, he kissed her gently. "Let's see how long that lasts." Moments later, they'd drifted off to sleep.

When they woke up, Richmond and Alicia decided that it was past time to order dinner. "Why don't we cook," he said as he glanced at the clock. "By the time a delivery gets here, we might be busy—again."

"Really? Do you think you're going to be that lucky?"

"Oh, I know I am." Richmond pulled on a pair of boxer shorts and handed Alicia a T-shirt. "Let's get cooking."

"How about I pour the wine and you get cooking." She winked at him as she pulled the shirt on.

"I'm going to teach you how to make at least one meal. Just so we can have something else that we do in the kitchen together."

Alicia stood on her tiptoes and kissed the end of

his nose. "Umm, no. But I will always make sure your coffee is brewed to perfection."

"I couldn't ask for anything more," he said as he wrapped his arms around her waist. "So, when are we going to start waking up together?"

"Maybe that's something we should talk about later," she said. "You should never make a decision on an empty stomach."

Richmond shook his head, but let the conversation drop. Maybe he was getting ahead of himself asking her to move in right now.

Alicia sat at the bar watching Richmond prepare dinner. Was he serious about her moving in with him? This thing was moving too fast, and she couldn't help but wonder what his ex's appearance had to do with the sudden urge for him to invite her to live with him.

"You're quiet over there. Everything all right?" he asked.

"Yeah, just thinking about work."

Richmond shook his head. "Nope. Too soon," he said. "We're not worried about work or anything else until we eat. And maybe watch a full movie this time."

She grinned at him. "Really, Mr. Multitasker?"

"You know I had to give you my full attention." Richmond crossed over to her and wrapped his arms around her waist. "And you know that you always come before Bond."

"I better."

Richmond dropped his arms from her waist. "But

this food isn't going to cook itself, and since you're not going to help me, I better get busy."

"I tell you what," she said. "I'll take care of dessert. Just let me get dressed and I'm going to get you the best and sweetest Southern treat."

"You mean that's not you?" He winked at her and turned back to the food he was cooking. Alicia headed for the living room and grabbed her discarded clothes. When she pulled her pants on, she noticed his phone on the side of the sofa.

She wanted to ignore the message on the screen, but she couldn't help it. Alicia picked up the phone and saw the message was from Vivian.

Stop ignoring me and call me. We have to talk.

Alicia saw red. Everything that he said about his ex was a damned lie. Richmond was no different from Tyson. Why would she be texting him talking about they need to talk? No one does this if there isn't a reason. If he wanted his cake and ice cream, Alicia was going to bow out.

She snatched the phone up and stormed into the kitchen. "Tell me again how you don't have anything going on with your ex." She waved the phone in his face.

"What are you talking about?"

"Why is she texting you? You know what, it doesn't even matter, because I'm not playing this game with you two."

Richmond took the phone from her hand and set it on the counter. "No one is playing a game. If there was something going on, do you really think

I'd be stupid enough to leave my phone out so you could see it?"

"Accidents happen. When you get things together with your ex, let me know." She stormed out of the house, leaving Richmond confused and pissed off.

Once she was in her car, Alicia broke down sobbing. She hadn't wanted to believe that Richmond was lying to her, but things just weren't adding up. The last thing she wanted to deal with was a man who had this much baggage. She came to Atlanta to start over, and she would be damned if she'd fall into the same trap again.

Richmond listened as the door slammed and wondered if he should go after Alicia or just wash his hands of this madness. If she wanted to believe the worst about him, what could he do to change her mind? Moreover, why did he have to be the one to explain what was going on when he hadn't done a damned thing wrong? Richmond was sure there were some demons in Alicia's life that she was making him pay for. This was a check he wasn't willing to cash. But he wasn't willing to lose this woman, either.

Putting the knife down, Richmond decided that he needed to make this right with Alicia and get Vivian out of his hair. One way or another, he was going to get peace tonight. He headed upstairs, dressed, and then called Vivian.

"It's about time that you gave me a call back," she snapped.

"We're ending this tonight. I'll meet you at your hotel and we're putting this to bed—forever."

"Richmond," she said, her voice a little softer. "I'm in trouble and I don't know what to do."

"If this is some sort of game or some—"

"Please, it pains me to need you right now," she said.

Part of him wanted to believe that she was telling the truth, but Richmond couldn't help but wonder if she'd just added another layer to her game playing. "Where are you staying?" he asked.

Vivian told him the hotel she was staying in and he hung up the phone. He called Alicia, but her voicemail picked up. He knew he was being ignored, but right now he was going to give her time to marinate in her feelings.

It was time to put Vivian in her place once and for all.

Chapter 20

Alicia sat in the bar of her hotel, nursing a vodka and cranberry juice. She hadn't wanted to go up to her room when she arrived at the hotel. Then Richmond called and she ignored him. What took him so long to come up with an excuse? She was about to take another sip of her drink when her phone rang. Seeing that it was Serena, she answered.

"Hello?"

"Have you let Richmond up for air?" Serena laughed. "How was Paris?"

"Paris was a lie and Richmond can kiss my entire black ass," Alicia said. "So, what's going on with you?"

"Whoa. I wasn't expecting that at all. What happened?"

Alicia took a sip of her drink, then sighed. "I don't want to talk about that right now. Are you and Antonio pregnant yet?"

"Don't try to change the subject, but since you asked, there is a possibility." Serena's excitement seemed to bubble through the phone. "I'm going to the doctor in the morning to confirm the six pregnancy tests that I've taken this week."

"Six? Really?" Alicia laughed.

"My period is late. Antonio is cautiously optimistic about it."

"And how do you feel?"

"I'm scared as hell. What if I'm not pregnant or I can't get pregnant?"

"Don't think like that. You and Antonio are going to be great parents. I'm going to be the best fairy godmother ever, because I'm going to have nothing else to do after I get off from work but spoil other people's kids."

"Okay, so what happened with you and Richmond that has you drinking and throwing in the towel?"

Alicia raised her right eyebrow. "How do you know I'm drinking?"

"I hear the ice clinking in the glass and you don't normally have ice in wine. What is it? Vodka or whiskey?"

"Vodka and cranberry."

"You are really in your feelings. What happened?"

Alicia downed the rest of her drink and told Serena what happened with Vivian showing up at the office and then finding her text message after they'd made love.

"Wow," Serena said. "I can't believe he would be that dumb."

"Me either," Alicia said. "I thought things were going to be different with me and Richmond. He—"

"You don't understand what I'm saying. I can't

believe that he would slip up like that if he was trying to have both of you."

"Why would *you* say that?"

Serena sighed. "Because Richmond is Solomon Crawford's brother. I think he would've hidden his tracks a little better. And of course his ex is sniffing around. Think about it, she had New York in the palm of her hand and now she has nothing. Please, she's going to pull out every trick in the book."

"What if those tricks work? They were together for a long time and—"

"People move on. I did."

"But how long were you and that creep together? You didn't marry him and—"

"Will you stop! You keep making every excuse in the book to believe the worst of him. Every man is not Tyson."

"I can't tell, because I've yet to be proven wrong."

Serena groaned. "I was scared to have a baby and look at me now. I've been doing everything I can to get pregnant. Do you know how many yams I've eaten?"

Alicia laughed. "What do yams have to do with getting pregnant?"

"Yams are a natural fertility food. I ate so many. I don't want to see another one for a while," Serena said with a laugh. "But back to you, don't write Richmond off all the way yet. Remember this is the same man who knocked out a stranger for you."

Alicia started to tell Serena that it didn't mean anything that he was good with his hands. "Maybe you're right," she finally said. "Or maybe I should've listened to Kandace all along. This man had been married for years and I was just a rebound so that he could get his feet wet and get back into the game."

"So, you've made up your mind and you're not going to consider anything else?"

"Yes! I'm tired of being some man's victim and getting hurt in the end. This whole love-conquers-all bullshit isn't for me."

"Bitter much?"

"You don't get it," Alicia said. "And how can you? You've always gotten what you wanted."

"And you always ran from things because . . . Why do you do that? When it comes to business, you can't be stopped. You're a beast. Were it not for you, Hometown Delights would've closed down after everything that happened there. But you let anything—any little thing—ruin a relationship. It's been that way since college."

Alicia shivered as her mind went back to that night with Felix and how it changed her life. All of the self-doubt that she carried for years and how she tried to get over it, but it haunted her into adulthood.

"Something happened in college that I never told you all about and I guess the more that I think about it, the more that I've been affected by it because I never reached out to get help."

"What happened?"

Alicia sighed and recounted the night that Felix attacked her. And how he told her if she ever told anyone they wouldn't believe her.

"That son of a bitch, and he had the nerve to seek you out at the reunion. Did he try to apologize?"

Alicia sucked her teeth. "No. He was disrespectful, and that's why Richmond punched him."

"Damn, had we known, Felix would've—"

"I know, and that's one of the reasons why I didn't tell you guys." Alicia sighed. "But I have to stop living in the past and—"

"Give Richmond a chance to love you the way you deserve to be loved?"

"I don't want to make another mistake and end up the one with the broken heart."

"Well, if it makes you feel better, if Richmond breaks your heart, I'll break his nose."

"It's good to know that you're still ready to resort to violence in a pinch," Alicia said. "I'm going to go now."

"All right. Let me know what happens and I hope that means you will end up in his arms tonight."

"Whatever. I'll talk to you later." After hanging up the phone, Alicia pushed her empty glass away and waved for the bartender.

"What can I do for you, beautiful?" he asked.

"Just let me cash out and have a glass of water," she said.

He nodded and smiled. Alicia spun around on her bar stool and was immediately disappointed when she saw Felix walking toward her.

"Fancy meeting you here," he said.

Rolling her eyes, she kept her mouth closed. She wasn't going to let this bastard ruin her already shitty night. When he sat beside her, Alicia knew the silent treatment might not be enough.

She rose to her feet and Felix grabbed her arm.

"You mean to tell me that two college classmates can't share a drink together?"

"Get your damned hands off me," she snapped as she snatched away. "We're not having anything together."

Felix grinned and tilted his head to the side. "You didn't always feel that way. Maybe it's time for me to make your dreams come true. Let me make love to you so that you can get over your silly feud with me."

The bartender brought over Alicia's bill and her glass of water. He looked from Alicia to Felix. "Is everything all right?" he asked.

"Yes," Alicia said as she grabbed her glass of water. "This guy here is just a little overheated." She tossed the contents of the glass in Felix's face and threw the glass at him. "There. Everything is better now."

"Bitch," Felix muttered.

"And you're the same bastard that you've always been. I guess you're here trolling for women in a hotel bar tonight?" Alicia kicked off her heels and stood up on the bar. "Excuse me, excuse me! Ladies and gentlemen, I have an announcement to make." She pointed her finger at Felix. "This man is a predator. I let him get away with assaulting me years ago and I'm always going to regret that. But if I can save anyone from his filthy clutches tonight, then it will be well worth it. Don't be fooled by a pretty face and a nice smile, this man is a snake and just like any snake, given the chance he will strike at you." Alicia hopped off the bar and Felix glared at her.

"This isn't over, and you and your new boyfriend are going to pay dearly for this," Felix growled before storming out of the bar. Alicia was baffled for a minute. Was he just trying to save face? Then she realized that was a dig at Richmond.

Boyfriend. Yeah, right, she thought as she paid her bill and gave the bartender a huge tip for not calling the cops.

"Miss," he said as he handed her the credit card back, "I've always had a bad feeling about the guy. He comes in here like he has a room, but he never does. I saw him put something in a woman's drink once, so I believe you."

"Why didn't you call the police?"

"No proof. I just accidentally spilled the drink. Maybe now I can get my manager to ban him from the place."

"That would be a good start." Alicia headed for the elevators, looking over her shoulder just to make sure that Felix was nowhere around. Seeing that he wasn't, she pressed the button on the elevator and stepped on quickly.

Richmond stood in the lobby of Vivian's hotel, waiting for her to come down. He wasn't going to meet her in her room because he didn't want to set himself up to be caught in a compromising situation. He already needed to get things straight with Alicia, which he was going to do tonight.

Before Vivian came down, Richmond saw a familiar sight—Felix. Ducking behind a tall potted plant, he listened as Felix made a call.

"Hello, New York. I'm still waiting on my money, and I'm not a patient man. I'm in your lobby, so you either come down here or give me your room number so that we can have some more fun . . . What do you mean, you're waiting for someone else? Bitch, we have a deal, and I'll release that video if I don't get my money. This is not a game."

Richmond wondered if he was talking to Vivian. Was this what she needed help with? And how did she get involved with this jackass? Pulling out his phone, he called Vivian. While the phone rang, he listened to what Felix said.

"No, I will not hold on. You're playing games, lady, and you don't want to play with me."

Richmond sent Vivian a text and asked for her room number. *I think I know what you need help with.*

After she gave him her room number, he headed for the stairs. Part of him wondered if this was a setup or if Vivian was really in over her head with Felix. Why did she get involved with him anyway?

Richmond knocked on the door and waited for her to open it.

"Thanks for coming," she said.

Richmond walked in and folded his arms across his chest. "What's going on with you and Felix?"

"How do you know about that?"

"He was in the lobby talking about the money you owe him. What's going on?"

Vivian inhaled sharply, then threw herself on the bed. "I met him when I arrived here," she began. "We had a drink and recognized that we had a common link."

"Me?"

She flipped over on her back. "Yes. Richmond,

I told him that I would be able to get a million dollars from you and I'd give him a cut."

Richmond shook his head and laughed sarcastically. "You're a . . . Vivian, you're the biggest fool I've ever met in my life. So, you decided that this stranger was going to help you bilk me out of a million bucks and now you have nothing."

"And he has a video of us having sex. He's threatening to release it."

Richmond ran his hand across his face. "My God. Why should I care or help you with this bullshit that you've gotten yourself into?"

Vivian rose to her feet and shook her head. "Whether you like it or not, we're linked for life, ex-husband. So, my skeletons are going to bring yours out."

"That's where you're wrong," he said. "I can write my own story without you in it. You just don't want your ass spread across the tabloids. You came to Atlanta to ruin me, and you're the one who's suffering. It would be funny if it wasn't so pathetic."

"Are you going to help me? Richmond, if you ever loved me . . ."

He placed his hand on her shoulder. "That's not going to work, love. We haven't had any love between us for a long time. You know that. I don't clean up your messes anymore, and after the crap you pulled with Alicia—" Richmond shrugged. "I don't give a damn if your sex tape is broadcast on every network and cable channel out there."

"You bastard," she said as she pushed him in the chest.

"We're divorced, our marriage has been over for years, and you wanted to come down here and ruin my real chance at love. Turns out that you're the one who got played. You need to figure this thing out with Felix and leave me alone."

"I think he drugged me," she blurted out.

"Okay, call the police. But leave me and Alicia alone."

Vivian snorted. "You think that . . . She's only with you because you're the new shiny thing in town. Richmond, women don't want you. They want what you can do for them. That's why I married you."

"I thought it was for the baby. And it's so good to know that all women aren't as trifling and conniving as you are. You made your bed, time to get comfortable in it." Richmond turned to the door and headed out of the room.

Now, he was going to find his woman and clear everything up.

Chapter 21

Alicia stripped down to her boy shorts and bra, then hopped in the middle of her bed. Though she would have loved a real dinner, she was going to settle for a bowl of popcorn and a glass of dry chardonnay. Of course, drinking the cheap hotel wine made her think about the wine she and Richmond shared. Then she thought about Paris and making love to him, and finally, Vivian's text.

Downing her glass of wine and shoveling a handful of popcorn in her mouth, Alicia decided to do some channel surfing until she went to sleep. She paused on a classic movie and smiled. Maybe her night could be salvaged.

About twenty minutes later, her phone rang and Alicia nearly jumped out of her skin. "Okay, this better be good, because *What Ever Happened To Baby Jane?* is on," she said without looking at the caller ID.

"So, Baby Jane is more important than I am?" Richmond asked.

She sucked in a deep breath. "I didn't realize it was you," she said. "I thought . . . What's up?"

"I need to see you."

"Richmond, I'm—"

"I'm outside of your hotel in the parking lot. I'll stay here all night if I have to, because we need to fix what's broken between us."

"Come on up," she said as she looked around the bed. A few popcorn crumbs littered the bed and her half-empty bottle of wine was on the nightstand. Sprinting to her feet, she cleaned up the popcorn and stuck the wine in the refrigerator. Then she grabbed the plush robe and wrapped it around her body. Seconds later, there was a knock at the door. Alicia closed her eyes and walked over to the door. When she opened it and saw Richmond standing there, she wanted nothing more than to fall into his arms.

"Can I come in?"

"Sure," she replied as she stepped aside.

Richmond closed the door behind him and drew Alicia into his arms. "I don't like fighting, especially when we've been set up."

"What are you talking about?"

"Can we sit down?"

Alicia nodded and led him over to the bed. "Am I going to need a drink for this?"

"Probably so," he replied. "Plan on sharing?"

"Depends on what you have to say," she said as she crossed over to the refrigerator and pulled out the wine. "What's going on?"

"Vivian came to Atlanta because she wanted me

to give her a million dollars. Somehow, she spilled her guts to Felix Thompson."

Alicia tilted her head to the side as she filled her plastic cup with wine. She poured the rest in a cup for Richmond. "How do they know each other?"

"Random meeting in a bar. When he found out she was getting this big windfall, he took her to his house or they went to her hotel room and had sex. He filmed it and is now holding it over her head."

"That slimy bastard. Not that she doesn't deserve to have a house dropped on her like the wicked witch she is, but that is the lowest thing he could've done to her. I wonder how many other women he has done that to."

"Why does it matter?"

"He works in education and he obviously trolls hotel bars for victims. Hell, he was here tonight. He has to be stopped. Maybe Vivian should go to the police."

"Good luck on that. She doesn't want that tape to get out, and I'm willing to bet she's not going to stick around to see the case through."

"So, we're just supposed to ignore this?"

"Yes," he said. "What are we supposed to do? That woman tried to blackmail me for a million dollars. And let's not forget that she almost cost me you. She is just as guilty as he is."

Alicia downed her wine and shook her head. "That's not the point," she said. "Felix is a—"

Richmond grabbed her chin. "Let's not talk about them right now. I want you to know that I'm all yours. Totally yours." He brushed his lips against hers. "But if you ever give me a cheap chardonnay again, I'm going to have to reevaluate how much I love you."

Alicia froze in place. "What did you say?"

"No more cheap chardonnay," he said.

"Stop it."

"Oh, you mean the I-love-you part? Alicia Michaels, I love you."

Alicia felt faint and wanted to fall into his arms. Love? Could she say the same thing? She wrapped her arms around him and kissed him slowly. They fell backwards on the bed. Richmond slipped his hands underneath her robe and smiled. "This is beautiful," he said as he slipped the robe off her shoulders.

"Great, now I can stop buying lingerie."

"Don't you dare," he said, then kissed her shoulders. He slowly moved down her body using his tongue as the tour guide. Pulling her boy shorts off, Richmond spread her thighs and stroked her wetness until she purred.

"Richmond," she moaned as his tongue replaced his fingers. Alicia arched her body into his kiss, feeling every bit of pleasure that his tongue provided.

Pulling back from her, he looked into her eyes and smiled. "You're simply amazing."

"Takes one to know one," she said. Richmond rose from the bed and stripped out of his clothes.

Alicia ran her finger down his chest as he got back into the bed. "I don't like to fight with you."

"Me either, but the making up is always fun." He took her hand in his and kissed it slowly. "Believe me when I say this, you're the best thing that's ever happened to me."

"Richmond."

"You're sweet, smart, beautiful, and kind. I don't know what I did to deserve you, but trust me, I won't be letting you go."

She pushed him on his back and mounted him. "I like the way that sounds."

Richmond dove inside her and Alicia moaned in delight. She rode him slow, as if she was breaking in a wild mustang. He gripped her hips and fell in rhythm with her. "Yes, yes, yes," Alicia cried.

"You feel so good," Richmond groaned as she ground against him with zest.

She leaned forward and kissed his neck. Richmond shivered and Alicia felt as if she was about to explode when he thrust his hips forward.

Richmond sucked her hard nipples and pushed her over the edge. She collapsed against his chest and buried her lips in his neck.

"I hope you don't plan on telling me to go home, because I can't move," Richmond said.

"I don't want you to leave, but I do have a question," she said.

"And I have an answer."

"Do you want to look at a couple of places with me tomorrow? I can't do the hotel living anymore."

"I told you that you could stay with me until you found a place of your own, or forever, whichever comes first."

"And I don't want to put that kind of pressure on us. Living together and working together could be too much," she said.

"Just admit it, you're afraid," he said.

"I'm . . . a little afraid. Are we moving too fast? Do you want to explore what's out there for a single man, and would I be standing in your way?"

"If I wanted to date every woman who crossed my path, then I wouldn't be here with you. You're the only woman I want and the only woman I love." He stroked her cheek. "Alicia, you're my everything. Don't ever forget that."

She smiled and let his words wrap around her. Maybe she could have it all and have her happily-ever-after. But why did she feel as if she was waiting for the other shoe to drop?

Two weeks later, Alicia had moved into Richmond's place while she waited for her condo in Midtown to be ready. They'd also set up the interview with *Atlanta Scene.* Alicia was particularly proud that they'd gotten the cover, and the photo shoot was going to be at the office and his home. Alicia was going to have to make sure that none of her belongings were visible.

And Richmond had found the perfect location to build the first hotel in Midtown. The land had been cheaper than he'd expected and Solomon was 100 percent on board with purchasing the land as soon as possible. Solomon and Kandace were going to come to Atlanta in the next day or two to see the property. But Richmond was sure that Kandace was coming to make sure he was taking care of her friend. Glancing over at Alicia, who was on her iPad, made him wonder, who would the babies look like, him or her?

"Why are you staring at me?" she asked when she looked up and caught his gaze.

"Because when you're in the midst of beauty, you stare at her." Richmond crossed over to her and took her face in his hands. "You're simply amazing."

"Remember that when you get my bill," she said with a wink.

He laughed, then captured her lips in a slow kiss. Alicia melted against him and lost herself in the sweetness of his kiss. Richmond pulled back from her. "Before we start something that we can't finish, I do have a meeting, and if we kiss one more time, I'm not going to make it."

"If you kiss me again, I'm not going to let you make it," she said, then stroked his cheek. "Besides, I have to get across town to do a soft launch of my client's online boutique and whatnot."

"Damn this work," he said. "If we were unemployed, we could just climb into bed and spend the day making love."

"And then be out on the streets in a month with no money to pay the rent. Not the life for me, darling," she quipped, then kissed him on the cheek.

"I know," he said. "It's fun to dream, though. But let's keep in mind that of all the problems I've ever had, money has never been one of them." Richmond looked at his watch. "We'd better get going."

As they headed out to their cars, Richmond watched the sway of Alicia's hips. She was the definition of beauty, and no one filled out a pair of gray slacks the way she did. He couldn't wait to peel them off later tonight.

"What are you thinking about for dinner?" he asked. "Because I know exactly what I want for dessert."

"Goodbye, Richmond," she said with a smile. "And I'll pick up dinner tonight. I'm going to be near the AUC, so I can get us something from the Busy Bee Café."

Richmond nodded as he opened his car door. "You're the best. See you tonight."

Heading to the office, Richmond was ready to get his day started. He'd expected it to be a good day until he saw Vivian waiting for him in the parking lot.

"Shit," he muttered. Richmond parked his car and slowly walked toward his ex. "Thought you were back in New York."

"He's threatening to release the video, Richmond. Please, let's pay him off. You don't even have to worry about me and what I need."

"I'm not," he said as he walked up the steps and headed for his office. Vivian grabbed his elbow.

"Please, if you ever . . ."

He turned around and faced her, angry and frustrated that she was singing the same song about a video he didn't believe existed. Vivian was a lot of things, but he didn't think she was this naïve and stupid.

"Sing another song because this one, like your begging, is played out. Find a way to deal with your own demons, because I'm done with you and your bullshit."

Vivian narrowed her eyes at him. "Typical. I'm not going down alone. So, if he releases this video, I'm telling all of your secrets."

Richmond stroked his chin. "Have you thought about going to the police? That way you could make sure he goes to jail and you won't have to worry about your goodies being shown to the world."

"Going to the police makes all of this public, and I don't want that to happen," she said as tears poured down her cheeks.

Shaking his head, Richmond couldn't help but remember how he'd been fooled by those tears too many times before. But not today. "Cut the water-works," he said. "It's not working and I'm not giving you money, but if you want to call the police, I'll help you out."

"You just want me to be embarrassed," she said as she wiped her eyes.

"No, I don't. You shouldn't be his victim. Do you think one payment is going to end this?" He placed his hand on her shoulder. "Don't open yourself up to being blackmailed for the rest of your life. He committed a crime and should pay for it."

"And you think he should pay for it because I could be hurt, or is this about Alicia? How long has this dalliance with her been going on?"

Richmond laughed and shook his head. "You have some nerve. How long were you sleeping with Robert McFaul, Thomas Greene, Damien Parker, and the artist with the name no one can pronounce?"

Vivian brought her hand to her mouth. "You knew?"

"Did you think I was a fool? I chose to look the

other way and tried to keep it a secret that my wife was behaving like a whore. For a while, I thought I could live with that, but I deserve better and I have better. While you're trying to stay in my pocket, I've moved on. Time for you to do the same, because if you show up here again—without being invited—I'm going to be the one calling the police."

"You son of—"

Richmond held up his hand. "Two choices. You can call the police and report what Felix did to you, or you can go back to New York and leave me the hell alone."

She rung her hands, then nodded. "Fine, I'll call the police. But—"

"But nothing, Vivvy. You're not my problem anymore. You need to learn how to budget the settlement you received, because I was more than generous with you."

She wiped her eyes. "What if we could give it another—"

"Not even if hell froze over tonight. Let me know when you and the cops need a meeting room and I'll get one prepared for you."

He headed into his office and slammed the door. Six months ago, he would've fallen for her tears and her sob story. But after knowing what real love feels like, there was no way in hell he'd return to being manipulated.

Alicia shook hands with her client as they wrapped up their business. The launch of the online boutique had been a success, over ten thousand hits and five thousand sales. "Alicia, you have to pick out one of these dresses, because without you, I'd still be doing trunk shows in the West End," Royal Jonathan, the designer, said.

"I can't do that, you're about to sell out," she said with a huge grin.

Royal walked over to the closet where he kept his newest designs. "I haven't even put these online yet. And with your figure, you would be the best advertisement ever." He held up a sea-green strapless dress with a wide yellow belt. Alicia was in love with the design and shape of the dress, but she wasn't sure that she could pull off the color combination. "I don't know," she moaned.

Royal crossed over to her and draped the dress in front of her. "Honey, this is beautiful and so are you. Imagine you and your boo, 'cause I know you got one, dancing at a rooftop restaurant and people snapping pictures of you with their camera phones. You'll be on Instagram, Facebook, Tumblr and YouTube." Royal gave her the dress. "You have to try it on."

"All right, I'll try it," she said as she took the dress into the fitting room and tried it on. As she looked at her reflection in the mirror, Alicia felt as if the dress had been made for her. It fit perfectly and the color actually looked good on her. "Never argue with a designer," she muttered as she spun around to get a 360-degree look at the dress.

"Come on out, let me see it!" Royal exclaimed.

"All right," Alicia said as she stepped out of the room.

Royal clapped his hands and jumped up and

down. "Yes, yes, yes! This is the perfect dress for you. I knew it was going to be amazing. Knew it! Oh my God, oh my God, I have the perfect purse to go with this dress and you have to get some gold sandals, the strappier the better!"

"You're amazing, Royal," she said as he handed her a yellow clutch. "You designed this too?"

"Eh, I wish I could say that I did, but this is the work of my ex-partner. The only thing he was good for was accessories. But that's a whole other story."

Alicia patted his shoulder. "Well, you can best believe that your phone is going to be ringing off the hook with exes and friends who've lost touch with you."

"And I'm charging those bitches double," he said with a laugh.

"That's a great business plan! I'm going to change, and I'll see you next week to go over your SEO rankings."

Royal shook his head and smiled. "I'm glad you know what all of that stuff means, because I have no clue."

"Oh, you need to start using the hashtag Royal-Designs, every time you post about your clothing line. And we'll put a plan together to get you trending." Alicia snapped her fingers. "We need a celebrity to wear one of your dresses. I have a great idea of who would give you a big boost."

"Please don't say one of those damned housewives. I don't want my clothes associated with that trash," he said.

"What do you think about Marie Charles-Harris? The *Mocha Girl in Paris* blog author."

Royal tented his hands around his mouth. "Are you serious?"

Alicia was sure that everyone in Atlanta and Decatur heard him scream. She nodded. "I went to college with her husband, and she loves fashion. I know she'll be perfect."

"That would be the best thing ever!" He pulled Alicia into his arms and gave her a tight hug. "You just made my day, honey!"

"Let's hope she says yes," Alicia said, then looked at her watch. "I have to go, but thanks for the dress. I can't wait to wear it."

"Pictures, make sure you take a lot of pictures."

As she left, Alicia was all smiles and ready to see Richmond. Before she headed to the office, she called Marie and told her about the fabulous new designer that she'd been working with.

"You know I'm all for new clothes. Where can I see his stuff?"

"RoyalJDesignsInc.com," Alicia said. "We launched the online boutique today and the response has been amazing."

"I have to check this out. And Richmond invited us to Atlanta. He wants to use some of Devon's recipes at the hotel, so we're taking a little break in the States. That's going to be so much fun."

Alicia was surprised that Devon was going to actually come to Atlanta. He didn't have a lot of good memories in his hometown since the death of his father and the revelation that the former NBA star had abused Devon's mother.

"Besides," Marie said, breaking into Alicia's

thoughts, "he wants to show the baby her roots, and that includes Atlanta."

"That sounds like Devon," she replied. "All right, Marie, this call is costing me a fortune, so email me when you check out the site."

"I will. Hey, how are things with Richmond? Wedding date set yet?"

"Ha! No, and no one is going to plan a surprise wedding either," Alicia said. "We'll talk soon."

Pulling up to the office building, Alicia was surprised to see a police car there. Fear flowed through her body. Had something happened to Richmond? She quickly parked her car and ran inside, expecting to see yellow tape and a crime scene.

When she saw Vivian and Richmond talking to a police officer, she was confused. What was going on?

Chapter 22

Richmond stroked his chin as he listened to Vivian recount her story about how she and Felix came up with their plan.

The officer turned to Richmond and tapped his pen against his pad. "I'm curious," he said. "This woman and Felix were trying to bilk you out of a million dollars. Why are you trying to help her?"

"Felix Thompson is an educator and he could be doing this to young girls who he's in charge of, and someone I really care about told me that he should be stopped. And quite honestly, I'm sick and tired of my ex-wife asking me for money to pay him."

The officer laughed. "I can appreciate your honesty." Then he focused his glare on Vivian. "You realize that Mr. Crawford could press charges against you."

She glanced at him. "I hope you won't," she said.

Richmond shrugged and looked out the door, locking eyes with Alicia. He waved for her to come in, but she shook her head and headed for her office. He didn't miss the smile on Vivian's face.

"Trouble?" she mouthed.

"Are we done?" Richmond asked the officer.

"For now. Ms. Crawford, don't leave town right away. We're going to have to find a way to prove the video exists and move forward from there."

Vivian grabbed a Post-it note from Richmond's desk and wrote her number down on it. "This is where I can be reached, and I'm going to be staying at the Days Inn on Spring Street."

Richmond raised his eyebrow, thinking how the mighty had fallen. As the officer and Vivian left the office, Richmond headed for Alicia.

"Knock, knock," he said as he opened the door.

She looked at him with a raised eyebrow. "Do I even want to know?"

"We're—Vivian—is going after Felix."

"Is she really going to actually go through the whole process? Or is your ex-wife just playing a role to get back in your pants and pocket?" Granted, Alicia wanted to get Felix, but she didn't want to deal with Vivian without a long-handle spoon.

"I told Vivian that this is it. She's not welcome here, and if she didn't press charges on Felix so that he would stop trying to blackmail her, I was going to press charges on her."

Alicia's eyes widened. "Really?"

He nodded. "I'm not going to let my past dictate my future anymore. She can try, but nothing and no one comes before the woman I love." He stood in front of her chair and noticed the garment bag draped across the back. "I thought you were just launching a boutique. Had no idea you were going shopping."

"And I was going to give you a fashion show," she said. "You're kind of messing that up."

"Let me straighten up and fly right, then. How did the launch go?"

"Amazing," she said. "Just amazing. As a matter of fact, the site keeps getting more hits and most of the inventory has sold out. Royal is over the moon, and I couldn't be happier."

"Wow. No wonder you got a new dress."

"And if you play your cards right, you'll get to take it off me." She winked at him.

"I have a lunch meeting with the developers to talk about when we're going to break ground on the hotel. Solomon and Kandace will be here in the morning."

"Great. Then we all go out tomorrow night and you can see my dress."

"Why do I have to wait?" he asked with a faux pout.

"Because I didn't freak out when I saw your ex-wife sitting in your office, and that's a win."

Richmond leaned in and kissed her gently. "I'm glad you know that she's nothing to me and not a threat to us," he said.

"But what do you think Felix is going to do when he finds out that he's under investigation?"

Richmond shrugged. "As long as he stays away from us, I don't give a damn."

Alicia offered him a nervous smile but didn't say anything.

When Richmond left for his meeting, Alicia wondered about Vivian going after Felix and if there would be repercussions that would come back to haunt her and Richmond.

"Shit," she muttered as she tried to keep an eye on Royal's web views. "I don't want to be involved in this crap with Felix and Vivian." Alicia rose to her feet and stalked back and forth in front of her desk. "I'm overthinking this. Felix probably will drop all of this once he finds out that the police are involved, and I won't have to deal with this bullshit."

She decided to call Jade and Serena on three-way to tell them about the latest development in the drama with Vivian and Felix.

"Alicia," Jade said when she answered the phone. "Royal Designs is your baby, isn't it?"

"Yes, but that's not why I'm calling," she said. "Serena, are you there?"

"I'm here, feeling like I'm in high school," she replied. "What's going on?"

Alicia sighed and recounted the story about Vivian and Felix making a sex tape and how he was using it to blackmail her. "She thought Richmond was going to give her a million dollars so that she could pay him off."

"Why is she in Atlanta?" Jade asked. "I thought she was all about making people's lives hell in New York only."

"She's broke, I guess," Alicia said.

"Or she's one of those slimy bitches who doesn't want a man until she sees how happy he is with someone else," Serena interjected.

"I don't care what kind of woman she is, I'm just tired of her being around. But Felix does need to be stopped. What if he does this to the girls at his school or their parents and . . ."

"How is that your problem?" Jade asked.

Alicia sighed and dropped her head. "Because I knew a long time ago that he was a . . . When we were undergrads, Felix nearly assaulted me and I kept quiet about it for years."

"Alicia, really?" Jade asked. Alicia could imagine the tears welling up in her friend's eyes. "Why didn't you tell us?"

"Because she knew you'd overreact," Serena said. "You're crying, aren't you?"

"And Serena, you still wanted to go and fight him some fifteen years later."

"Wait!" Jade exclaimed. "You knew about this and didn't say anything?"

"I've known for a few days, so calm down."

Alicia sighed. "I'm just worried that this is going to somehow hurt me and Richmond."

"So, you made up with him?" Serena asked.

Alicia smiled as if her friends could see. "He told me that he loves me."

"What?" Jade exclaimed. "Wait, wait. Why am I being left out of everything these days?"

Alicia kicked her feet up on the desk and leaned back in her chair. "Because, Jade, you overreact to everything. And you have a busy life with the kids and James."

"Well, Serena's pregnant!"

"Jade, that's why we don't tell you anything, you can't keep your mouth closed for shit!"

Alicia cheered for her friend. "That's awesome. And if it's a girl, remember our deal."

"What deal is that?" Jade asked.

"I'm ending this call right now," Serena said.

"I know she didn't tell you that she was naming the baby after you," Jade snapped.

"Yes, she did."

"Serena!"

"What? That was the only way to get y'all off my back. Jeez, you three made me feel like I was the most helpless woman in the world. But thank you for being there for me."

"So, your baby's name is going to be Alicia Jade Kandace?" Alicia asked with a laugh.

"Hopefully I'll have a boy," Serena said. "Look, y'all are stressing me out and Antonio just walked in."

When Serena hung up, Alicia and Jade burst into laughter. "I can't wait to see her with the baby," Jade said.

"That's going to be a special sight. I'm so happy for her."

"Me too. Antonio is over the moon. But I'm worried about you, though."

"I'm going to be fine, I'm sure of it," Alicia replied.

"Well, if Felix tries something, just know Atlanta is a short trip from Charlotte."

Alicia laughed. "Y'all love resorting to violence, as if we don't have everything to lose."

"Well, what are you going to do if he tries something? And don't say you aren't above violence, because I saw Richmond knock Felix on his ass."

Laughing, Alicia thought about that night and how everything changed with one punch. She was never the kind of woman who thought she needed a hero, and yet that was exactly what Richmond had become to her lately. But that night, all he'd been missing was a white horse and a shiny sword.

Maybe she did love him. But could she drop the fear and tell him how she felt?

"Hello!" Jade said, reminding her friend that she was still on the line. "Where did you go?"

"I was just thinking about this whole thing with Richmond. Jade, when did you know that you loved James and that telling him wouldn't make him run away?"

"You said Richmond told you that he loves you, so why are you too afraid to tell him the same?"

"Because I've never felt this way before and I've never had to respond to those three words."

"That's because you normally run away before you get to this part. Tyson doesn't count because he's a piece of . . . His wife finally left him."

"What?"

"Yes, and it was big news because he was having an affair with the new mayor, who just resigned. I wish you could've been here to see it."

Alicia sucked her teeth. "Please, Karma may not come when you want her to, but she is always right on time."

"I wish I was there to give you a high five."

Alicia glanced at her watch. "I have to go. I was so excited about the dress Royal gave me that I forgot to go to the Busy Bee and get dinner."

"Yeah, you better hurry."

After hanging up with Jade, Alicia headed to her car and drove back to the West End. She was going to make tonight special for Richmond and tell him how she felt about him.

She made it to the café just in time to get a chicken dinner box for her and Richmond, then she headed to the liquor store and picked up some top-shelf vodka so that she could make the famous "Serena Punch."

Alicia arrived home before Richmond did, which gave her a chance to prepare for dinner. She placed the chicken in the oven to keep it warm and moist. Then she mixed the ingredients for the potent drink. After the food and drinks were ready, Alicia headed upstairs and took a warm shower. She figured that she'd channel her inner Serena all the way and meet Richmond at the door in black lace.

Richmond was tired of shaking hands and drinking sweet tea, but was excited that he had the support of so many people in the community with the building of the hotel. He could only imagine what things would be like when the article in *Atlanta Scene* came out.

Richmond knew the success of this hotel launch would be the beginning of his new life in business, his chance to overcome all of the rumors about his paternity and if he was "Crawford" enough to take on a project like this. He'd been enjoying Solomon's hands-off approach, but Richmond couldn't imagine the groundbreaking without him. Especially since he was thinking that would be the perfect day to ask Alicia to be his forever.

"Richmond," Clover Hughes, owner of one of the city's biggest construction firms, said as they headed for the door. "You have to let me introduce you to some of the best contractors in the city. Being that this is the South, you don't have all of those union issues."

"We're going to pay everyone fairly, I want that to be clear, and my working conditions are going to be as safe as if it is union supervised."

"Whoa," Clover said. "I guess it is possible to find an honest real estate developer from New York. Still, I want to get you the best to build this hotel."

"I look forward to it. And thanks for the help."

"Do you know how long we've been trying to get a Crawford hotel in the city? You guys do luxury like no one else."

"Hopefully this will be the first of many. Atlanta is a magical place, and I look forward to making this place home."

Clover nodded. "If you do make Atlanta home, you better get used to writing checks to the big three."

"The big three?"

"Spelman, Morehouse, and Clark Atlanta."

Richmond smiled, thinking about how great he and Alicia were going to look at next year's AUC ball. "I can't wait to write checks and sign up interns. Besides, one of the best people I know went to Spelman. Depending on how we do over the first five years, I might endow a scholarship in her name."

"She must be a hell of a woman."

Richmond nodded. "You have no idea." He looked down at his watch. "She has dinner waiting for me, so I better get going."

After shaking hands with Clover, Richmond dashed to his car and headed home. While he was looking forward to the crunchy chicken from the Busy Bee, he couldn't wait to kiss his woman.

When he got home, Richmond was treated to a surprise he hadn't been expecting. Alicia answered the door in a black lace teddy with a can of whipped cream in her hand.

"Welcome home, Mr. Crawford," she said.

"I don't know what I did to deserve this kind of welcome home, but let me do it again tomorrow."

She squirted some of the sweet cream on her index finger and ran it across his lips. "So, you have a choice. We can eat dinner or have dessert first. And I have to say, Busy Bee chicken is so good cold. Now, it's in the oven heating and we can certainly eat dinner first."

Richmond slowly licked the cream from her fingers. "I'm all for cold chicken if you're going to be my hot dessert. Turn that oven off." Alicia covered his mouth with hers and before he could get in the door, Richmond knew that chicken was going to be ice-cold before he took a bite of it.

When he felt her tongue dancing against his, he knew that he was going to have to pull away from her or they would be making love in the foyer. Alicia's fingers dancing on the back of his neck as they kissed only seemed to fuel the passionate fire burning inside him.

He pulled back from her and stared deeply into her eyes. "We have to stop or . . ."

Alicia took his face into her hands and said, "What if I don't want to stop?"

Richmond groaned. "Don't we have things to talk

about? I don't want another misunderstanding to come between us."

"We can talk later." She moaned, then ran her tongue across his lips.

Before Richmond could answer, Alicia captured his mouth in a hot kiss. Stepping back, she placed her hand against his chest. "I'd better turn the oven off before we burn this place down."

She strutted to the stove and he drank in her sexy image. This woman had gotten so deep under his skin that he couldn't imagine a day without her. When she crossed over to him, Richmond wrapped his arms around Alicia. As he stroked her smooth skin, his dick stood at attention. Richmond swept Alicia into his arms, then brought his lips on top of hers as he carried her into his bedroom.

Gently, he laid her against the comforter and gazed down upon her. She looked so alluring, so demure and so sexy. Richmond quickly undressed, but he wasn't going to rush anything else as he parted her legs, slipping his finger inside her lacy lingerie.

Alicia moaned as he probed her hot body with his finger. It was as if he was on an expedition to discover what pleased her and how to make her revel in delight. Each touch made her hotter, wetter, and Richmond could barely contain his desire to melt with her.

"Richmond," she moaned as his tongue replaced his finger. He pressed her body closer to his lips so that he could taste every inch of her. Alicia grasped the back of his neck as waves of pleasure washed over her while he pushed her teddy off her body.

Richmond traveled up her body, spending time around her navel before reaching her breasts and sucking them until they swelled against his lips. Easily, he could have taken her. His hardness pressed against her thighs, and the heat radiating from her body made it difficult to control his desire. When she wrapped her legs around his waist, Richmond knew it was going to be hard to hold on to his restraint.

"Slow down, baby," he whispered. "We have all night."

"I want you," Alicia moaned. "Need you inside me."

"And you're going to have me." Richmond took her breast back into his mouth as she ground against him. Pulling back, he reached for a condom from his nightstand. Alicia stroked his chest with her fingertips as he slid the sheath in place. He pulled her against his chest and their lips met. Alicia took Richmond by surprise as she kissed him passionately, drawing his tongue into her mouth. As they broke off their kiss, Richmond found his way into hot wetness. He felt as if he'd gone straight to heaven as her warmth enveloped him. She kneaded his back softly as they fell into a sensual dance, fueled by passion and desire. Alicia matched Richmond thrust for thrust. He'd never felt like this before, and when she took control, rolling over so that she was on top of him, his body went into overdrive.

"Alicia, Alicia, Alicia," he moaned like a prayer as she rode him fast, then slow, then faster, and then slower. She leaned forward and nibbled on his earlobe and Richmond lost it. He climaxed and gripped her hips tightly as he spent himself. She fell into his embrace and they drifted off to sleep.

Hours later when they woke up, Alicia and Richmond headed to the kitchen in their underwear to eat chicken, cornbread, and cabbage. "You're lucky that they ran out of coleslaw," she quipped as she broke off a piece of his cornbread. She nibbled on it and realized that she still wasn't a huge fan.

"How are you going to ruin the mood like that?" he asked as he snatched a wing off her plate.

"Really?"

"Every time you say the C word, I'm taking prime pieces of chicken from you."

"I will fight you if you take another wing from me," she said with a wink.

"I tell you what, dessert was delicious and I want a second helping. This time with whipped cream on top."

She smirked at him. "Should we take it back to the bedroom or in the kitchen on the tabletop?"

"Let's start down here on the tabletop. I believe there's some chocolate sauce to go along with that cream."

Alicia pushed their empty paper plates on the floor and lay across the table, ready to give him another taste.

Chapter 23

The next morning, Alicia and Richmond woke up to the persistent ringing of the doorbell. Richmond wanted to ignore it since he had naked Alicia in his arms and was loving it. But when the ringing turned to banging, Richmond grabbed his robe and went downstairs to open the door. And if it wasn't a police officer or a firefighter telling him that there was a mandatory evacuation, there was going to be hell to pay.

When he pulled the curtain back and saw Solomon standing on his front step, he started to leave him there. But he knew he couldn't leave Kandace outside in the sweltering Georgia heat.

"Really?" Richmond said when he opened the door. "You couldn't call first?"

Kandace elbowed her husband in the side. "I told him to do that," she said. "Guessing Alicia's around here somewhere?"

"I cannot believe my brother isn't happy to see me," Solomon said. "And I brought breakfast."

"I have breakfast upstairs."

"Eww," Kandace said. "Walking away. That's my friend you're talking about. Or it better be."

"Why don't you take the breakfast you brought into the kitchen and I'll get Alicia," Richmond said after he ushered his brother and sister-in-law inside. Solomon looked at the discarded paper plates on the floor and a spot of chocolate on the table.

"Do I even want to know?" Solomon asked.

"Had some dessert last night, it got a little out of hand."

Kandace shook her head. "How old are y'all?"

Richmond dashed upstairs and heard the shower going. Stepping in the bathroom, he tapped on the shower door. "Guess you know we have company," he said.

"Yes, and I hope you at least picked up the plates from the kitchen floor."

Richmond dropped his robe and stepped in the shower with her. "Nope. And they brought us breakfast."

"Then we shouldn't take all day in the shower," she said, then splashed a bit of water on him.

Richmond wrapped his arms around her waist. "But I already know what I want to eat for breakfast."

Alicia didn't have a chance to protest before Richmond dropped to his knees and began to suck the hot wetness between her thighs. Her knees went weak as his tongue danced across her throbbing bud and his fingers played deep in her wetness. As much as she wanted to scream out his name in delight, the last thing she wanted to do was alert her friends to what they were doing upstairs. But

Richmond wasn't going to stop until she gave him a bit of a scream.

"Umm," she moaned. "You're so-so bad."

He tore his mouth from her and smiled. "And you taste so good."

"If we don't get out of here soon, they're going to know what we're doing," she said, then shut the water off.

"I guess you're right," he said. "And knowing my brother, half of the food is already gone. So, if you want something to eat, we better get a move on."

The couple dried off quickly and dressed, then headed downstairs. Just like Richmond had predicted, most of the biscuits and eggs were gone by the time he and Alicia made it downstairs.

"Well, well," Solomon said as he watched Richmond and Alicia walk into the kitchen. "Nice of you to join us."

"Hey, Solomon," Alicia said. "Kandace! Please tell me you're in the kitchen making coffee."

"Yes, I am," she said. Alicia turned the corner and gave her friend a hug.

"You and Richmond are nasty," Kandace whispered. "On the kitchen table, really?"

"You have no proof," Alicia said with a laugh.

Kandace raised her right eyebrow. "You just told on yourself. Y'all are so cute together. Jade and Serena are coming this afternoon too, and I can't wait to tell them about this."

"You better not."

"How much is it worth to you, doll face?" Kandace asked as she reached for the coffee mugs above the coffeemaker.

"Careful, you're starting to sound like a real New Yorker these days," Alicia said.

"I guess this is what happens when you live with the king of New York." Kandace poured the coffee and Alicia added sugar and cream, though she left hers black.

"So," Kandace asked. "What's going on with Vivian these days?"

Alicia shrugged, then told her about the meeting Vivian and Richmond had with a police officer. "Why would Richmond help her with that?" Kandace asked.

"Because Felix Thompson is blackmailing her with a sex tape."

Kandace covered her mouth with her hand. "I-I . . . What?"

"I can't believe he's out here victimizing women like that and working with children. I hope she sticks to her guns and goes after him." Alicia shivered. "He should've been in jail and on a sex offenders list years ago."

"Yeah, I heard," Kandace said. "I wish we had been able to help you out back then, because you shouldn't have had to suffer alone all this time."

"It wasn't easy to talk about," Alicia said. "But that's the past. Let's drink this coffee with our men and look forward to the future."

Solomon passed Richmond a biscuit and gave his brother a smirk. "Good to see you're happy and you haven't even had coffee yet," Solomon said.

"Don't need that much coffee when I have Alicia.

I'm glad I listened to you and told her how I felt, because this woman is magical."

"And you're sure this is your future and you want to make Atlanta home. Nice house, by the way. There are some beautiful houses out here, for sure."

"What are you trying to do, sell houses now?"

"Hell. No. But if I was going to move down South, I'd go Atlanta over Charlotte."

Alicia and Kandace walked in with the coffee mugs. "And what's wrong with Charlotte?" Kandace asked.

"No history," Solomon replied as he took his coffee from his wife's hand and gave her a playful smack on the bottom. "But don't worry, I'm going to leave the South to Richmond and just come visit."

Kandace sat on his lap. "But what if I want to be closer to my business and my friends?" She batted her eyelashes at her husband and stroked his cheek.

"I'm in trouble," Solomon said.

"Luckily, I love New York almost as much as I love you."

Alicia looked at Richmond and shook her head. "I will never feel that way about New York."

"Then I guess it's a good thing that I have fallen in love with you and Atlanta."

Kandace's mouth fell open and Alicia kissed Richmond's cheek. "I think it was the Dancing Goats that did that," Alicia said.

"Not just the coffee," he said as he kissed Alicia's cheek.

"At the risk of sounding like a cornball," Kandace said, "I have to say that this is the best breakfast that

I've had with my family since Solomon and I got married. And I'm so happy to see all of this love."

Solomon wiped a stray tear from her eye. "Baby, that was incredibly corny."

"Shut up," Kandace said as she elbowed him in the stomach.

As Alicia watched her friends ribbing each other, she couldn't help but realize that she and Richmond were well on their way to that kind of love.

"So," Richmond said. "How are Adrian and Dana doing?"

"They're in Los Angeles for the month. I think he's trying to make the family bicoastal for as long as he can."

"I was hoping they could be here for the groundbreaking. That way we show the media a true united front."

"Oh!" Alicia exclaimed. "Your interview with *Atlanta Scene* is going to be this afternoon. The pictures will start at the office and the groundbreaking. Then a shoot at the house." She hopped up and started looking for her cell phone. "I better call the cleaning service."

"Nah, let the cameras catch all of this freakiness," Solomon quipped. "Plates on the floor, empty whipped cream cans."

"Shut up," Alicia said. "I bet back in the day, a morning after with Solomon was much worse."

"Back in the day? Have you seen my wife?"

"Keep me out of your locker room talk," Kandace said before she downed her coffee. Then she winked at Alicia and mouthed, *Amateurs.*

Alicia found her phone, called the cleaning

service, and then took Kandace upstairs to show her the dress she was wearing to the groundbreaking, while Richmond and Solomon started talking business.

"Oh my, this dress is sexy and classy. Is this a Royal?"

"Brand-new, not even online. He loved how the online launch went and gave me a dress. He is about to be the next great thing in fashion."

"I know, I went online during the launch and everything I wanted was sold out. Look at you doing the damned thing out here."

Alicia shrugged. "Well, this is how I do it," she said, then shimmied her shoulders.

"I can't believe it, we finally have it all." Kandace smiled and ran her hand across the dress. "Well, you have it all, because I don't have a Royal dress."

"We'd better get ready for the groundbreaking. I know Richmond is excited about everything and how he broke into the culture here."

"He had help," she replied. "And I'm glad I was wrong. You two are perfect for each other."

Alicia hugged her friend tightly. "I think I love him."

"Girl, bye. You do love him and he is crazy about you. And when Crawford men fall in love, they don't let go."

"So you think he never loved his ex-wife?"

Kandace shrugged. "Maybe on their wedding day. Hell, you've had more interaction with her than I've ever had. And it seems as though her heart has always been with the money."

"And now she's here, wrapped up in a sex tape scheme. I just don't want this to hurt Richmond."

"She's in love," Kandace sang. "'Cause that don't sound like business to me."

Alicia tossed a pillow at her friend. Kandace ducked, then asked, "So, where are you staying?"

Alicia hid her smile. "Here. I mean, I hit the ground running, stayed in the hotel longer than I meant to, and Richmond has the best wine ever."

"You're blaming it on wine? Girl, stop! I guess I better check and see if my husband is ready to go check into our hotel so we can get dressed."

"Why don't you guys stay here?" Alicia asked. "There's plenty of room."

"Well, umm, this is the first trip in a long time without Kiana, so we need a little more privacy." Kandace winked at her friend as she headed for the stairs. "And someone else can clean up our sensual aftermath."

"Get out of here, nasty."

About an hour later, the Crawford clan and what seemed liked every camera in the city of Atlanta was at the future sight of the boutique hotel. Alicia and Kandace stood in the background as Richmond spoke to the media. Solomon looked on proudly.

"Atlanta is one of the most vibrant cities in the country. Hollywood of the South. And Crawford Hotels is happy to be a part of the Atlanta community. From the history of this beautiful city, to her bright future, Atlanta is the place to be. What we're bringing to the city is a vibrant hotel that will give visitors a unique place to stay and a restaurant that will become one of the favorites of the residents of this great city. Superstar Chef Devon Harris is going to create the menu for the restaurant."

Cheers erupted from the press corps. "Now we don't have to go to Paris or Charlotte for that cake," a photographer exclaimed.

Richmond and Solomon laughed. "But," Solomon said, "until the hotel is built, keep in mind that Charlotte is a short trip away and my wife owns that restaurant in Charlotte."

"Master marketer," Richmond quipped.

Kandace shook her head as if she could feel all the cameras now focusing on her. Alicia nudged her friend and told her to smile.

After the cameras focused back on Richmond, Kandace whispered to Alicia, "Now we're going to see stories about Carmen's death and the restaurant again."

"Maybe not. The way Richmond is charming everyone out there, maybe they will cut Solomon's advertisement for the restaurant out of their reporting. But you have to give the man an A for effort."

Kandace shrugged. "There are things that you never live down, and that's my little red wagon."

"Are you all right?" Alicia asked.

"Yeah, I'm fine. I just get tired of my past cropping up so much."

Alicia nodded. And wondered if you could ever give up the past or if that was something that would always haunt you. Had she dealt with her past, and would she be able to move forward with Richmond with it lingering over her head?

Then the craziest idea popped into her mind. She was going to have to help Vivian bring Felix Thompson down. She just wondered if Richmond would be okay with that. He was trying to get that woman out of his life, and Alicia was about to pull her right back into their lives.

"Ladies and gentlemen, thank you for coming, and we look forward to seeing you when the hotel opens." Richmond's voice snapped Alicia out of her thoughts. When he reached for her hand, Alicia smiled and joined him in front of the cameras. "I have to thank one of the brightest minds in the city for helping me learn about Atlanta. Alicia Michaels, thank you for all of the work that you've done to help Crawford Hotels get here. You've also helped me understand that Southerners don't know how to make hot dogs, but I digress. Alicia, I love you."

"Richmond?" She locked eyes with him.

"Will you make me the happiest man in Atlanta and be my wife? Will you marry me?"

"I-I," she stammered, then swayed from side to side. Next thing she knew, everything was black.

Richmond had anticipated a few different reactions to his marriage proposal, but Alicia collapsing in his arms hadn't been one of them. He rushed her to the car and allowed Kandace to drive to the closest hospital. Solomon closed out the press conference and then took an Uber to meet his family at the hospital.

With Alicia in his arms, Richmond rushed into

the emergency room of Piedmont West. "We need help. She passed out."

The charge nurse helped Richmond lay Alicia on a gurney that an orderly brought over. "And what's her name?"

"Alicia Michaels," Richmond said.

"Any known allergies?"

Richmond turned to Kandace. "Allergies?"

"Penicillin and ibuprofen," she said.

"Okay," the nurse said as they rushed Alicia back to an examination room. Richmond wanted to follow them back, but Kandace grabbed his arm.

"What the hell is going on? Has she been feeling all right? Has this happened before?"

"No. As far as I know she's been fine. I got to get back there and be with her."

Alicia's eyes fluttered open when she heard all the beeps. Wasn't she just standing outside listening to Richmond propose to her? *Wait, he asked me to marry him and I fainted. In. Front. Of. The. Press.*

"You scared us," Richmond said.

Alicia looked around the room and saw Kandace and Solomon standing there as well.

"What happened?" Alicia asked.

"This one scared the hell out of you, asking you to be his wife," Solomon said with a laugh.

Before Alicia could reply, the doctor walked in with a smile on her face. "Ms. Michaels, glad to see that you're awake. Your family was really worried. Now, I'm going to need to do an exam and go over some test results with Ms. Michaels. And I need some space."

"We'll be outside," Kandace said as she, Solomon, and Richmond started for the door.

"Mr. Michaels, you can stay," the doctor said. Alicia hid her laughter.

Richmond crossed over to her bed and held her hand as the doctor opened Alicia's file.

"Well," she began, "congratulations are in order. It looks as if you're pregnant."

"What?"

Richmond brought his hand to his mouth.

The doctor nodded. "And you got a little dehydrated, so we're going to keep you here for a little while and get you hydrated. You're going to have to leave the coffee alone."

Alicia was trying to focus on what the doctor said. Pregnant. How? Well, she knew how it happened, and it made her feel as if wanting to help Vivian bring down Felix was now going to be an idea that Richmond wouldn't be behind.

"Any questions?" the doctor asked.

Alicia shook her head.

"Well, I'll leave you to it. Once we get that bag of fluids in you, we'll check your levels and then you can go home."

"Thank you, Doctor," Richmond said, then turned his attention to Alicia. "So, what are we going to do?"

Her heart pounded and she couldn't think of anything to say. A baby hadn't been in her plan. Marriage hadn't been in her plan either. But she couldn't live her life without Richmond, and the look on his face told her that he wasn't going to leave without knowing where they were going.

"We're going to have a baby and a wedding," she said with a smile.

Richmond leaned in and gave her a kiss. "I love you so much."

Chapter 24

Several hours after the groundbreaking, Alicia was wrapped in a blanket lying on the sofa, surrounded by three Crawfords. Solomon flipped the channels on the TV like a kid looking for cartoons before Kandace took the remote from him and handed it to Alicia.

"Can we let the sick and shut-in have the remote?" Kandace said.

"So, what's wrong with you?" Solomon asked as Richmond walked into the living room with three glasses of wine and a bottle of grape juice.

Alicia sat up and smiled. "I got a little overheated and . . ."

"My baby didn't like that," Richmond said as he handed Alicia her grape juice.

"B-baby?" Kandace and Solomon said in concert.

Richmond nodded and handed out the wineglasses. "Now, I'm going to have to keep my fiancée hydrated and rested for a few days."

Kandace sat on the edge of the sofa beside Alicia and gave her a tight hug. "You and Serena are about to be mothers at the same time. This is perfect," she said. "And we're officially going to be family."

Alicia squeezed Kandace's hand. "We need to talk, alone," she said.

"Guys," Kandace said. "What are we going to eat? You know pregnant women and their friends need to eat. And Houston's. That would be great."

Solomon and Richmond glanced at each other. "Are you guys trying to get rid of us?"

"Nah, we're just trying to get some food," Alicia said, then winked at them.

Richmond nudged Solomon in the side. "Let's go."

"Text us what you want to eat," Solomon said as they headed out the door.

Once they were alone, Alicia sat up and exhaled.

"What's going on?" Kandace asked.

"Before all of this, I thought the only thing that I was going to have to talk to Richmond about was how I want to help Vivian bring Felix down."

"Do what? Why do you want to get involved in that?"

"Because I feel like that's a part of my past that has been clouding my future. To know that he's still out there victimizing women makes me ill. What if I had turned him in while we were in college? And he's in education. Kandace, I can't just sit back and let this happen."

"All right, I can understand that, but how can you trust that she's a real victim?"

Alicia shrugged. "But if I go into this with good intentions and it turns out to be a fraud, then it's not my fault. But I don't think she'd fake a sex tape."

"So, how are we going to do this and what are you going to tell Richmond?"

"The truth. There's no way that I'm going to be able to hide this from him. Hell, I need to get her number from his phone."

"I think this is a bad idea, but what are you going to do if Richmond doesn't want to get involved?"

"I hadn't thought about that," she said. "But I have to do this for me—not for Richmond, not for Vivian, but for me."

"I got your back, but we're not doing anything that's going to put you or the baby at risk."

"Did you text them what we wanted from Houston's yet?"

Kandace shook her head and pulled out her phone. "Biltmores, red cabbage, and extra onions."

Alicia laughed. "Don't forget extra cheese on the sandwiches."

"What do you think those two are up to?" Richmond asked as they pulled up to the restaurant.

"Who knows, but it's something," Solomon said. "Quite the turn of events today."

Richmond nodded. "For a second there, I thought when she passed out it was because I asked her to marry me."

"Are you sure that you're ready to go down this road? Instant family."

"Never been more sure in my life." Richmond smiled. "This is what love is supposed to feel like."

"I told you Alicia was a great woman and you

couldn't be luckier, especially after that thing that you married the first time."

"And she keeps popping up. I think that she's still in Atlanta because of that so-called sex tape thing."

"Wait a minute, she made a sex tape? What in the hell is going on?"

Richmond shrugged and told his brother about Felix's scheme and how he was still pressing Vivian for a percentage of the money he thought Richmond was going to hand over.

"Why does he have such a hard-on for you? This seems more personal than anything else. He's risking his career. I know that kind of money wouldn't do shit for me," Solomon said.

"Spoken like a man who grew up with a silver spoon hanging out of his mouth. This may have something to do with the fact that I decked him at the Atlanta University Center ball."

Solomon dropped his head. "So, you came to Atlanta and started living your Lennox Lewis fantasies?"

"No, but something was going on with him and Alicia. The look on her face just made me want to pummel that fool. He wouldn't leave her alone, and she clearly wanted him to get lost."

"Do they know each other?"

"From college, I think."

Solomon shook his head. "Seems like you've opened a can of worms, brother."

"That's why I've washed my hands of it. The Atlanta Police Department and Vivian can handle that."

"Hopefully he won't try to come after you now

that we've announced the groundbreaking. This would be prime time for him to try and start a scandal. Knowing his shortsighted ass, he'd try to get money from the company, and I don't want to get involved in that."

"It's not going to go that far. I'm sure once the police talk to him, he's going to let all of this go. Like you said, it's not a huge amount of money and he has a reputation in the community."

"And what does Alicia think of this?" Solomon looked down at his phone. "The food order is finally here. What's a Biltmore?"

"As long as there's no coleslaw involved, I'm good."

"There's red cabbage and extra cheese on it," Solomon said. "Guessing the Biltmore is a sandwich."

After ordering the food and waiting for what seemed like an hour, they finally got the food and headed back to the house.

"It sure took you guys long enough. I'm starving over here," Kandace said as she crossed over to her husband and took the bags from his hands.

"It took you long enough to send me what you ladies wanted, and we have to eat too," Solomon said.

"And I had to make sure there was no coleslaw hiding in any of this food," Richmond quipped.

"You're going to end up loving coleslaw like I've fallen for lox."

Kandace shook her head. "That is the one thing I can live without. I want my salmon cooked and in a croquette."

"That sounds delicious," Alicia said. "Forget all of this, we need salmon croquettes."

Richmond and Solomon looked at each other and burst into laughter. "You two play too much," Richmond said. "And I was going to break out a good bottle of wine, but Kandace, you messed that up."

"Hold up," Solomon said. "Why do I have to suffer because my wife is being bad? Alicia can't have any wine, so that just means more for us."

"Solomon! I can't believe you would do me like that. I can withhold things, too." Kandace shot him a saucy look.

"I think it's wrong for all of you to be drinking wine knowing that I love it and can't have it."

Richmond threw his hands up. "Coke for everybody." He crossed over to Alicia and kissed her on the forehead. "How are you feeling, babe?"

"I'm a lot better now that you're here." She reached up and gave him a quick peck on the lips.

Solomon unpacked their dinners and he took a seat on the floor beside his wife while Richmond snuggled up with Alicia on the sofa. They fell into a comfortable silence as they ate dinner. Richmond couldn't help but think of all the time he'd wasted in misery and jealousy. He and his brother could've had this kind of relationship for years if they hadn't been used as pawns in a game they had no business playing.

Alicia polished off the last bite of her cabbage and turned to Richmond. "I have to say something." She stroked Richmond's cheek. "This whole thing with Vivian and Felix is giving me pause. He can't get away with this, and I feel like it's my responsibility to help her get justice."

"Why?" Richmond snapped. "You don't owe her a damned thing."

"Damn right," Solomon interjected. "If anything, she should be glad that we didn't press harassment charges against her. Every time she can't get into a restaurant or a Broadway show, I get a call from that crazy . . ."

"Listen, I don't care about all the things she did in the past, I just know that what Felix is trying to do is wrong. Part of me feels like I could've stopped this years ago."

Richmond and Solomon exchanged confused looks. "What do you mean?" Richmond asked.

"Until recently, I never told anyone what happened in college between me and Felix. He tried to . . ."

Kandace inched closer to Alicia and held her hand. "Take your time," she said.

Richmond's face was a brick of anger as Alicia continued her story. "He tried to assault me, and I never reported it. Finding out what he did to Vivian just had me thinking, what if he's been doing this for years? What if he's made victims of the girls at his school? I can't stand by silently anymore."

"So, what are you trying to do?" Richmond asked.

"I want to reach out to her and help her put that bastard away."

Richmond leapt to his feet and shook his head. "I want you to stay as far away from this as possible. Again, you don't owe anyone a damn thing!"

"I owe this to myself."

"You have more than yourself to think about," Richmond said, then looked down at her flat belly.

"Do you think I'm going to put our child at risk?"

"I think this is a bad idea, and I don't trust that Vivian is innocent in all of this," Richmond said. "Let her and the police handle it."

Kandace nudged Solomon. "Let's give them some privacy," she said as they rose to their feet.

"Alicia," Solomon said, "I'm not going to tell you how you should feel about anything that happened to you, but don't allow this to hurt you by reliving a painful part of your past. Vivian is a con artist, and you don't have to give her anything."

"Just like I said," Alicia responded, "this isn't about her. This is about me."

Kandace nodded. "Come on, babe," she said.

Once Kandace and Solomon had moved to the kitchen, Richmond turned to Alicia and drew her into his arms. "I'm so sorry," he said. "I'm sorry he hurt you."

Alicia cried silently as Richmond hugged her tighter. She hadn't cried about that night in years. But there was something cleansing about these tears, and knowing that Richmond had her back made her feel as if she had everything she needed to heal properly.

"I can't wait to be your wife," she whispered in his ear.

"Want to go get married tomorrow?"

She bit his bottom lip. "Now, you know I can't do that. Jade and Serena would kill us all."

Solomon walked into the living room holding up

a bottle of merlot. "Kandace wants to know if this is the good stuff from Paris. Are you two all right?"

Richmond nodded. "We're all right and that is the good stuff from Paris, so put it back. We're not drinking that until my son is born."

"Your daughter, you mean. Girls run in my family and I can't imagine how you and Solomon would ruin a boy," Alicia said.

"And you and your girls won't spoil a little girl?" Richmond said with a laugh.

"We won't be any worse than you are with Kiana," Kandace said, then stuck her tongue out at her brother-in-law. "You better hope for a boy or you're going to have a houseful of giraffes."

The couples laughed and Richmond headed down to the wine cellar to get another bottle of wine.

"All right," Solomon said. "I have to do the brother thing here. Don't hurt Richmond. He's a really good man and deserves the best. This is pretty much the same thing I told him when he came to Atlanta."

"Really?" Kandace asked. "I think I told him to leave Alicia alone, period. But neither one of them listened."

"And I'm glad I didn't," Alicia said.

Kandace winked. "Me too."

"Me three," Solomon said. "I've never seen him happier and I hope it stays that way."

"That is the plan," Alicia said, then patted Solomon's cheek. "I love him more than I thought I could ever love someone."

Richmond walked into the room with a bottle of pinot noir and glasses. "What did I miss?" he asked.

"Nothing," Alicia said. "Just these two telling me I'd better not break your heart."

Richmond nodded. "I heard something like that before. And there was a threat." He shot Kandace a smile.

"Whatever," Kandace said. "Is it my fault that I wanted two of my favorite people to be happy?"

"Let's watch a movie," Alicia said as she grabbed the remote. "I bet there is a James Bond movie on somewhere."

"As long as it isn't *A View To A Kill,*" Solomon said.

Chapter 25

Two days later, against Richmond's objections, Alicia and Vivian were sitting across from each other at Trader Vic's.

"Why do you want to help me?" Vivian asked. "I have the police looking into this video, and Richmond doesn't want to give me what I need to get this creep off my back."

"You don't think giving him money is going to keep him from coming back?"

Vivian took a sip of her tea and frowned. "I don't see how everyone in Atlanta doesn't have diabetes." She pushed her tea aside and Alicia tried not to forget why she was there.

"Vivian, you shouldn't be blackmailed and you never agreed to have that *day* videoed."

Vivian rolled her eyes and picked at her food. "I don't even remember having sex with him. I think he slipped something in my drink."

Alicia shivered. This was worse than she thought. "Did you tell the police that he drugged you?"

Vivian sucked her teeth. "I get the feeling that the police don't give a damn about what's going on."

"Why do you think that?" Alicia asked.

"Because I've been here for two weeks and they haven't said anything to me since I left Richmond's office. Unless you know something that I don't."

"I know this man works in education, and if he's making secret videos of women he's having sex with, he's committing a crime."

Vivian folded her arms across her chest. "Why does any of this matter to you? Seems as if you and Richmond could be sitting back getting your laugh on about it."

"Vivian, I know Felix from college, and he's a son of a bitch. I feel as if . . . I don't want you to be victimized by him."

"And what are you going to do, set a sting or some stupid shit?"

Alicia was ready to back away from the table and tell Vivian how quickly she could go to hell. But she was going to give it one last shot. "Do you really want that video to be held over your head for years to come, or worse yet, do you want him to leak it because he feels like it?"

"And what am I supposed to do?" Vivian asked.

"Call him, tell him that you have the money, and we'll get him on tape talking about the video."

Vivian took another sip of her tea. "I've done that whole thing with *I have the money, let me see you delete the video.*"

Alicia handed her a check for five hundred thousand dollars. "Now you have proof that you have the money."

"And suppose I take the money and run?" Vivian fingered the check and smiled.

"If you did that, then you'd be the trifling bitch that everyone says you are. And I will stop payment on the check."

Vivian laughed. "Guess you've been talking to Richmond about me, huh?"

"No, but I see how you operate."

Vivian tented her hands underneath her chin. "Really?"

"I'm not here to argue with you. Either you want my help or you don't."

"All I want is for that video to disappear. If that means I have to work with you, then what choice do I have?" Vivian folded the check and slipped it in her purse. "So, what's the plan?"

Alicia smiled. "Send him a picture of the check and set up a meeting. He needs to bring the laptop and give us access to his cloud server to make sure the video is gone. But since we will have him on video admitting that he committed a crime, the police can search his place for additional copies."

Vivian nodded. "I can do that."

"And make sure this meeting is in a public location. I'll make sure that everything is recorded."

"If he doesn't bite? Then what?"

Alicia sucked her teeth. "He will."

"The food's on you, right?" Vivian asked as she rose to her feet.

Alicia nodded, then watched Vivian saunter out of the restaurant. She really didn't like her. *This isn't about her,* Alicia thought as she finished her meal.

* * *

Richmond paced his office wondering how things were going with Alicia and Vivian. What if Vivian went all crazy bitch on her and they got into a fight? *Nah, Alicia wouldn't let that happen,* he thought as he paused for a brief moment. *And Vivian wouldn't want to cause a scene in public.*

Richmond had given Alicia the fake check, but cautioned her not to tell Vivian that the check wasn't real. He still believed that his ex would run off with the money. And if she did that, Richmond would know that everything everyone said about Vivian was true and he'd wasted too many years of his life trying to make that woman love him.

He couldn't help but be happy to have Alicia in his life and in his heart now. But if she didn't hurry up and give him a call, he was going to go out of his mind.

Solomon walked into the office and shot his brother a questioning look. "What's going on? You heard from Alicia yet?"

"Nope."

"You think Vivian kidnapped her?"

Richmond glared at his brother. "When are you going back to New York?"

Solomon sat across from Richmond's desk and shook his head. "You need to calm down. I know you're worried about Alicia doing this, but once this thing works, you get Vivian out of your life."

"But if anyone hurts Alicia, there won't be a hole in hell where they can hide."

Solomon threw his hands up. "Damn, who knew you were a gangsta like that?"

"Would you let Kandace do this?"

Solomon leaned back in his seat. "I almost lost

my wife before I had a chance to spend forever with her. We're with two strong women, and we have to trust that they know what they're doing."

Richmond nodded and then his phone dinged.

She took the check.

"Well, Vivian did the one thing that I knew she'd do," Richmond said. "She took the money."

"Like that was ever a question," Solomon quipped.

A few minutes later, Alicia walked into the office looking exhausted. "What did you ever see in that woman?" She crossed over to Richmond and gave him a kiss on the cheek.

"That's the million-dollar question," Solomon said. "And we could never get the answer to that question."

"We all make mistakes so that when we find forever, we know," Richmond said. "So, what's next?"

Alicia perched on the edge of his desk. "She's going to send him a picture of the check and set up a meeting."

"And I don't give a damn what you say, I'm going to be there," Richmond said. "No arguments, and I'm not taking no for an answer."

Alicia smiled, then leaned in and stroked his cheek. "Yes, sir."

"Ooh, I like the way you say that."

Solomon cleared his throat. "Hey, guys, I'm still here."

"Then you should leave," Richmond said. Solomon rose to his feet and smiled at the couple.

"You guys are nasty," he said as he walked out the door.

"Glad we're alone now," Richmond said as he

slipped his hand underneath Alicia's lace shirt. "I've been wanting to do this all day." He brought his lips down on top of hers, kissing her slow and deep. Alicia wrapped her arms around his neck and pulled him closer as their tongues danced.

Richmond pulled back from her. "I don't know what I'd do without you."

"You don't have to worry about that. I'm not going anywhere."

He kissed her again. "I don't want to have to worry about someone taking you away from me either. I'm worried about you getting involved with this thing."

"Richmond, everything is going to be fine. You don't have to worry."

One more kiss. "What do you say we get out of here and spend the rest of the day in bed?"

"Sounds good to me. Oh, and I brought you takeout from the restaurant, so we don't have to get up for anything."

"Make sure you text Kandace and tell her to keep Solomon away from the house for at least four hours."

Alicia pulled out her phone and sent the text. "Done," she said.

"All right, let's go."

Richmond sped to the house, parked the car, and scooped Alicia out of the passenger side. They barely made it to the foyer before Richmond started undressing her. "God, I want you," he moaned as he dropped his pants and wrapped her leg around his waist.

Thrusting forward, they melted together. "Yes," she moaned.

"I love you, I love you," Richmond said as they ground against each other.

"Are we even going to make it to the bed?" she breathed against his ear.

"Eventually."

She bounced against his hardness, getting wetter and wetter with each thrust. Alicia exploded and Richmond lifted her in his arms.

"Now, we take this to bed."

After spending the next two hours making love, Alicia and Richmond shared takeout from Trader Vic's.

"This is good," he said. "And needed, because you wore me out, woman."

"Right back at you. I don't think I'm going to be able to walk for a few days. But I like it."

He held out a spring roll to her. "When you're the boss, you can work from home. And home can be right here in this bed."

She bit the roll and he placed her hand on his chest. "Not until Felix is in jail," she said after chewing and swallowing her food.

"Yeah," he said. "I'm still not sold on this."

"Richmond, I don't want to fight about this. I've made up my mind, the plan is in motion and . . ." When her phone dinged, indicating that she had a text message, Alicia reached for it. "And Felix is ready to meet for his money."

"There goes staying in bed for days. All right, where are we going?"

She looked down at the phone. "It looks like he wants to meet at Amélie's."

"Let's go."

They got dressed and headed to the pastry shop. Richmond and Alicia found a table in the back of the shop where they could see Vivian and Felix walk in. Alicia set up her iPhone so that it could capture the image of the two when they arrived.

"Are you sure that they're coming?" Richmond asked after they'd been waiting for about ten minutes.

"Well, if they try to cash that check, then both of them will be going to jail," Alicia said.

Richmond nudged her. "There she is."

"And here he comes," Alicia said when she noticed Felix. "Smug bastard."

"Relax. Today, he gets what he deserves."

"Maybe we should move a little closer," she suggested.

"You do that. I'm going to stay out of sight," he said. Alicia nodded and headed to a table closer to where Felix and Vivian were sitting.

"Nice to see that some people keep their word," Felix said. "Where's the check?"

Vivian folded her arms across her chest. "Where's the video? I'm not going to give you anything until I know that video is gone."

"You're still pretending that you didn't know what was going on?" He laughed. "Vivian, you came to me mad as hell about your ex. I just wanted to give you a little leverage to get that million dollars that you wanted."

"By drugging me and having sex with me while I was unconscious? You're a real great guy."

Felix laughed. "Say what you want, but you got what you wanted. You should be thanking me."

"I should be stabbing you with a rusty knife. And I didn't get a million dollars. Cheap bastard."

"Temper, temper." Felix pulled out his laptop and turned it toward Vivian. "Just look at the beauty of this video."

Vivian slammed the lid of the laptop down. "Don't do that. Not in public."

"Maybe we should try again and go for two million this time."

"Delete it."

"Hell, maybe I want a million now. Never knew how important this was to you." Felix leaned back in his chair. "Coffee or an éclair?"

"This isn't a date," she exclaimed. "You made an illegal video of me and you want to act like we're sitting here on a date? Go to hell."

Felix smiled. "Well, if you could get half a million, I'm sure you can get the rest. Say, in seven days? Now, give me the check or I'm uploading this video to my favorite porn site. Hashtag Vivian Crawford."

"You bastard." She reached into her purse and slid the check across the table.

"And you know that I did shoot the video where I didn't show my face. So, it's going to be all about you."

She leapt to her feet and started to storm out of the bakery, then she saw Alicia and smiled. "You're going to wish you never met me," she spat at Felix.

Alicia could've killed Vivian when they locked eyes. Was she trying to ruin their plan? But she was able to get back to the table with Richmond without Felix seeing her. "That woman is a piece of work."

"Tell me something I don't know."

"Do you still have that cop's card, or did you give it to Vivian?"

"I think I have a card back at the office. He wanted me to press charges against her because she'd been trying to blackmail me."

"Then let's call this guy so that he can get the real criminal." They headed out the back and Alicia figured that their nightmare with Vivian and Felix would be over sooner, rather than later.

Chapter 26

Two days later, Felix Thompson walked into Richmond's office expecting a million dollars. The police had monitored a call between Felix and Vivian where she'd told him that Richmond would give him the money. Atlanta Police were going to be at the ready to take him down if he showed up.

And there he was. Alicia stared him down as she opened the door.

"Aww, black beauty," he said. "Good to see you."

She folded her arms across her chest. "You're a piece of shit, you know that?"

He stroked her cheek and Alicia recoiled at his touch. "Don't you ever fucking touch me again! I can't believe you did this to someone and you're here to get paid for it. There is a special place in hell for you."

Felix kissed at her. "And you can join me."

Alicia would've kneed him in the balls if she didn't know what was waiting for him when she moved out of the way. Finally, he was going to pay for everything that he had done to her and, she assumed, other women. Stepping aside, she waited to hear the magical words that she'd wished she had heard as an undergraduate.

"Felix Thompson, you are under arrest for extortion. You have the right to remain silent. Anything you say can and will be used against you in a court of law. You have the right to an attorney. If you cannot afford one, one will be provided for you at government expense. Do you understand these rights as I have read them to you?"

Alicia smiled as the Atlanta police officers ushered Felix out. "Felix," she said. "Make sure you smile for the cameras." She nodded to the media presence out in the parking lot. "Now, everyone will know what a son of a bitch you really are."

He glared at her and before he could say anything, one of the officers nudged him forward and out of the building.

Richmond walked up behind Alicia and wrapped his arms around her waist. "I'm glad this is over," he said. "Do you know what a remarkable woman you are?"

"Do you know how scared I was?"

"I couldn't tell because you kicked ass, babe. Let's get out of here."

She nodded. And as they headed home, Alicia was looking forward to a future with her man, her baby, and their amazing life.

Six months later

The hotel was about two weeks from opening. And Alicia felt as if she was as big as a house. She and Serena had taken to sending each other belly pictures every morning to see who was bigger. Jade thought they both were ridiculous.

Kandace and Solomon, along with Devon and Marie, had come down to Atlanta for the opening. Devon had wanted to show Marie his hometown through his eyes. His wife had been used to coming to the A to party back in the day. Their daughter was going to spend the week with her doting grandfather in Charlotte.

"She's going to be totally rotten when she comes home," Marie had said over dinner one night.

"Like she wasn't before she left," Devon said. "It's hard to say no to my baby, though."

"Get ready, Alicia," Marie said. "When a baby comes along, we lose the ability to say no."

Richmond placed his hand on Alicia's belly. "I can say no," he said.

"I've seen what you do for Kiana. You can't say no," Alicia said, then kissed him on the cheek.

"Devon, this is delicious," Richmond said. "What is it?"

"It's a new take on my Orleans chicken, because I'm sure a certain restaurant in Charlotte might not like it if we shared recipes. So, this is Sweet Auburn Chicken and spinach."

"I'm in love," Alicia said.

Marie smiled. "I told him that he better not let Bobby Flay tell him to put more peppers in everything."

"This has a little bit of kick to it, but it isn't overpowering," Alicia said. "The spinach and onions are delicious."

"And a good thing about this is you can switch it out for shrimp or salmon," he said.

Richmond nodded. "How long will you be here to train the cooking staff?"

"Two months," Devon said. "The recipes are simple and delicious."

"I can't wait to open this place and have it become another icon in Atlanta."

Marie sipped her wine and smiled. "With all of us working together? How can we lose?"

Alicia reached across the table and gave Marie a high five. "Sounds like we're getting a shout-out on your blog?"

"Absolutely. Are you guys going to do weddings at the hotel?"

Richmond shrugged. "I'm thinking we're going to be all about the honeymoon at this hotel. Sensual rooms with big soft beds. A lot like the hotel we stayed in while we were in Paris."

"Probably where y'all made that baby," Marie quipped.

They all laughed, and then Devon rose to his feet to get the dessert. And to everyone's surprise, it wasn't his signature chocolate cake.

"This is my ivory delight, buttercream and moist yellow cake," he said as he cut everyone a slice.

Alicia decided that she wanted to eat the whole cake. "Oh my God. This is the most delicious thing that I have put in my mouth today."

Richmond raised his eyebrow and reached for her plate. "I will stab you with my fork," Alicia quipped. "Taste it."

He put a forkful of his own cake into his mouth. "This is good."

"And will be an exclusive dessert for the hotel," Devon said.

"That's not fair," Alicia said. "This would be so good at Hometown Delights."

Richmond tilted his head to the side. "Don't you live here now?"

She pointed her index finger at him. "You're right. Never mind."

After dinner, Marie took her husband to her favorite club in Buckhead just to show him that she still had a little bit of party girl in her. Richmond and Alicia decided to share a quiet night on the sofa, creating a social media buzz about the new hotel. Alicia created a Facebook page for the new hotel and it already had five thousand likes.

"Let's just hope we can get that many reservations for the first three months," Richmond said as she showed him the page.

"We will, it's the new and shiny thing."

Richmond closed the lid on her laptop and set it on the coffee table. "Enough work," he said. "It's time to relax."

"Fine, but I have to get a picture of that cake and post it to Instagram."

"Tomorrow."

"It might not be here tomorrow, because I want another piece, now," she said with a wink.

"I'll get the cake, you take the picture, and then we relax. No arguments."

She gave him a mock salute. "Yes, sir." While Richmond headed into the kitchen to get the cake,

Alicia picked up her laptop and Googled Felix Thompson. She and Richmond had been so busy with the hotel opening that she hadn't had a chance to pay attention to what had been going on with his case.

When the news story popped up, she read it with rapt attention.

Former educator Felix Thompson pleaded guilty to making an explicit video of a woman without her knowledge or permission. Then he tried to blackmail her for a million dollars. The woman, who was not associated with the charter school where Thompson worked, turned the camera around on Thompson and filmed his blackmail attempt.

The guilty plea allows Thompson to avoid being listed as sex offender. But he does have to surrender his teaching license and he has been fired from the charter school. He will be spending ninety days in jail.

"I thought we were supposed to be relaxing?" Richmond asked when he returned to the sofa.

Alicia closed the laptop and smiled. "You know me, sometimes it's hard to turn off."

"And you wanted to see what was going on with Thompson, right?"

She nodded. "He pleaded guilty, lost his job, and all of Atlanta knows he's a piece of shit."

"Good. Now we can put that behind us." He handed Alicia her cake. "Have I told you that I love you?"

"Yes, but I don't mind hearing it again."

"I love you."

"Love you too," she said, then leaned in and gave him a slow kiss.

Epilogue

The lobby of the Crawford Bistro and Hotel had been transformed into a chic starlit night. Twinkling lights gave the room a beautiful glow that made it seem as if time had stopped. Richmond, just like the one hundred guests in attendance, held his breath as Alicia appeared in the doorway, holding Solomon's arm. She was a vision in her yellow-white gown and her hair pulled back in a tight bun. A small tiara adorned her head in lieu of a veil. The "Wedding March" began to play and the guests rose to their feet.

Richmond had never seen a more beautiful sight than his future wife. Her smile lit up the room and made his heart skip more than just a beat. His mouth watered with the anticipation of kissing her lips, which were shimmering with a hint of lip gloss. *Damn, I love this woman,* he thought as she joined him at the altar. He was happy that Solomon had agreed to walk Alicia down the aisle. This was the first time that either man had been at the other's wedding.

Solomon beamed as he looked from Alicia to Richmond. Seeing his brother this happy almost brought him to tears. This was the kind of love that Richmond deserved after the nightmare marriage he'd had with Vivian and everything else that he'd been through since Elliot's death.

Alicia handed her bouquet of white roses to Jade, who had tears shining in her eyes. Jade had never seen Alicia looking more beautiful than she did at that moment, even with her huge baby bump. Her skin was glowing and her eyes gleamed with happiness. She never thought that she would be so happy for Richmond. He wasn't the nicest person when Kandace and Solomon were first married, but the evolution of Richmond Crawford had been wonderful to watch. And since he'd been taking great care of her friend, Jade was rooting for this marriage.

Serena wouldn't have squeezed her pregnant body into a bridesmaid's dress for anyone other than Alicia. She couldn't tell if her tears were from joy or her hormones. But looking at her best friend standing there getting ready to marry the man who loved her, made her smile and cry at the same time. She reached out and touched Alicia's shoulder. *I'm so happy for you,* she mouthed as her friend looked back at her.

Alicia looked into Richmond's eyes as the minister asked, "Who gives this woman away?"

"We do," the entire clan said, eliciting giggles from the crowd and the bride and groom.

Solomon cleared his throat. "Well, Alicia, you are a loved woman and God loves the institution of marriage. He loves for his children to become one and join together as husband and wife," he said in a booming voice. "What God has joined together, let no man put asunder. Marriage is not to be entered into lightly. And with all of these witnesses, these friends and family, Alicia and Richmond are vowing to love, cherish, honor, and pledge their lives to each other until death does them part.

"The couple has written their own vows to express their love and devotion to one another. Richmond, will you recite your vows to Alicia?"

Richmond nodded and took Alicia's hands in his, then gently kissed them. "Alicia, you blew into my life and turned it upside down and I couldn't be happier about it. I thought that you were something special the moment I laid eyes on you, and when I got to know you, I knew that to be true. You made my life better, you expanded my heart, you made love more than an abstract feeling, but the focus of my life. Because of you, I'm a better man, a man who plans to love you forever and a month. God brought us together for a reason, and we're standing here fulfilling a destiny that neither of us could've ever dreamed of. I love you more than words could ever say, and the rest of my life will be devoted to showing you how much I love and need you," Richmond said. His eyes glistened as he spoke.

Alicia was unable to hold her tears back, even though she'd promised herself and her sisters that she wasn't going to cry because brides who cried on their wedding day were just so cliché. But there she stood, looking into the eyes of the man she would spend the rest of her life with, and hearing him describe their love, the only thing she could do was cry.

Alicia was afraid that an alarm clock was about to go off and this perfect day was going to be just a dream. She opened her mouth, but nothing came out. It wasn't that she'd forgotten her vows, she was simply making sure that clock didn't start buzzing.

"Alicia," the minister said in an effort to urge her to speak. "Your vows."

She nodded, as Richmond wiped away her tears with his thumb. "Never have I known a man more gentle and loving than you. When we met, I was a mess, but you took the time to get to know me and show me what it feels like to be loved, and made me unafraid to say *I love you.* I didn't want to fall for you and I tried to fight it, but thank goodness I lost that battle. You're the best thing that's ever happened to me and I'm going to enjoy spending my life with you and building our family. The thought of you makes me smile, and because of you, I know what it feels like to cry tears of joy instead of pain."

Richmond kissed her hands again.

"The rings, please," the minister said.

Alicia turned to Jade to retrieve Richmond's white-gold wedding band with three small diamonds embedded in it. Her hand trembled as she took the ring. This was it, the symbol of their union. She was going to be Mrs. Richmond Crawford. Never in her wildest dreams did she think when they met outside of the library at her college reunion that she'd end up standing in this spot, about to become the happiest woman in the world. Not only had he showed her how to love, Richmond had taught her that when you give your love to the right person, it doesn't hurt. His love made her feel as if the world was her oyster and together they could accomplish anything. Alicia barely heard the words that the minister said as she slipped the ring onto Richmond's finger.

"With this ring, I thee wed," she said breathlessly. Her eyes were like two damp diamonds glittering in the sun as she looked into Richmond's eyes. Once again, Richmond wiped her tears away. Alicia kissed his hand as he moved it away from her face.

"Please join hands," the minister said to thc couple. "With the power vested in me, I now pronounce you husband and wife. Richmond, you may kiss your bride."

Richmond took Alicia into his arms and kissed her as if they were the only two people in the room, causing her to swoon in his arms.

The audience hooted and cheered, bringing the couple out of their embrace.

"Ladies and gentlemen, Mr. and Mrs. Richmond Crawford," the minister said as Alicia and Richmond joined hands.

Kandace reached for the decorative broom at her feet and placed it in front of the couple. Then the bridal party gathered around the couple as they joined hands and leapt across the broom. The leap, to Alicia, symbolized a clean sweep of the past heartache, men who didn't love her as deeply as she thought that she'd loved them. The leap was a jump into her new life, new joy, and more happiness than her heart and hand could ever hold.

ALSO AVAILABLE

I Heard a Rumor

Chante Britt is nobody's fool—and she's definitely not standing by her cheating ex-fiancé and current mayoral candidate, Robert Montgomery. Too bad he chose to tell the media otherwise. To escape an onslaught of prying reporters, Chante flees to her grandmother's South Carolina beach house. But when she meets Zach Harrington, she may be out of the frying pan and into the fire. The man is arrogant, way too forward—and way too sexy . . .

Enjoy the following excerpt from
I Heard a Rumor . . .

Chapter 1

Chante Britt filled her favorite pink and green mug with Ethiopian blend coffee, which had been a gift from her best friend and sorority sister, Liza Palmer-Franklin. *That girl knows coffee,* she thought as she inhaled the fragrant aroma. She almost didn't want to pour the creamer into the coffee. She took a sip and realized that it was perfect black. Reaching for the remote to the small TV set mounted over the stove, she sighed as she turned it on. This was her morning routine, and it was getting on her last damned nerve.

Chante was bored, mad, and tired of the purgatory her life had become since her suspension from the law firm she'd worked for, Myrick, Lawson and Walker.

She had been considered a distraction, according to managing partner Taiwon Myrick, because of her relationship with former senatorial candidate Robert Montgomery, who lost his bid for a senate seat after she and Liza exposed the fact that he was a liar and paid for sex with prostitutes. When Chante and Robert had been dating, she'd lobbied for her firm to support his candidacy, which they did. Taiwon liked Robert's pro-business stance on several issues and threw a lot of money his way, even after Chante had expressed her doubts. But as always, Taiwon chose not to listen to Chante. Over the last two years at Myrick, Lawson and Walker, Chante had been working herself ragged to become a partner. But she'd been constantly looked over—despite the fact that she'd delivered over a million dollars in billable hours, boasted a ninety percent winning ratio, and brought in more than a third of the firm's new clients.

Taiwon was from the old-school law community and just didn't believe a woman could be a partner with the firm his family had started. Though she couldn't point to any provable sexual discrimination, she knew it was her gender that had been holding her back at the firm.

So when Jackson Franklin won the senate seat after it was revealed that Robert had been involved with a hooker during the campaign, Taiwon had been happy to blame her for the firm being mixed up in the controversy.

Bastard, she thought as she lifted her head and saw Robert's image on the screen. Chante started to turn the set off. But curiosity got the best of her, so she unmuted the set to hear what he had to say.

"Wonder if he's still out there buying sex," she muttered, then took another sip of her coffee.

"I'm standing here today because of grace and forgiveness," Robert said into the camera. "I made mistakes in my quest to become senator, and I hurt a lot of people. But those people, including the love of my life, have forgiven me. And their forgiveness has given me the courage to throw my hat into the ring to be Charlotte's next mayor."

Chante spit her coffee across the kitchen. Was this man daft? Who was going to support him to be mayor, let alone the city's dogcatcher? And who was the love of his life? Poor woman. She didn't know what kind of mess she was going to be in as the pretend love of Robert Montgomery's life. The only person Robert loved was Robert.

She reached into her robe pocket and pulled out her smartphone to text Liza.

"Last night, as I talked to my future wife, Chante Britt . . ."

"What the . . . !" Chante exclaimed. Forget texting Liza; she was going to have to call her friend and hope that she wasn't interrupting anything going on between the newlyweds.

"This is Liza," her friend said when she answered the phone.

"Robert has lost what's left of his blasted mind," Chante exclaimed. "This fool just . . ."

"Calm down," Liza said. "I'm sure no one is taking him seriously."

Chante's phone beeped. "Hold on, I have another call coming in," she said. Clicking the TALK button, she answered the unknown number.

"Chante Britt."

"Ms. Britt, this is Coleen Jackson. I'm a reporter

with News Fourteen. I wanted to ask you a few questions about Robert Montgomery."

Click.

"People were paying attention, Liza," Chante said. "That was a reporter."

"Oh my goodness. While you had me on hold, they showed a clip of his announcement on the news here. He really called you the love of his life. Have you two been seeing each other?"

"Hell no! I haven't spoken to that man since two days after the election, and that was last year."

"I can't believe him. What does he think is going to come of this, and why would he think that you would agree to being . . . ?"

Chante's phone beeped again. She looked at the incoming caller's number and saw it was another unknown one. "I'm guessing that's another reporter," Chante said. "What am I going to do?"

"Issue a statement. I'll write one for you to e-mail to all the media outlets in Charlotte. This will blow over. Let's just take control of the narrative and wait for the next news cycle. Everyone will move on to the next thing and you can get on with your life."

"Thank you, Liza. I'm going to go for my run now."

"Has your suspension been lifted yet?"

"No. And I'm guessing this latest stunt from this asshole is going to give them another reason to keep the suspension going."

"I still think you should start your own firm," Liza said. "You don't need them."

Chante sighed. Part of her agreed with her friend, but there was something about the security of becoming a partner at an established law firm.

Maybe she wanted that partnership so that she could prove her mother wrong.

Allison Louise Cooper-Britt had grown up as the ultimate Southern belle. She attended South Carolina State College for one reason—to obtain her MRS. That happened when she'd met and married Eli Britt. He'd been the crucial catch: wealthy family, right complexion, and a member of all the right organizations.

When Chante had graduated from college and decided that law school was more important than a husband and a family, her mother wished her failure. Thankfully, her smarts and a few of her father's connections had given her the blueprint for success.

She and her grandmother, Elsie Mae, had a much better relationship than she had with Allison. Probably because they were so much alike. Elsie Mae Cooper had carved out her niche in Charleston, South Carolina, by selling her handwoven baskets to tourists. In 1972, she began adding unique pieces of South Carolina culture to the baskets and opened a gift shop on Folly Beach. Elsie's Gifts and Goodies became one of the beach's most popular tourist attractions.

When Elsie Mae retired from running the shop, she sold it to a historical group while keeping a forty-nine percent stake in the company. The residual income allowed her to travel the world at will. Of course, Allison thought her widowed mother should spend her time in a rocking chair on the front porch. That was not Elsie Mae's style at all, and her world traveling and adventure seeking became a bone of contention between mother and daughter.

Chante wished she had her grandmother's fearless nature. She knew for a fact that Elsie Mae would've started her own firm without giving it a second thought. Her grandmother wouldn't have taken all the grief she'd subjected herself to for that partnership. Part of her knew she'd be fine if she struck out on her own. She had a huge client base, and she was a proven winner who'd made millions for her clients. But she was afraid. Afraid that if she failed, her mother would lord it over her, just as she'd always done with the fact that she isn't married.

As if that was the only thing she was supposed to do with her life. Rolling her eyes at the ringing phone, Chante hit the IGNORE button on another unknown call, then shut the phone off.

When she received Liza's e-mail with her statement and a list of contacts to send it to, Chante was ready to pound the pavement and Robert's face. Lacing up her sneakers and popping her earbuds in, she opened the front door and was blinded by flashbulbs.

"What the . . . ?"

"Ms. Britt, have you forgiven Robert?"

"When is the wedding?"

"Will Senator and Mrs. Franklin be there? Have all of you kissed and made up after such an ugly election cycle?"

"Get off my doorstep!" Chante exclaimed. When the members of the media took a step back, she thought they had heeded her demand. That was until she saw Robert walking her way. Narrowing her eyes at him, all she could think was that the media had just saved his life.

"Chante, darling, I didn't mean for this to happen," he said with a huge smile on his face. She watched in abject horror as he walked up the steps and stood in her face.

"You son of a . . ."

Robert wrapped his arms around her and attempted to kiss her. Chante kneed him in the family jewels before storming into her house and slamming the door. All she could hope was that the cameras had caught every minute of it. One thing was for certain: she wasn't going to stick around to be harassed by the media or Robert freaking Montgomery!

Zach Harrington downed a mojito as if it was a glass of water while he sat on the white shores of Folly Beach. It felt good to be an anonymous man in the crowd. In South Carolina, he was just a man on the beach. Back in New York, he was the ex-husband of the "Harlem Madame." Just thinking about the moniker the media had given his ex-wife made him cringe. And the circus! Cameras followed him around the city and camped out at his office building and his temporary home.

He couldn't even meet with the Crawfords about a tract of land they wanted to purchase in Manhattan for new office space. He was sure that Solomon and Richmond Crawford wouldn't want to be photographed outside his office after what their family had gone through in the media lately. Solomon and Richmond had discovered that their father, Elliot, had a son—Adrian Bryant—before his death. Adrian had taken the story to the media around the same time that Richmond had been arrested in Los Angeles for solicitation of sex.

Then there had been Richmond's messy divorce. The businessman in Zach knew that any partnership they'd enter into right now would be a disaster. And he hadn't told the Crawfords that he and Adrian had been friends long before the scandal broke.

Just thinking about the media circus and the money it was costing him made him crave something stronger than a sweet rum highball. When he'd filed for divorce from his wife, Natalie, he thought she'd been having an affair. He had no clue that she was running an escort service from their home on Long Island. It had taken three months for him to clear his name and prove to the district attorney that he didn't have anything to do with Natalie's illegal empire.

She'd been clearing about a million dollars a year. At least she was sleazy enough to hide the money in an account that had nothing to do with his business or their personal accounts. Shaking his head, Zach brought himself back to what was in front of him: a beautiful shoreline, women in barely there bikinis, and the blazing Southern sun.

Digging his toes into the warm sand, Zach tugged at his Brooklyn Nets ball cap and grinned. For the next seven days or more, he was going to be anyone he wanted to be, without worrying about the glare of the New York media. Just as he was about to close his eyes, his cell phone vibrated in his pocket. Grabbing it, he smiled when he saw it was his assistant, Kia Clarke.

"What's up, Special K?"

"Your final divorce decree just arrived. You are officially unattached."

"Been unattached. I'm just glad the state has approved it," he said. "Have the reporters stopped calling yet?"

Kia sighed. "You haven't heard the latest?"

"I've been listening to ocean waves. Do I even want to know?"

"She claims there's a black book and you know where it is. We've had a few agents stop by the office, but I told them that without a warrant they couldn't come in. And three more clients have dropped us."

Zach muttered curses that caused a few people to give him the side eye. "Why does she keep tarnishing my name?"

"She doesn't want to let you go, and she isn't trying to go down without taking a lot of innocent people with her. I've never liked Ms. Shady Boots, and I told you that from the beginning."

"I wish I'd seen her true colors years ago," he said, then expelled a sigh.

"Tried to warn you, boss. But you were blinded by something else."

"Don't remind me. How's the baby?"

"Still baking. I'm two weeks overdue, and Dave is stressing me out. That's why I came into the office today."

"Please don't give birth in my office," he quipped.

"I'm so happy for you and Dave. I wish I could be there to celebrate with you guys."

"Zach, I'm not mad at you for staying away and getting your head together. And why not have some fun while you're out there?"

"That's my plan. When I come back to New York, hopefully this news cycle will be over and I can get back to my business and spoiling my godson."

"Excuse you, I'm having a daughter. So, you better get some of the Southern girly-girl stuff while you're in Charleston."

"I'm bringing football helmets and shoulder pads," he said with a laugh.

"Anyway. Unless anything major happens, the next time you hear from me, I'll be calling with the news of your goddaughter's entrance into the world," Kia said.

When they said good-bye, Zach turned his phone off, leaned back in his lounge chair, and closed his eyes. The warmth of the sun did little to ease the chill he felt creeping up his spine. Even though he'd divorced his criminal wife and had had nothing to do with her sex peddling, his boutique real estate firm was suffering. A couple of clients had taken their business elsewhere, costing him fifteen million dollars. The loss hurt, but his company was strong—for now. If he kept losing the big clients, then he would be hurting, as well as his employees.

Part of him wanted to push Natalie into the Hudson River with a hundred pounds of weights attached to her Louboutins. But he was nonviolent, and he just planned to let everything blow over. He was going to have to diversify, and maybe he would find a great investment down South that would make up for his losses. Down here, he wouldn't be cast as the husband of the "Harlem Madame." He could create a Southern branch of his business, buy some cheap land, and turn it into gold. After all, he knew his Midas touch was still intact. At least, he hoped so.

Groaning, Zach decided it was time for another drink and some more girl watching.